THE
HOUSE
SWAP

THE
HOUSE
SWAP

A NOVEL

REBECCA FLEET

PAMELA DORMAN BOOKS
VIKING

VIKING
An imprint of Penguin Random House LLC
375 Hudson Street
New York, New York 10014
penguin.com

A Pamela Dorman Book/Viking

Published by arrangement with Transworld Publishers, a division of The Random House Group Ltd.

Title page photo: robinimages2013/shutterstock.com

ISBN 9780525558835 (hardcover)
ISBN 9780525558842 (ebook)

Printed in the United States of America
1   3   5   7   9   10   8   6   4   2

Set in Berling LT Std
Designed by Nancy Resnick

ACKNOWLEDGMENTS

Writing *The House Swap* was something of a leap of faith for me, and I've been lucky enough to find many people along the way who have been willing to take the leap with me. First was my brilliant agent, Caroline Wood at Felicity Bryan Agency, who saw the potential in the book straightaway, helped me to craft and polish it, and got on with the complex business of "agenting" with astuteness and aplomb to ensure that it landed in the best hands. Thank you, too, to the amazing team at Transworld, who have championed the book with such teamwork, energy, and passion from the start— and above all to my editor, Frankie Gray, who has combined an exceptionally keen editorial eye with a real understanding of what I was aiming to do with the novel. *The House Swap* has also found a home in several territories around the world, and more thanks must go to Pam Dorman and Jeramie Orton in the United States in particular for their editorial input and enthusiasm along the way.

Closer to home, I'm very grateful to all the friends and family who have helped me stay positive about the often up-and-down nature of writing. Special mentions go to Charlotte Duckworth for beta reading and empathy by the bucketload; Jenny Duggin for cheerleading and relentless belief; the Book Frisbees for being voices of expertise and sanity in the wilderness; my parents, Nigel and Elaine, for their rock-solid support; and my husband, Daniel, for never letting me lose sight of what mattered. Last, thank you to Saskia for reminding me that living is just as important as writing.

THE
HOUSE
SWAP

*T*he key slides and turns in the lock, as smooth and slippery as a silverfish. Lying in bed last night, staring at the trembling shadows of the branches grazing the window and thinking of this moment, I thought it would be harder. I imagined scratching metal. Jarring resistance. After everything that has led me here, it feels as if it should be more of an effort. But it's easy—an anticlimax, even. An eggshell cracked in the hand and tossed aside.

The door swings open and the pinewood boards of the hallway unfurl ahead, gleamingly polished and clean. Just inside, stiff dark branches studded brightly with plastic-looking berries protrude from an ornamental vase. Reflected in the mirror, I can see a row of framed photographs lining the far wall. Stepping inside and closing the door softly shut behind me, I move fast through the hall, keeping my back to the wall. I won't look at them, not yet. Soon.

The country-style kitchen—oddly out of place in this third-floor city flat—is decorated in pale green, artfully hung with saucepans and dried bunches of herbs. On the oak table lies a torn-out piece of paper, darkly scrawled with ink.

Welcome! it reads. **Instructions for all appliances in the green**

folder in the lounge. Bread, milk etc. in the fridge—help yourself. Do call if you need anything. Enjoy your stay and make yourself at home! Caroline. I stare at her name for a long time. The confident slash of the C, the spatter of ink where the dot of the i has bled across the page. I touch that spatter with the ball of my thumb, half expecting it to rub off on my skin, but of course it has long since dried up.

At last I get up and make a cup of coffee. I will do as Caroline invites. I will make myself at home. I drink it sitting at the table, imagining the rooms still to be explored. The secrets that might be tucked inside them, tightly curled up in her possessions and ready to be extracted. I remember the fox I saw crouched by the roadside as I drove past this morning, digging into some unidentifiable corpse—the sharp flash of bloodied silver on its claws as it teased out what it wanted. This will be like that. Dirty, unpleasant. That's the way it has to be. The way I want it. It's the only way to get under the skin.

AWAY

Caroline, May 2015

When we turn into the street my first thought is that the houses around here all look the same. Neat whitewashed rectangles with boxy little windows and flatly sloping roofs. They almost all have window boxes, too—lined up along the lower sills and filled uniformly with white and purple pansies, like they're subject to some sort of dress code. There must be around thirty of these houses, all prettily popped off the production line.

"Welcome to suburbia," Francis says, squinting through the setting sun that strikes the windscreen as he steers the car down the road. "I hope you're happy." His voice is deliberately grumpy, self-mocking.

"It's not so bad." The reply is automatic, made before I have had the chance to consider whether or not I mean it. It happens between us a lot these days, this kind of conversational fast-tracking. Cut and thrust, back and forth. Adversarial but nonthreatening, like two children mildly squabbling in the playground. Francis glances at me out of the corner of his eye, makes a face.

I stare out of the window, taking in the line of houses again as we crawl down the narrow road. Now that I look more carefully,

I can see the little touches of individuality that some of the owners have tried to impart. A garishly painted garage door here, a smart gold number plaque there. One of the houses, number 14, is a little less smart than the others—its walls scuffed faintly with dirt, the lawn longer and more overgrown, tangled with weeds.

"They're letting the side down," I say, gesturing out of the window. "Neighborhood Watch'll be on to them." Francis smiles faintly, not really listening.

"Twenty-one, right?" he asks, already swinging the car into the driveway. I scan the house, looking for distinctive features, but there are none. The lawn is precisely clipped, and the windows are framed with little bunches of curtain, white and spotless. The lights inside are off, and for an instant I see the reflection of the car bounced back at us from the downstairs window in the glare of the headlights, our shadows inside darkly outlined side by side. For some reason, the sight gives me a tremor of unease—a slight, irrational pulse that slips away as soon as it comes.

"Looks all right," I say, wriggling out of my seat belt and pushing open the car door. It's colder outside than I imagined, the wind prickling the hairs on the back of my neck. Francis is climbing out of the driver's seat, making a pantomime of his aching legs. The drive down from Leeds has taken a little over four hours—not a bad run, but long enough to breed that fusty, lethargic sense of having been enclosed and motionless for too long. In the old days we would have shared the drive, but not long after I stopped offering, he stopped asking.

"Yeah, as far as it goes. Couple more hours and we could have been in Paris," Francis says mournfully, grinning at me. "Romantic walks along the Champs-Elysées. Nice cup of *café au lait* and a croissant would have hit the spot right about now."

"I know," I admit, "but it just felt too complicated, and a bit far to go, leaving Eddie and all that. Think of it as a trial this time 'round, see how it works. Maybe next year."

This is old ground. Right from the start, Francis's plans for this week away had been more ambitious than mine. Still, his enthusiasm had spiraled out of nowhere when I had tentatively floated the idea of a house swap, lurching from apathy to manic energy in the space of seconds. He had been so appreciative of what he saw as my initiative that I had shrunk back from telling the truth: that I had signed up to the house swap site on an idle whim months ago and forgotten about it. I had only seen the message notification by chance, sifting through my spam folder in search of a mislaid communication from a friend. *Someone wants to swap with you!* It was an intriguing little hook, tugging me forward. I clicked on the link and there it was: a polite, featureless message from someone who signed themselves S. Kennedy, expressing an interest in our Leeds city-center flat and offering their Chiswick house in exchange, if a suitable time could be found.

I had flicked through the pictures of number 21 Everdene Avenue—the unremarkable décor and the cool, pale walls, the nicely kept front lawn—but in truth I had barely taken them in. All I could think was that here was a chance for a change of scene at minimal expense, a week away for just the two of us, if my mother could take Eddie. Close enough to London for sightseeing day trips, far enough out of the center to feel like a break from city life. We had toyed with the idea of a holiday in Spain months ago and abandoned it. Too much money and too much effort, or at least so we had told each other. Perhaps Francis, too, had been secretly daunted by the implications of an exotically hot hotel room and candlelit evenings on a mimosa-scented terrace.

Francis is ferreting beneath the plant pots at the side of the house, locating the key. "Brace yourself," he says, brandishing it.

"This is where we find out they've left a load of dead bodies festering in the kitchen."

I roll my eyes, ignoring the sudden decisive shudder that passes down my spine. Ridiculous as his words are, I can't help feeling all at once that it is a weird thing to be doing—squatting in the house of a stranger. I remember a program I watched months ago: some crackpot psychic floating around a supposedly haunted house, wittering on about how its past tragedies were ingrained in its walls. I had scoffed, but that night I had dreamed of walking through silent rooms and cool dark corridors, breathing in the infected heaviness of their air.

Francis unlocks the door and lets it swing open, and we stand there in silence for a few moments on the threshold. "Well," he says at last, "we needn't have worried. The cops have already been here and cleaned the place out."

I half smile, intent on taking in our surroundings. It's the emptiest house I have ever seen. Nothing on the walls, not even a mirror. Pale pine floorboards and smooth blank doors opening into near-vacant rooms. A lounge containing a black leather sofa, monolithic and stark, and a sparsely filled bookcase. At the end of the corridor, I glimpse the kitchen—the bare pinewood table and a gleaming oven that looks as if it's just been installed.

"Is this . . . normal?" Francis asks, moving gingerly through the hallway and peering into the rooms one by one, then following me up the stairs. "I mean, it's not very . . ."

"Cozy," I finish, as we reach the bedroom. It's like an exhibit in a modern-art show. The double bed is made up neatly with a dark chocolate–brown duvet and two pillows, and there is a bedside cabinet, as well as a wardrobe looming in the corner of the room, but it's just as devoid of personal possessions as the other rooms.

There is a sheet of white paper lying on one of the pillows, folded precisely in half. I cross the room and unfold it; it's type-written, in a small centered font. **Dear Caroline,** it reads, **I hope you enjoy your stay. Information in kitchen folder. Please help yourself to anything you find. S.**

I read the note out to Francis, who starts wheezing uncontrollably with laughter before I have even finished. "What?" I say irritably. "What's so funny?"

Francis takes a moment to compose himself. "Where do I start?" he says. "The way it's only addressed to you, like I'm chopped liver. The idea of you helping yourself to precisely fucking nothing, which is all that's on offer as far as I can see. The fact that it's been left on the bed like some sort of love letter, only it's the least romantic note I've ever had the pleasure of receiving by proxy. The whole thing is—"

"All right, all right." I screw the note up into a ball and throw it at him, laughing despite myself. "I'm sure the intention was good. And yes, it's a bit basic, but it's not like we have to spend all our time here, is it. We can go up to London, go out for dinner. That was the point, wasn't it?"

Francis shrugs. "Yes, I suppose so. Well, one of the points."

I glance at him across the room, and just like that the atmosphere shifts and changes, our laughter sucked up into the space between us. The silence lasts a little too long for recovery, and I let it stretch, leaning back against the bedroom wall and shifting my gaze to the chilly brightness of the sun striking the skylight window. I don't have to look at him to see the expression on his face: lost and vacant, a strange mixture of mutiny and regret.

"OK . . . ," I say, just for the sake of speaking, and as I do I can feel panic starting to rise. I'm already missing Eddie, and the bridge he provides between us, the shared love and focus we can turn on him. Now there's only the sudden claustrophobic terror of being trapped in this strange house with my husband for seven whole days, with each hour feeling like a potential land mine that we will have to tiptoe around, avoiding anything that might explode the still-fragile truce we have woven over the past two years. It feels oddly apt that this house is so empty: stripped back, with nowhere to hide. And that was the point, of course. We're both tired of hiding. Sooner or later, we will have to take a step back into the light and take a look at what we have, and find out if it is enough or not. When I rub the flat of my hand across my face my palm is damp.

"Better get unpacked!" Francis's tone is casually cheerful. He is busying himself with unzipping our suitcases on the bed, pulling out clothes and briskly shaking out their creases. "Might as well get it out of the way." He's smiling, his eyes full of warmth, but I think I can read the message behind it. Time to move on and bury the moment back where it came from.

"I'm going to the bathroom," I say, "and then I'll come and help you." I need a few moments to smooth my frazzled nerves. Heart thumping, I walk down the corridor toward the bathroom. My footsteps sound surprisingly loud on the polished floorboards, sharp echoing bursts of sound in the silent air, and I find myself speeding up. For an instant, I'm oddly reminded of the way I used to hurry down the corridor between my parents' room and my own as a child—the vague supernatural sense that I wasn't alone.

I shake the memory off and push open the bathroom door. It's another gleamingly untouched room, polished to perfection: marble surfaces and metallic fixtures. The window has been left open an inch or two. Light gusts of air are blowing through the gap, ruffling my shirt collar.

I want to move forward, but I am rooted in the doorway, staring at the vase on the windowsill. It's a bunch of pale pink roses, beautifully arranged and just coming into flower. I try to fight the thoughts, but they're too quick for me. A pulse of despair thudding through my body—the split second of inevitability before the memory hits and explodes, too vivid to ignore. All these months of careful suppression and denial, and all it takes is the sight of some curled pink petals. Just like that you're back in my head.

HOME

Caroline, December 2012

I wake up alone again. In my sleep my limbs have uncurled and stretched, sprawling across onto his side of the bed. The sheets are smoothly cold. I can't remember if we started the night sleeping together or apart.

The bedside clock reads a quarter to seven and the room is filled with dull gray light seeping through the curtains. I lie there for five or ten minutes, listening for sounds inside the silence. Nothing. Slowly, I clamber out of bed and pull on my dressing gown. An ache is already spreading across my temples and I reach for the glass of water I keep on the bedside table, but it's empty. I fumble for the little packet of painkillers anyway. Swallow two down, wincing at the scrape of chalk against the back of my throat. The sight of my own face, briefly caught in the tilted mirror by the door, brings a strange throb of vertigo. Pale skin, eyes stained with rubbed mascara. I seldom bother to take it off before bed these days. Like so many things, the point of it seems lost, sucked up into the effort of existing.

I step quietly into the hall. Now I can hear the tinny, relentless waves of sound ebbing from the living room: dramatic music, the staccato murmuring of voices. I push open the door and peer inside. Light buzzes from the computer, faintly illuminating the darkness. He's sitting there, head propped on one hand, elbow resting on the arm of the sofa. Staring at the screen. Some kind of Scandinavian cop show: cream and beige furnishings, haggard men in uniform speaking a foreign language in clipped miserable tones.

"Francis," I say, but he doesn't react.

I'm shivering as I perch on the edge of the sofa. "You didn't come to bed," I say. It's a guess but he doesn't challenge it, his shoulders moving almost imperceptibly in a shrug.

"Fell asleep here," he says at last. "Then woke up." His eyes are flat and glazed, still focused on the screen. These days he seems to do little but sleep, and yet to look at him I am reminded of nothing so much as the black-and-white photos I have seen of torture victims, kept awake for days on end by their captors.

"That's a shame," I say uselessly. If anything is shaking him awake in the middle of the night, I have no idea what it is. His head is no longer the open cave it once was. I used to be able to climb inside it as easily as breathing, read and touch the quality of his thoughts as if they were my own. Now it's a fortress. I spend my time fumbling in the dark for a key that isn't there.

The episode on the computer ends. Credits roll, small and blurred against a gray-washed background. A wall of sound unfurls bleakly behind them; the kind of sinister, relentless music that makes me feel as if I am suffocating. I realize that my skin is hot. For a moment I think I might faint. Blinking hard, I press the tips of my fingernails into my palms. "Are you working today?" I ask. "Any appointments?" As I ask, I realize that I can't remember the last time he definitely went to the clinic. I try to imagine the man next to me sitting in his therapist's chair, listening to his patients. It's worryingly hard to do.

Francis looks vaguely jaded, as if I have reminded him of something unpleasant. "No."

"OK." I hesitate, knowing I shouldn't continue. It's too late; the words are rising to the surface and pushing themselves out of my mouth. "So what are you going to do, then? Any plans?"

He slams the laptop shut, and with it the light snaps out of the room, plunging us into near darkness. "No," he says again after a while. I watch his profile for a few minutes, willing him to turn his head and look at me, but he doesn't move, and in the end I just get up and leave.

In the bathroom I wipe clean last night's makeup and put the new day's on. I focus on my face in fragments, minutely scrubbing and rebuilding one small area after another. I smear foundation thickly over my skin, trace shadow carefully over my eyelids, run black liner to the corners of my eyes. Last, I choose a dark pink lipstick and apply it slowly across the width of my mouth, pressing my lips together to set the color. Only then do I step back and stare at my reflection. I look good. Better than I should. Even so, I don't like looking myself in the eye these days. I'm afraid of seeing something there that I don't want to transmit. Disappointment, maybe, or sadness. Anything at all.

"Mummy, Mummy." Eddie's voice drifts from down the hallway, amicably querulous. I glance at my watch. Already half past seven, and I only have an hour to get us both ready and out of the house. Then the hurried journey to nursery, the bus back into town to the office, eight hours of sitting at my desk turning over the mental picture of Francis on his own in the house and wondering what he is doing, what he is thinking. The thought of it all is exhausting.

I could go back to bed. The idea falls into my head, as clear and sweet as water, as I walk down the hall and push open Eddie's bedroom

door. Call in sick, pull the covers over my head, and sleep for another eight or nine hours. But I won't.

"Good morning!" I sing, opening the curtains. I bend down by
his bed and pull him into a hug, feeling his hot little fingers closing
around the back of my neck.

I start the routine. Clothes, breakfast, toothbrushing. First one
thing, then the next. This is how you get through life. This is how
it goes.

"Nursery today," I tell Eddie. "What do you think you'll be
doing?"

He cocks his head to one side, an exaggerated parody of thought-
fulness. "Don't know," he says slowly. "Playing, I think."

"That sounds about right." I smile and he beams at me, aware
he's somehow made a joke. "Well, make sure you have fun," I add.

At half past eight I brush his blond hair carefully twenty times,
counting each stroke in my head. He is murmuring quietly to
himself, moving two plastic animals across his lap in some complicated game. "What are they doing?" I ask, but he doesn't reply,
swiveling his gray eyes up to mine and narrowing them in what
looks like amused mistrust. Sometimes, his expressions strike me
as oddly mature, brewed for far more than the two and a half years
they have had to arrange themselves on his face.

I finish the brushing and straighten his T-shirt. "Go and say goodbye to Daddy," I say, and he trots eagerly off to the living room. I hear
Francis's voice, complimenting him on his smartness, advising him
to be good and have a nice day. He sounds pleasant, doting even.
Completely normal. The thought lifts me for a moment, and I hurry
down the hall to join them. Sure enough, he's smiling, stroking the
top of Eddie's head with the flat of his hand.

"We'll be off then," I say. Eddie slips out of the room, knowing
the drill, clattering down the hallway toward the front door to wait

for me. The instant he is gone, the atmosphere drops and folds in on itself. Francis sits down again, wrenching the lid of the computer up and intently focusing on the screen.

"Yeah," he says.

"You won't forget to pick Eddie up? I've got that work party tonight, remember?" I ask.

He glances up, irritation flashing across his face. "I know," he snaps. "You told me already. Three or four times."

I bite back the retort that springs to my lips—the accusation that what he remembers these days seems to be entirely arbitrary, filtered through some invisible system that can hang on to the slightest perceived misdemeanor or thoughtless word for years, but let dates, times, and appointments drift through it like clouds of finely spun sugar. "Fine," I say, knowing my voice is harsh and unkind. "Well, don't wait up." The petty cliché falls uselessly between us.

Francis leans back in his seat and sighs, a short, defeated exhalation that raises the hairs on the back of my neck. "See you," he says flatly, and all at once I'm thinking about touching him, wondering how it would change things if I walked over and knelt in front of him and pressed my hands to his forehead, smoothing his hair and kissing his lips. The idea is strangely compelling, but I don't move.

I tell him goodbye, and search my head for something else to say. But there's nothing.

~

The bar is hot and dark, its walls prickled with flashing Christmas lights. Glancing at my watch, I realize it is already almost ten o'clock. I've been dreading this party for days, unable to imagine getting into any kind of festive spirit, but now that it is here, I am flooded with relief. Lately it seems that I have shuttled between the house and the office like a rat on a wheel, the cycle broken only by the odd halfhearted dinner with a friend filled with platitudes and lies that ends by 9 p.m. It has been a long time since I have been out with a group, and dressed in the short sparkly dress that I brought to change into.

Glancing down, I smooth it over my thighs, watching it shimmer, and for some reason I find myself giggling. It strikes me that I am already quite drunk. My head feels pleasantly fuzzy, anesthetized. Across the table, Steven is raising his voice in some vague attempt at managerial authority, rambling out a toast. "We've all worked hard . . . ," I catch. "Time to celebrate and look forward to another year of . . ."

Whatever it is we have to look forward to is drowned in a general chorus of agreement and clinking glasses. It doesn't much matter what it is in any case; in the world of media sales there's only so good it's going to get. I snatch my own glass up and join the toast, not caring that the liquid sloshes over my hand. I tip the rest down, wincing at the burn of alcohol. I don't drink much these days. My head spins, and I decide to go to the bathroom. I nudge Julie next to me, indicating that I want to get out, and she shifts across the bench, half falling into the lap of one of the junior salesmen, who looks none too displeased. "No need to hurry back," she calls, winking at me. I roll my eyes good-naturedly, but I can't help feeling a brief prick of something like envy.

I make my way across the bar. The music throbs loudly around me, but I can hear the smooth click of my high-heeled shoes on the polished floor inside my head, neat and rhythmical, each click vibrating through my body. Spotlights glimmer above me, reflecting and blurring on the smooth metallic bar. As I draw closer I see that

Carl is waiting there, jostling in the throng. He's checking his phone, head bent, squinting at the lit-up screen.

"You'll never get served like that," I say as I pass, and he looks up and laughs, tucking the phone away into his pocket and glancing back toward the bar.

"Yeah," he answers, "got distracted. It's taking fucking ages. I can't even remember what anyone wants."

"Just get a few lemonades," I shrug, grinning.

"Right," he says. "They're all so pissed they wouldn't notice anyway."

"Not like you," I fire back.

"Or you. We're the sensible ones," he says.

"You got it." It's easy to fall into this kind of banter with Carl, as easy as breathing. Eighteen months of walking around on the same bit of carpet for five days a week has created a friendship between us that I have grown to value. He's almost a decade younger than I am, but we have the same attitude toward the job we're in—the same mix of bored familiarity, frustration with our colleagues, and occasional flashes of excitement and interest.

"Having a good night?" he asks, angling himself away from the bar and toward me, the attempt to attract the barman's attention forgotten.

"Yeah—it's great," I say, leaning forward earnestly for emphasis, and as I do so the heel of my shoe twists under me and I trip slightly, lurching against him, the sleeve of his blazer brushing against my bare skin.

"Steady on." He rights me, his dark eyes amused, flashing in the beams of light glittering across the bar.

"Sorry," I say, laughing. "I didn't, um, I didn't mean to throw myself at you like that." It's meant to be a joke, the kind of lightly flirtatious banter that we're well used to making in the office, but somehow in this setting—the dark, perfume-scented air, the red-tinted spotlights, and the crush of people around us—it sounds different. Loaded. Frozen by sudden embarrassment, I find myself staring into his eyes, and I have just a second or two to register that there is something strange in this mutual silence before he shrugs and smiles.

"No worries," he says. "Must be all those lemonades." He twists away from me suddenly, motions toward the barman, and reels off a long list of drinks, seemingly at random. I take a few deep breaths, composing myself. "So," he says when he has finished, "how are you doing?"

"Er. I'm all right." The question is too vague to be worth replying to in any detail. "On the edge of mental collapse," I elaborate lightly. "That was a joke," I add a moment later, though it wasn't really.

Carl leans back against the bar, his arms folded. "Things still bad at home?" he asks.

I shrug. The implicit reference to Francis stabs me unpleasantly, and I realize I have barely thought of him all evening. The picture slides into my head—his body slumped apathetically on the sofa, lost in sleep or oblivion, the lamp burning in the corner of the cold, gray room—and out again. "Not great," I admit. I think about saying more, but I can't quite find the words. Carl knows more than most about the way things are, and we've always been good at striking a balance between friendly intimacy and respectful distance, but tonight I can't trust that I can find that balance. I have the vague, worrying sense that if I started talking, I might not stop.

He's watching me closely, but when he speaks his tone is light. "Well," he says, "if you need a shoulder to cry on you know I'm around."

I nod. I know I should say something, but my mind is suddenly blank. "Better get to the bathroom," I say, and turn abruptly away, realizing that my legs are shaking.

In the bathroom I splash cold water onto my face and watch my reflection in the mirror as the drops trickle down my skin. My eyes look wide and intense, sparkling in the glowing red light. I turn my head slightly, monitoring my profile, evaluating myself from this angle and that. The room lurches around me, and I blink hard, trying to drag myself back down to earth. One more drink, and then I'll go home.

For the next hour I sit in the tight little circle of my workmates, listening to the conversations flowing around me, barely in the room. When I get to my feet and say my goodbyes, Carl comes 'round to wish me a happy Christmas.

"See you in the New Year," he says, "have fun." His hug is friendly, vaguely affectionate. It lasts about two seconds, and yet it sends something unfamiliar ricocheting through me, something I can't quite pin down and examine before it's gone.

"You too," I say, "bye then," and then I'm ducking out of the bar, my heart beating fast again, and my bones rattling under my thin jacket as I step into the icy cold air.

All the way home those few minutes at the bar replay senselessly through my mind. I lean my head against the steamed-up window of the bus. I've never thought about Carl this way before—not really, not seriously—but right now I can't drag my mind away. A harmless little fantasy, I tell myself. No one could begrudge me that. And suddenly the gates swing open and I'm wondering what it would be like to kiss him—to kiss anyone, after all this time. The thought is strange and violent. I press my fingertips against my forehead, which is already aching. I'm going to be in no state to be the perfect wife and mother tomorrow.

When I reach home I unlock the door quietly, and as soon as I do so I can hear Francis snoring. I tiptoe to the half-open door of the lounge and see him sprawled on the sofa, fully clothed, dead to the world. Silently, I turn away and go into the bedroom, closing the door behind me. I pull off my short silver dress, feeling the sequins scratch against my bare skin; peel off my underwear so that I'm standing naked in front of the window. The curtains are open, and I hesitate for a few seconds before pulling them shut, a half-formed thought lurking darkly in the back of my head: a sudden wanton desire to be watched, to be seen.

Throwing myself down on the bed, I reach for my handbag and pull out my phone, seeing at once that it is flashing to signal a new message. I bristle with instinctive knowledge, and sure enough it's Carl's name that appears on the screen.

Good to see you, the message reads. **You'll be glad to know I decided to go home soon after you left. Got to stay sensible, right?**

I try to think of something to reply, but my thoughts slip through me and I can't hold on to what I want to say. I throw the phone onto the bedside table, roll over to turn off the lamp, then lie back and close my eyes, feeling my head swim. It's not unusual for us to text each other, but it's rarely so late at night. In light of my fantasies on the way home, it feels significant. It isn't, of course. It won't change anything. All the same, as I lie there in the darkness and think about him I do something that I haven't done for a long, long time, and when I wake up hours later, dragged out of sleep by dreams that I can barely remember but that leave me hot and frustrated and confused, I do it again.

I't's another day and a half before I look at the photographs in the hall. They are what I expected: luminously filtered snapshots of marital and familial bliss. Caroline holding Eddie and laughing against a sparkling snowy backdrop, both of them wearing woolly hats and gloves; Caroline and Francis strolling hand in hand down a sandy beach and squinting amiably into the sunset, the photo presumably taken by some roped-in onlooker; the three of them seated in the chaos of what must be Christmas morning, surrounded by the debris of multicolored wrapping paper and ribbons. Eleven photographs. They all show different moments, different landscapes, but they've got one thing in common: they all seem to have been taken within the past year. There's no progression, no sense of history. Everything that came before is blank space.

I don't spend as much time looking as I had thought I would. When it comes down to it, they're just pictures. They don't hurt in the way I thought they would either. The happiness in them doesn't feel real, and whoever said the camera never lies clearly never set foot in this place.

I go back upstairs to her bedroom and look around at the mess I've *created. Anyone walking in here would be forgiven for thinking it had been the victim of a senseless raid—possessions thrown helter-skelter across the floor, cupboards and wardrobes stripped and gutted. I haven't bothered to clear up after myself, but I've been very thorough. Any fool knows that if a woman has things she wants to keep secret, she hides them where she sleeps. So far I haven't found much, but I know that will change. I know in my gut that Caroline isn't the type to erase the past, despite the image she tries to portray. She isn't the type to make a choice. She wants it both ways.*

You can't have your cake and eat it. Strange expression. It makes no sense, unless you know that in the past, "have" was used to mean something more like "keep." You can't keep your cake and eat it. You can't hang on to something and destroy it, too. Wanting to keep your memories safe, and at the same time wanting to wake up one morning and find that they've been wiped out of your head . . . Wanting to nurture what you've got, and at the same time wanting to light the blue touch paper and stand back to watch it burn and explode . . . yes. That's something Caroline and I can both relate to.

AWAY

Caroline, May 2015

I get up early and make breakfast in the gleaming show kitchen. Its emptiness is surprisingly restful; at home I can barely move for clutter. Sometimes I fantasize about doing what I occasionally read about in magazines and throwing out everything we own, starting over again with an entirely clean slate. The people who put themselves on record to talk about this kind of thing always look liberated to the point of insanity—smiles manic, eyes wide and evangelical. When it comes down to it, though, I can't imagine doing it. Francis is a hoarder, and I wouldn't even know where to start.

There are eggs and milk in the fridge, if nothing else, and a quick scout through the minimalist kitchen cupboards reveals a bag of flour, so I make a pancake batter and heat a frying pan on the hob. I'm keeping myself busy, but as I stir and pour I can't help thinking about the flowers on the windowsill in the bathroom. Their image hangs there like an eye mote, glimmering pinkly at the corners of my mind.

This sort of thing happened a lot, in the early days. I'd be caught out at almost every turn by a song playing in a shop or an idle turn of phrase from a stranger. Everything reminded me of you, because

I was so quick to make the connections—you were at the very top level, all the time. In the same way, back when Francis and I first got engaged, I found myself noticing other newly engaged women everywhere I went. They were easy to spot, because they wore only one ring on that finger, and often it was slightly too big or too tight, making them fiddle with it. It was like that, only it wasn't a good feeling. It was like it in the worst possible way.

I thought I'd got past that. It was because it was unexpected, I suppose. As I prod at the edges of the batter in the frying pan, watching it bubble and harden, I'm thinking of that afternoon in the market, and the way you grabbed the roses from that stall, saying you wanted me to have them even if I couldn't keep them. The way the petals felt on my fingertips. Cool and smooth. And the scent of them that lingered on my skin, long after I'd left them lying on the station platform and taken the train back home.

I'm still staring at the frying pan, turning the memory over in my head, when I become conscious of a creeping sensation across the back of my neck—a wordless warning. I glance around me, registering the smooth blameless surfaces, the evenly spaced spot-lights. There's nothing here to unsettle me, but I can't shake the feeling that I'm being observed; the instinct urgent and strong, in the same way that the presence of a stranger in the house at night might be sensed, even through closed eyes.

Outside. I swing 'round to face the window, and it's barely half a second—the smooth gliding of a shadow, something half seen and snatched away. It could be a trick of the light, but it's enough. I peer out, looking for something, anything. The neat little square of lawn is empty, but I think I catch the faintest ruffle of the leaves at the far side, the kind of tremulous movement that could be the aftershock of someone pushing past and through.

"I was going to do that!" The sound of Francis's voice makes me jump. He is suddenly behind me, putting his arms around my waist and briefly kissing the back of my neck. "I don't want you to be slaving away over a hot stove all week."

"I know," I say. "Don't worry. I just woke up and couldn't get back to sleep, so I thought I might as well."

"Something on your mind?" His expression is anxious, solicitous. "You look a bit rattled."

My eyes stray back to the kitchen window. The garden is empty and the leaves are still again. I shake my head. "No. It's fine."

"Good," he says. "If you're sure. Well, shall we have these and then go up into London in a bit, when we're ready? I thought maybe we could go to a museum or something, have some lunch out, then, I don't know, do something else. Is there anything you fancy doing?"

"Not sure . . . I'll have a think." Even a year on, it feels new to hear him making plans and suggestions. It has the curious effect on me of wanting to relinquish responsibility completely and be borne along on the tide of his enthusiasm. There is no need for me to steer and control our days now. I don't want to decide what we do or where we do it.

We eat the pancakes at the wooden breakfast table, joking about how Eddie would commandeer them all if he were here. I miss the sound of his voice, and I think about calling Mum, checking that he is all right. I'll do it this afternoon; he'll be at school now anyway, and I'm supposed to be relaxing and enjoying myself.

"I miss him, too," Francis says, reading my sudden silence. "He'll be fine, though. He'll probably want to go and live with your parents permanently by the time we get back."

"I know," I agree, and lean in toward him for a kiss. It lasts longer than I had intended, and for a moment I wonder if we should go back upstairs to bed. Tired by the journey and shaken by the sight of the flowers, I hadn't felt like sex last night, but all at once the idea feels interesting, tangible. I hesitate a little too long, and the moment passes. Francis collects up the plates and takes them over to the dishwasher, talking about an exhibition on light and sound he has heard about that he thinks I might like to visit. It does sound good, actually—the kind of thing I used to go to on my own in my early twenties, wearing my most carefully selected artistic clothes in an attempt to fit in. It also sounds like the kind of thing that Francis would see as entirely inane and pointless.

"We could do something that you want to do, too," I venture.

He laughs. "Whatever you want to do is fine with me," he says. "That's what I want."

I wait in case anything else is forthcoming, but he just stares at me expectantly. "OK, then," I say finally. "Great." For a moment, I experience a strange pulse of nausea—the sense of some veneer cracking. Who is this Mr. Perfect busying himself with the cleaning and tidying up, chatting about taking me out to exhibitions? Not my husband, or not the one I thought I had.

I breathe in deeply, steadying myself, waiting for it to vanish, and it does. "I'm going to pop up the road to that newsagent we saw," I say. "I can pick up the paper and a few bits and bobs while you have a shower?"

"Sure," he says casually, to my relief. I need to get out for a few minutes to clear my head. I want to enjoy this week, and to do that I need to be in the right frame of mind. It's not easy yet, not automatic. I'm not sure it ever will be.

~

I take my time on the way back from the newsagent, knowing that Francis will still be getting ready. Turning back into Everdene Avenue, I stroll down the pavement, glancing at each of the houses as I pass. They are boxy and self-contained, neatly spaced along the road in terraces of three. Occasionally, I see the shadows of their inhabitants moving past windows, gliding in and out of view like fish in darkly lit aquariums. If I moved a little farther away from the road, I would be able to stare into their living rooms. In the tall, narrow tower block we live in now, we're suspended in midair. Beyond the occasional bursts of music and noise that filter through the ceiling and floor, we might as well be living alone in the building. Here, it feels odd to have other people's lives so near that I can almost reach out and touch them.

As I approach number 14, I find myself slowing down even further. This was the house I noticed yesterday—the one with the relatively unkempt front lawn, the trails of dirt and dust running in fine lines along the outside walls. As I come closer I see that there is a silver wind catcher hanging from the front porch, tinkling gently in the breeze; the sound soft and clear, almost menacing. It reminds me of something for an instant, a split second of barely remembered, uneasy meaning that soon twists away.

All at once the front door swings open and a woman is standing there, peering out into the street. She's in her mid-twenties, wearing a dark khaki dress, with long, carelessly tangled blond hair that spills over her oversized black cardigan. "Are you Heather?" she calls out abruptly.

"I—no." Awkwardly, I smile and shake my head, feeling my cheeks flush. "Sorry," I add.

The woman laughs, leaning back against the doorframe and folding her arms. "Well, it's not your fault," she says. "I'm expecting someone from St. Mary's to come 'round about the fund-raising event. Thought you might be her."

"Right," I say, shifting away. "No worries."

"Actually," the woman says, and I have already turned away

from her when I hear her voice pulling me back, "I think I saw you arriving yesterday. You went into number 21, didn't you?" Somewhere along the line, she has drifted away from her own doorway, and is halfway across the front lawn toward me, standing in her bare feet. Her face is open and innocent, and yet I catch a sly, conspiratorial look in her wide green eyes, as if she is intimating that she and I both know that her initial query was a pretext.

That's suburbia for you, I think, glancing back up the street. She seems a little young for a curtain-twitcher, but I suppose this environment breeds it early. I imagine a hotline of coded radio signals, pulsing along the street in secret and tapping into each home one by one—*newcomer alert*—and I can't help smiling. "Yes," I say mildly. "Just staying for the week. House-sitting." Some obscure little scruple stops me from saying *swapping*, rather than *sitting*. I know absolutely nothing about the person whose house we are staying in, have no idea if they would want their movements and their choices relayed to their neighbors.

The woman perches on the edge of the low brick wall flanking the front lawn, fumbling in the pocket of her dress. The movement briefly pushes her breasts out against the material, and as she bends her head, I see the sweep of her long eyelashes and the angle of her cheekbones. She is unusually pretty.

She fishes out a packet of cigarettes and tilts it in my direction, raising her eyebrows inquiringly. I laugh, uncomfortable. "No, thanks." The woman seems unperturbed, putting one to her lips and bending her head to light it.

It feels like a natural end to the encounter, and I start to move away again, but she glances up. "Well, if you find yourself at a loose end," she says, "I'm at a bit of one myself this week. If you fancy a coffee or something? . . . Two lonely women and all that."

Her voice is lightly mocking; for a bizarre moment I wonder if she is flirting with me. There is something unsettling about her proposal—the directness of it, an invitation to play. I look at her; the way she is perched on the wall with her knees drawn up to her chest, the inquisitive tilt of the head. She reminds me of something, or someone. I can't quite catch on to the thought, but the trace it leaves fizzes with significance. It's the same sense of déjà vu that I felt when I looked at her front doorway, and I don't like it.

"Actually I'm here with my husband," I say, a little more sharply than I intended. "But thanks. I'd better get on."

The woman half smiles. She eases herself off the wall, smoothing down her dress, then abruptly turns and walks wordlessly back to the house. I watch her as she goes back inside without a backward glance and closes the door. Guilt is starting to prickle over my skin. I was a little rude to her; she was only being friendly, however bizarre it seems considering that we have never met before. A vague idea stirs—an apologetic note through the door, a conciliatory proposal to meet—but I tell myself I am being stupid. We are only here for a week, and we've come to spend time with each other, not to make friends.

Lost in thought, I find that I am already at the front door and that I have pushed the key into the lock with as much familiarity as if this really were my house. As soon as I open the door I realize that something is wrong; a split second of instinctive recoil even before I have heard the first note. Music is drifting down the staircase. It takes me a few beats to recognize the song, but my body knows it before I do. My heart is thudding and my limbs feel weak and liquid, suddenly awakened.

I haven't listened to this song since the last time I saw you. But I remember the crowded bar where I first heard it with you; that magical sense that everything was fusing together, that it was a perfectly crafted soundtrack to what was happening in the tiny pocket of the room where we stood inches apart, your hands moving lightly to my waist and pulling me toward you.

Francis appears at the top of the staircase, rubbing his hair dry with a towel. "What's wrong?" he asks instantly.

"Nothing," I say with an effort. "Why have you put that on?"

"The music?" He glances inquiringly behind him. "I just found a few CDs in the bedroom, behind the stereo, and it was the one on top. I thought I might as well stick it on while I got ready. Got a bit overexcited, you know—stuff! Possessions! If we keep looking we might even find a book or two."

"Right . . ." I'm not in the mood for lighthearted repartee. I walk quickly up the stairs and into the bedroom. The song is only halfway through, and I am shocked by how hard it is to reach out and switch the stereo off. When I do, a fierce sense of loss rips through me.

Francis is standing behind me, his face anxious and alert. "What is it?" he asks. "Did I do something wrong? Was it . . ." He doesn't carry on, but I know what he's thinking.

"No," I say, but even as I say it, I'm thinking that I'm sure he knows this song is loaded for me. I'm sure I've mentioned it in our long, exhaustive conversations over the months, when the spirit of confession has seized me and his desire for self-torture has been matched by my own savage compulsion to purge these details from my head. Can he have forgotten? "I just . . . ," I say uselessly, looking at him as he stands there unblinking, waiting for me to continue.

"It's nothing," I say at last. We stand in silence for a few moments, and I put my arms around his neck and hold them there, pushing my face into his chest and listening to his heartbeat. When I pull back, I realize my eyes are wet, but I don't blink, and after a short while I feel the tears shrinking back unshed.

"I'll go to the bathroom," I say, "and then let's get out, yes? Take the train up to town and go to that exhibition." I watch his face relax into a smile, and I try to take some comfort from it. Small things can remain small. They don't have to inflate until they suffocate all the life out of the room.

Feeling stronger now, I give him one last squeeze and then gently extract myself, heading for the bathroom. I cleared the flowers out this morning, telling myself that they were beginning to brown and curl at the edges, so the windowsill is blamelessly clear. I go to the window and push it open. Leaning out, I stare down at the street with its cloistered lines of identical houses. A little ripple of sound and movement catches my eye—the sense of a door or window banging shut—and I find myself glancing instinctively across at number 14, but by the time my eyes have settled on the house everything is silent and still.

HOME

Caroline, February 2013

I'm walking along the riverbank with the wind lashing wetly into my face, flattening my hair against my scalp. My fingers are curled whitely around the handles of the buggy, pushing it forward. Eddie is shifting restlessly under the rain cover and I can see his profile darkly through the plastic as he twists his face upward, staring at the rivulets of water that run down the canopy. Next to us, Francis is moving as if he is barely awake. His face is sulkily clouded, eyes staring straight ahead. His hands are shoved into his pockets, and the wind is catching his shirttails, whipping them back and forth in the cold air.

"You must be freezing," I say for the second or third time. He refused to take a coat when we left the house, muttering something about not needing anything. I had argued back, but it had only had the effect of entrenching his position. We had made our way to the bus stop in morose silence, avoiding each other's eyes. Already, before we had even lost sight of our road, I knew the excursion was a mistake.

"I'm not," he says now, shooting me a glance of mistrust, as if he suspects me of some underhanded motive in showing concern. "Just shut up about it, will you?"

"Charming," I snap, increasing my pace, although I know he won't bother to keep up with me. Marching along the bank, I try to imbue my steps with enough righteous indignation to warm me from the inside out. It doesn't work. Despite my long coat I am shivering, and the rain is starting to soak through and settle on my skin in a damp clingy film. Last night, when I had conceived this plan, I had imagined a bracing riverside walk in crisp winter sunshine, a chance to clear the cobwebs. I try these kinds of strategies maybe once a fortnight. Half the time, the dice fall in my favor. The other half, I'm left feeling that I am trying to move an unwilling puppet into action, contorting its limbs into a semblance of life.

After a while I realize that Francis isn't even walking anymore. I look back and see that he is leaning on the iron rails, looking out onto the churning river. For a brief, nauseating instant I see him as if he were a stranger: the disheveled hair and clothes, the strange shuttered expression. I push the buggy quickly back to where he is standing and put my hand out to touch his wet shirtsleeve.

"What is it?" I ask. I had meant to sound concerned, but my voice is harsh and accusatory.

He shrugs, still staring out at the gray lurching water as it rises and falls with the wind. "I think I'm going to go home," he says. "I'm knackered. And this isn't really working anyway, is it."

Even though I cannot disagree, fury surges up in me at losing the day I had planned. I glare at Francis, torn between rage and worry. And above it all, settling grayly, the flat blanket of weariness. It's all piling up: the sleepless nights, the short-tempered moments, the distance in the way he looks at me, the emptiness. We had a few good weeks, but lately it's becoming more and more clear that nothing has really changed.

He's back on the pills. The thought lands like a stone in my gut. I've been trying to paper over the cracks, but it's impossible to ignore. We're back on this same old grinding merry-go-round. His pointless denials and the increasing loss of control. The refusal to admit that this is still happening. My tears and recriminations and supplications that count for fuck-all because trying to reason with addiction is like trying to hold back the tide with the palm of your hand.

"You know," I say, "maybe you should go back to the doctor. He might . . . might be able to help you." I can taste the irony in my own words. This was how it started, more than three years ago now— with my well-intentioned suggestion that he should visit the doctor, maybe get something to help him through a tough few weeks at work. An image of him returning home the next day, jauntily waving a little prescription slip. *Got me some happy pills!* "I mean, sort out some counseling," I say carefully. "Not just a quick fix."

Francis shoots me a look of heavy scorn. "Fuck off," he says wearily.

My mouth opens in shock. It's not the words themselves, but the way in which they seemed to be so close to the surface, so ready to push me away. "Fuck off?" I repeat. "Believe it or not, Francis, I'm trying to help you."

"You seem really fond of that word," he says. "*Help.* I don't need any fucking help. All right?"

"Yes, you do," I bite back tightly, struggling to keep control. "Yes, you do. You're like a bloody zombie most of the time, and I'm sick of it. I'm sick of pretending not to notice—" I cut myself off, seeing a middle-aged couple ambling toward us.

Francis follows my gaze, and his lips twist unpleasantly in an approximation of a smile. "Don't mind us," he says loudly, fixing his gaze on the couple. "We can even speak up if you like, if you're feeling curious?"

"Francis," I hiss, "shut up." I'm flooded with embarrassment, my cheeks hot, clothes prickling damply against my skin. The couple give us a look, half pity, half alarm, and move swiftly away, muttering inaudibly to each other.

"Fucking rubberneckers," Francis says, turning to me with eyebrows raised, and with a light shock I realize that he thinks we're on the same side, complicit. He doesn't understand at all.

"I've had enough of this," I say. "I'm tired of you showing me up, and I'm tired of living like this. What would you do if you were me, Francis? Seriously, what the—" Somewhere along the line, my voice has risen out of control and I realize I'm shouting across the rapidly widening space between us. I watch him amble away with his head down, his interest in the conversation lost, pushing through the crowd of tourists and heading for God knows where. I'm crying, tears running down my face and mingling with the rain, and my left hand is still automatically rocking the buggy. I glance down and see that Eddie is oblivious, a fist pressed to his mouth and his eyes starting to glaze with tiredness.

It's almost an hour before I get him home, and I already know from the nine abortive calls I have made to his mobile that Francis won't be there. Sure enough, the hallway is dark and cold, and I don't even bother to call out his name. I peer at Eddie, checking that he's asleep. He is tightly curled up, his knees drawn against his chest, and his head drooping lazily to one side, blond hair ruffled against the fabric of the buggy. When he is sleeping, he looks so like Francis that it gives me a confused pang of love and longing, sorrow and loss.

I park the buggy in the hallway, then go to turn the thermostat up and peel myself out of my sodden clothes. I put on my fluffy dressing gown, light the candles in the lounge to try to make the room feel cozy, and make myself a hot chocolate. I drink it slowly, curled up in a blanket, feeling warmth seep gradually through me.

I lean my head back against the cushion, and as I do so something catches my eye—a long white envelope, poking out from beneath the basket next to the sofa. There's something about it, the way it seems to have been hidden, that makes me lean across and pull it out. It's bulkier than I had expected, and inside are several metallic strips, each containing ten little blue pills. No prescription slip, no official packaging. Source unknown.

I weigh the envelope in my hand, and it isn't shock that I feel, nothing as sharp as that; a blunted weight of nausea pressing rhythmically at the back of my throat. *No, no, no.* I've known for weeks now, expected it, but it still hurts to be confronted with the reality.

I think about throwing the pills away, maybe confronting him, but in the end I push the envelope back where it came from. I know by now that throwing them away achieves nothing; there will always be more. And besides, if he doesn't know that I know the envelope is there, I can monitor it. See how fast they disappear.

I force my thoughts down, turning away, and I see that my mobile is blinking green on the sofa beside me. At first I think that Francis may have texted, and my hand tenses as I pick it up and jab at the screen, but it's a WhatsApp message from Carl. **Hey there. Good weekend? Looking forward to tomorrow? X**

I stare at the text, unsure at first about what it is that bothers me, and then my eyes drift to the kiss at the end of the message. I scroll back through our conversation, confirming what I already know. It's the first time either of us has ever ended a message this way. Ridiculous though it is, I can feel my heart fluttering lightly, a knee-jerk teenage reaction. I know I shouldn't be feeling like this. It reminds me of the early days with Francis, when it seemed

I was always waiting with bated breath for a communication from him. For a moment I remember those days, and the memory is bittersweet, shot through with guilt and sadness.

Slowly, I type a reply. **Crap weekend, actually. Had a row with F and feel like shit. But yes, am looking forward to it! Should be good.** Grant from the office is playing a gig with his band in a local pub after work, and Carl and I have promised to go and support him. I hesitate, then type an X. My finger lingers over the send button as I look at the kiss, unsure if I'm doing the right thing, unsure of exactly what message I'm sending. I'm on the point of deleting it when I hear the key in the lock, the front door pushing open, and in a panic I hit send, then stuff the phone into my dressing gown pocket and stand up.

I brace myself, gathering myself and standing quite still in the center of the room, waiting to see the look on Francis's face. He appears in the doorway, and there is a dazed, shameful apology in his eyes. "Sorry," he mutters.

"That's OK," I find myself saying. It's cold comfort, but it's something. Enough to make me feel a pang of guilt about the message I've just sent, and to make me want to try to claw this day back to normality. I go over to him and slip my hand into his, and so it begins.

~

The next morning in the office Grant is a ball of nervous energy, full of talk of his gig and his fears over how the new tunes will be received. He checks more than once that Carl and I are still coming, and we assure him that we'll be there. I can't help but look forward to it, especially since Eddie is staying with my parents for the night. I don't have to worry about anything or anyone, not today. The knowledge is seductively light and freeing.

I can't concentrate on my work, and when the clock hits midday I decide to go out early and pick up lunch. I slip out unnoticed and hurry down the high street, hugging my jacket around me for warmth and ducking my head down as rain starts to spit lightly. I'm waiting at the traffic lights, shivering, when I feel the pressure of hands around my waist, a quick hard squeeze before the release. "Boo."

I spin 'round and Carl is there, grinning at me. "You bastard," I say, "you startled me," but I can't help laughing.

"Sorry," he says, not sounding it. "Saw you duck out and thought I'd follow you. Thought you might want to grab a sandwich."

"Yeah, all right." We fall in step together toward the nearby café. I can still feel the sensation of his hands on my waist, the electric jolt it gave me. In the weeks since that night at the bar, it's as if something has been unlocked. We touch each other more often, brief teasing connections that I would see as no more than friendly if they were with anyone else. I tell myself I'm being stupid. I'm a married mother, eight years his senior—hardly fantasy material for him. As for me, it's not the first time I've had one of these little crushes, and Carl fits the mold; married to a man seven years older than me, it's probably no surprise that I gravitate toward the novelty of uncomplicated younger men. These crushes always pass. There's no reason it should feel any more dangerous than before.

We go into the café and pay for our sandwiches, then settle into a table by the window, watching the steady increase of the rain. "Lovely weather," Carl remarks. "Really lifts the mood, doesn't it."

"Yes," I agree, "I can't think of anywhere I'd rather be." We deal in this kind of sarcasm on a regular basis but it strikes me that right now, shielded from the rain in this cozy cocoon, and hanging out with someone with whom everything comes so easily, there's more than a hint of truth in my words.

"I'm getting a bit worried about tonight," Carl says as he attacks his sandwich. "I don't know if you've ever actually heard Grant's stuff, but it's not exactly what people 'round here might expect."

"You're saying it's crap," I state.

"No." He frowns, feigns offense. "Of course not. It's just a bit, well, a bit alternative." He catches my eye, and we're laughing together uncontrollably, hunched over the table in incoherent mirth. My body aches with the release.

"For God's sake," I say, wiping my eyes as I straighten up, "I'm not going to be able to keep a straight face now. Come on, eat up. We should get back, I've got a shitload to get through."

We wander back to the office, and when we get there something makes me say that I'm going to the toilet first, leaving him to go in alone. I barely want to voice it to myself, but I don't want them to see us come in together. In the bathroom, I look myself in the eye, squaring up, telling myself to snap out of it. No one would think anything of it anyway if they knew that Carl and I had been out to lunch. We're friends. Friends.

Back at my desk, the afternoon passes slowly. I work on autopilot, my thoughts elsewhere—shifting, rationalizing. It's almost four o'clock when I look up and across the office to where his desk is. His eyes are already on me, and when he sees my gaze catch his, he doesn't look away. He isn't smiling.

～

Grant sets down two pints of lager and a glass of white wine on the table, then flops into the chair opposite mine. He's flushed with recent exertions, sweat shining on his forehead. "Tell you what," he says, "that was a pretty good one. I think the crowd went for it, didn't they?"

"I think they did," I agree. Underneath the table, I feel Carl's knee nudge against mine for an instant, and when I turn my head to glance at him he's smirking down into his pint. Ten minutes earlier, we had been laughing about the fact that we had never seen a crowd of pubgoers so perplexed by what was going on in front of them. As Carl had predicted, Grant's band had been a fairly radical departure from the usual folksy, gentle outfit that this venue generally attracts: a lot of wordless shouting, a lot of discordant guitar and seemingly random bursts of percussion. "As did we," I elaborate.

"Certainly did," Carl chips in. "When's the next one? Gotta get our tickets booked."

"Oh, no need to book," Grant says modestly. "Just turn up. I think we're playing in Kentish Town next Friday, actually. And after that . . ."

He starts to recite his diary, ticking off dates and venues on the fingers of his hand, complete with a precis of what to expect from each night and some background on the other bands that might be playing. I struggle to concentrate, but all I can focus on is the sudden sense of bodily warmth at the edge of my left hand as it rests on the bench beneath the table. Carl's hand is next to mine, only millimeters away, and then somehow some movement is made—I have no idea by whom—and our fingers are touching lightly.

The contact sends a small, decisive shiver through the length of my body. I look across at him again. He's scratching idly at the side of his face with his free hand, ruffling his dark hair. His attention is seemingly entirely fixed on Grant; he's nodding, making the occasional humorous interjection. The words flow over me like water. All I can think about is the tiny circle of warm air where my hand is touching his, and all at once I realize, with a clarity that shakes me, that this could really happen. It could happen tonight.

I try to work out how this makes me feel. I try to think of Francis, and the home we share with our child. But the happy pictures I want to conjure up feel far away, and all I can think of now is the rising tension in my chest whenever I step through the front door; the clutter that neither of us can find the headspace to clear up, our jagged nerves that brush up against each other whenever we are in the same place for more than a few minutes, and the unbreakable wall that the pills are building up between us.

I have assumed that if this situation with someone like Carl ever got out of hand then I would pull myself back from the brink as easily and smoothly as breathing. Now that it is happening, I find that I can't. I catch Carl's eye for an instant and he looks back at me with a flash of intensity that makes me catch my breath, and I know that there is trouble brewing and I feel it in waves, closing over me and dragging me down, impossible to resist.

Grant is gathering his stuff, fumbling with his coat. "Anyway, sorry," he says amiably. "I'm going on and on about this shit, you're probably bored stiff. I'm going to head off—busy day tomorrow, right? Are you coming?"

I hesitate. "I probably should, yes," I say. "Carl? What do you think?"

Carl shrugs, draining his pint glass. "Can do," he says. "Or I wouldn't mind staying for one more, if you want."

I find that I am nodding casually and automatically. "Sure."

"OK, well, I'll be off then," Grant says, buttoning his coat and slinging his guitar onto his back. "Thanks a lot for coming, guys. See you in the office." And then he's gone.

We sit in silence for a few moments. Despite what we've said, neither of us makes a move toward the bar. I can feel the pulse of my heartbeat, battering lightly and insistently against my skin. His hand has slid fully into mine and our fingers are loosely linked. It is the most innocent caress that we could be sharing, but it feels shocking, almost dirty. I can't remember ever having been so conscious of touching someone, of the nakedness of my skin.

"So," he says eventually, "this is interesting."

I nod, staring intently at the tabletop. I can see the shadow of his reflection in the smeared glass, the lines of his shoulders and his face turned toward me in profile. "Interesting," I agree, "and not very sensible, eh."

"Well, we can stop it if you like," he says.

"Do you want to?" I fire back.

He sighs, leaning his head back against the bench. "Oh, Caro," he says, "what do you think? You know I . . ." He lets it trail off deliberately, letting the echo of the words linger. And as he speaks I realize that of course I do know that I've been lying to myself, for weeks now. The offhand tone is belied by the sudden dampness of his hand in mine, the glimmer of uncertainty that sparks in his eyes as he takes in my reaction. He is not sure either, I realize, exactly what is happening here, or how it will go.

"I don't know what to do," I say softly, and I mean it, no matter how pathetic it sounds.

"Nor do I," he replies. His voice is low and gentle, almost sad, and it strikes me that this may be difficult for him, too. Whenever I have tried to talk myself out of my thoughts in recent weeks, I've told myself that he's nothing but a youthful sexual predator, wanting to carve another notch on his bedpost, but right here and now, nothing seems further from the truth. He cares about me, I think—he likes me. The thought is simple and incredibly powerful. Heat flushes up inside me, making me flushed and dizzy. The music emanating from behind the bar seems to swell and rise, vibrating through the walls.

"I can't hear myself think," I say. "Let's get out."

We walk to the tube station together side by side. I fold my arms across my chest, shivering in the night air. From time to time, we chat about Grant and his band, laugh about something that happened at work last week. It is as if the conversation in the pub has not happened, and as the thought strikes me I realize fiercely that this is not what I want. I want those moments back. I want that intimacy, the meaning that buzzed between us in the silence with his hand in mine. I can't see past it, can't get 'round it. My head is so full of it that I can barely think.

We stop outside the tube and for a moment we look at each other in silence. "Are you coming?" he asks at last.

I shake my head. "I'll walk on to the next one, get on the Northern line." We face each other in the cold, the wind blowing between us. Desire is making me faint, and the whole world blurs before my eyes. He says something that I don't quite catch, but I know that it's a question and I am nodding, moving forward into his arms and tilting my face up to his. My fingers are running through his hair as he holds me against him. His lips are cold. We kiss for maybe twenty seconds. A bunch of teenagers lurch past, whooping drunkenly and appreciatively as they do so.

He releases me and I let my eyes slide up to meet his for an instant. "Don't feel too guilty," he says quietly.

"I'll try." I can hardly form the words in my head, let alone talk. I mumble a goodbye and twist away from him, walking fast down the street. I am still shivering with adrenaline. I turn those few seconds over and over in my head, trying to understand what I am feeling. A strange sense of anticlimax is trickling through me. Whatever it was, it wasn't enough. And it's already gone.

*W*hen I find it, it's in a place so obvious that I hadn't even bothered to look at first: a dark red notebook with nothing printed on the spine, pushed in between two novels on the bedroom bookcase. Hiding in plain sight—it's her all over. I should have made more effort to think the way she does, but it doesn't come easily.

I sit down on her bed and flick backward through it, watching the dates at the top cycle back in time until I reach January, and then I read every page she has written for the next six months. The words are crammed in, crowded almost on top of one another, as if she has had difficulty in squeezing her thoughts into the narrow lines. She writes from the heart, holding nothing back. And yet the first thing I feel when I come to the end is a crushing sense of disappointment. It's so pedestrian, all of it. She's an intelligent woman, and she can talk a good game, but when it comes to emotions Caroline clearly paints by numbers. Some of the phrases she uses are so worn and universal that it makes me wonder if she even realizes that this diary could have been written by pretty much any woman in the country. I think about him all the time. I want to be with him, even when he's only just gone. I can't think about anything else, can't even step back to understand what I'm doing or why. I can't get enough of him and it scares me. *Things like that. Put slightly differently, twisted an alternative way, over and over again, for six months.*

As I expected, the last entry comes on July 8th, and then there's nothing. Just blank space. I read through the whole thing one more time, and then I do what she should have done long ago and light a match to the pages one by one by the open bedroom window, watching the charred black fragments drift down to the pavement below the tower block and disappear into nothing. It takes a long time. Halfway through I feel a strange little pang of guilt, because it doesn't sit well with me to destroy something that someone else cares about, even if that someone is her. I get over it, though.

When it's done I sit there for a while, thinking again about the words I have just burned and their prosaic simplicity, how far they fall from anything that really matters. I suppose it shouldn't surprise me. When it comes down to it, what she's writing about isn't important. It isn't a matter of life and death. It's just love.

AWAY

Caroline, May 2015

I see her coming from the top of the street; a tall slim figure strolling in jeans and a bright blue tank top, her hands pushed casually into her pockets. I'm on the way back from the daily ritual of my trip to the newsagent to pick up the paper. It's obvious that we're on a trajectory toward each other, that our paths can't avoid crossing.

I'll just keep my head down and pass by quickly, I decide. The carrier bag feels slippery in my hand and I can feel my cheeks burning. It's ridiculous—I don't even know the woman. It doesn't matter if she thinks I'm the rudest person she's ever met, or sends a bulletin to all her neighbors saying that they should batten down their hatches and ignore me on sight. I'm only here for a week.

"Hi. How are you doing?" I hear the words coming out of my mouth with a kind of detached incredulity, unable to pinpoint exactly what nuance of social nicety has compelled me to say them.

She smiles brightly at me, seemingly delighted. "All right, thanks," she says, stopping dead opposite me in a way that makes it impossible to nod and hurry on by. "How are you?"

"Fine, fine," I say, and suddenly I'm talking fast, conscious that

I am going to do this, and seeing no point in delaying. "Listen, sorry if I was a bit rude yesterday. I'm not used to strangers being friendly." I laugh in what is meant to be a self-deprecating way, although to my ears it sounds positively unhinged. "I live in a city, you know, not much interaction between the neighbors."

The woman nods, and I see her eyes flick over me subtly and curiously. "Don't worry about it," she says. "I can see it might have seemed a bit weird. To be honest, I'm just bored. I don't know many people around here, and I'm not working at the moment. When I saw someone new, well, I got a bit overexcited." She gives a short, humorless bark of laughter.

"I see," I say, to fill the silence. I find myself staring at her small diamond stud earrings, and the pale pink lipstick she is wearing. I often wear a similar shade, but I don't think it looks as good on me. She looks put together with that sort of effortless elegance that is as rare as it is artful, as if she has just stepped out of a glossy fashion spread from a high-end fashion magazine. She's not the sort of person I would expect to be lonely.

"I was just on my way to a café," she cuts into my thoughts. "You don't fancy a coffee, do you?"

Just as I did the day before, I feel jolted—the directness of the invitation, the oddness of it. Faced with it a second time, it feels impossible to say no. I think for a moment of Francis waiting back at the house, but he was still in bed when I left, nowhere near ready to leave for the trip to Greenwich we have planned. I could send him a quick text from the café, let him know I'll be a bit longer. "OK," I say.

The woman is already walking briskly on, clearly expecting me to follow. "Great," she throws back over her shoulder as I hurry to catch up. "It's not far. I'm Amber, by the way."

"Caroline," I say. "Nice to meet you," I add lamely.

Part of the reason this feels so strange, I realize, is that I am not used to making new friends. That process of laying my quirks and foibles out for inspection and seeing if they are accepted or not is something you do less as an adult. I can remember doing it only once in the past few years. As the thought crosses my mind I wince and dig my fingernails into my palms, trying to fend it off, but before I can slam the door on it I'm back in your bedroom with you lying next to me, watching you watching me with my heart in my mouth, and seeing that look in your eyes that tells me that you see me. *You know me.*

I am following Amber blindly, with no idea of where we are heading. We are turning onto a bijou little high street: a collection of small independent stores and charity shops, and a green-fronted coffee shop toward which Amber walks, pushing the door open and elbowing inside. "What do you want?" she asks.

"Oh, I'll get it . . ." I start to reply, but she shakes her head.

"Don't be silly," she says. "I invite you out, I pay. You can repay me another time." She is looking at me teasingly, almost coquettishly. There is an indefinable charisma buzzing around her that I can't help but be attracted toward, perhaps all the more for its slightly manic edge.

"OK, thanks. Just a filter coffee, then," I say, sinking into one of the armchairs arranged by the window as she heads for the counter. While she gives the order, I rummage in my handbag and realize, with a sinking feeling, that I have left my mobile back at the house. Francis won't like not being kept informed, and I feel a pang of compunction that makes me wonder if I should make my excuses and leave.

Before I can decide, Amber brings the coffees over and sets them down with a flourish, gesturing at the intricately piped pattern of white foam that spirals out geometrically. "Pretty, eh," she comments. "It's the little things, right?" Her left eye flickers in what might be a wink, but it's over so fast that I don't have time to react. "So," she continues, settling down opposite me, "what brings you to these parts, then? Seems like a funny choice for a holiday."

"Well . . ." I hesitate, unsure of how much to say, or even of what the answer is. I choose my words carefully, weighing them up. "I suppose it is funny, in a way," I say. "But we wanted a week away, and didn't want the hassle and the expense of going abroad. I don't particularly know this area, but it's pretty close to central London, and, well . . . The opportunity came up."

"Sure," Amber agrees, shrugging. "Why not. And actually it is nice 'round here, of course. I'm just too used to it to notice, most of the time."

"Have you lived here long?" I ask.

She glances up and to the left in the way people do when trying to access a long buried memory. "About . . . ten months. So not really, no," she adds, grinning. "Seems longer." She leans forward in her seat, lowering her voice to an intimate murmur, excluding the people around us. "Kind of like a prison sentence," she says.

I know I should laugh, but the words set something off in me, and I just nod, not trusting myself to speak. "It's not that bad, surely," I say eventually.

She shakes her head, leaning in farther so that her elbows are resting on the table. "No, of course not," she says. "I like it mostly. It's just—a little stifling at times. A little strange, when you think about it. Living here, you get to know everyone by sight really fast. I see the same people around all the time and we smile and say hi, and you end up wondering what they're thinking about you. Because of course you don't *really* know them, and they don't really know you. You only know what you can see. Little pockets of the same things. You know—mums on the way to the school run, old ladies digging up weeds in their front garden, husbands washing the car on a Sunday. Bits of people's lives. And sometimes I wonder what bits of mine they see, and what they think about them. That's all." She settles back in her seat and blows carefully on her coffee. The foam spreads and scurries, sinking down into the cup.

"I see," I say, to fill the sudden silence. For some reason the hairs on my arms are prickling, sending a shudder down my spine. "So you don't generally invite the people you see out for coffee?" I ask, trying to lighten the mood.

She smiles, a little awkwardly. "No. Not usually. Maybe I'm getting desperate."

"What about the people who live in the house I'm staying in— number 21? Do you know them?" I ask. All of a sudden it seems crazy that I am staying in this, this S. Kennedy's house, when I know so little about them.

Amber looks quickly at me, a frown creasing her perfect forehead. "Well, don't you?" she counters.

Too late I remember that I have told her I am house-sitting, implicitly painting it as a favor to a friend. "Not exactly," I hedge. "We're more friends of friends, I suppose." As I speak, I am aware that she has not answered the question, and so this time I deliberately let the silence stretch.

"Oh," Amber says flatly at last. "Well, no. Not really. Like I say, you see people 'round. But that's about it." She folds her arms across her chest and stares out of the window, watching the cars patrolling slowly past with an intentness that seems disproportionate. There's something about the way she bites the words off, as if she's stopping herself from saying more. I look across at her, eyebrows slightly raised, a smile on my lips. She looks back at me levelly, but she says nothing.

It strikes me that she is unusually self-composed, clearly feeling none of the twitchy compulsion to fill the silence that is currently spreading through me. Perhaps I should admire this, but I can't help finding it strange. It's only a few more seconds before I break. "OK," I say brightly, "sure . . ." and I steer us back onto safer waters.

We chat for a while about the best things to do in the neighborhood, discuss the church fund-raising event that she has been unwillingly drawn into, and after a few more minutes I feel justified in glancing at my watch and saying I should get back to my husband. Amber greets the news with equanimity, draining her coffee cup and getting to her feet before I have even had a chance to pull on my jacket. She bestows another of her smiles on me as we emerge back into the sunshine. "Thanks for coming," she says. "Breaks the day up. Maybe see you around again before you go?"

For a moment I feel childishly disappointed; her words are vague and noncommittal, delivered with no real impetus behind them. "Yes," I say. "That would be nice."

"OK." She backs away from me, gesturing up the high street. "I'm going to carry on and pick up a few things. See you!" She raises her hand in a little wave, waggling her fingers, and then she turns and hurries up the street, her blond hair swinging jauntily in the breeze. I watch her go; the easy seductiveness of her walk, the chain reaction of men's heads turning. A little catch of recognition snags on me.

I walk slowly back to Everdene Avenue, thinking about who it is she reminds me of. I am almost back at the house before I realize, and when it comes to me I give a little snort of surprise. It's myself. Our coloring and our hairstyles are similar, though I don't think I ever looked so glamorous and put together, even when I was her age. But it's something deeper than appearance; there's an energy in the way she moves, the fluid confidence of it, that makes me remember the way I was when I was full of the electricity of being with you and it spilled out of me everywhere I went. It's a light that got switched off almost two years ago, but I can remember clearly how it felt. If I could slip inside her body, I could bring that Caroline back to life.

The thought is tantalizing and sad. The past twenty-two months have been ones of regrouping, restabilizing, but they have also been ones of suppression. I lost the old me—that woman with the in-built confidence, the conviction that life was going to be OK—the night I last saw you. After that, I didn't deserve her anymore.

~

Francis is there as soon as I open the door, fully dressed and clearly agitated, brandishing my mobile like a weapon. My heart drops, and I feel that sickening, scattergun sense of impending discovery. It takes me a few seconds to remember that I have nothing to hide.

"Where were you?" he asks immediately. "You left your phone, and you've been ages. I was really worried."

"I'm sorry," I say, slipping inside and shrugging off my coat. "I bumped into the woman up the road I told you about yesterday. We went for a quick coffee. I know it sounds a bit weird, but . . ." I trail off, aware that there is really nothing more to say.

My eyes meet his, and I see the unspoken question in them—the one he can't seem to stop asking, even after all this time. A great sense of weariness sweeps over me, sucking my energy with it. Maybe it's unreasonable, but I can't help feeling exasperated. Angry, even. It's as if it has been accepted that at any given moment, every few minutes that we spend apart, I might well be filling the time by fucking someone else. In the early days, I would try to fight this with denial. *It's over. It's over.* I said it again and again, and it sounded more unconvincing every time, although it couldn't have been more true. At times I had wanted to explain—to say the words that would make him believe me—but whenever I opened my mouth to try I thought of how his face would change, the way he would look at me and realize what I was. And those words wouldn't come.

Now I face him head-on and speak clearly and quietly. "There is nothing to worry about," I say. "I bumped into this woman. We went for a coffee. That is it." I let the space collect around my words, careful not to overjustify.

Francis nods, his face hardening with the effort it costs him to believe me. "I know," he says.

"Well, thanks for the vote of confidence." It comes out without my wanting it to—a petty, ill-judged thought, pushed into reality by that small defiant part of me that can't seem to stop fighting. As soon as I hear the unpleasant ring to my voice, I want it back.

"Caroline, why are you being like this?" he asks, his expression wounded and uncomprehending. "I didn't accuse you of anything. I was just worried. I've come here to have a good time with you. To have fun. Is that too much to ask?"

"Of course not," I say, trying to soften my tone.

We are standing very close together in the hallway, our faces almost touching. I put my arms around his neck and dip my face into the hollow, breathing in, talking myself down. It's understandable that he is still suspicious, and that it can make him anxious and needy. Even if what I did was explainable, it wasn't excusable. I can't expect its impact to disappear overnight.

"It's OK," he says, "I'm sorry," and he draws back a little and smiles with the familiar mouth that I have kissed for fifteen years. It isn't easy, now, to remember the sullen lines in which it is still sometimes set. That mouth belongs to someone else.

"I'm sorry, too," I murmur, trying to fight the irrational, unreasonable burning in my chest. Sometimes, the better he is, the more enraged I feel.

We stay there in each other's arms for another full minute, loosely clasped, feeling the rhythm of our breathing. His heartbeat against mine is quick and strong. The closeness slowly does its work and calms me. I lean my head onto his shoulder, staring emptily at the wall opposite me.

There's a little alcove that dips just past the front door. It seems to be designed for a coatrack that isn't there. Now there is just a small framed picture, hanging in the middle of the whitewashed wall. A stylized photograph of a park, a river curling diagonally along the edge of the frame and the edge of an ornamental garden beyond. I stare at it for what feels like hours before I realize what I am looking at, and when I do the shock grips me. It's Hyde Park, the bank of the Serpentine where it runs close to Kensington Gardens, the small stretch I once visited with you. It's impossible not to imagine us there, lying next to that riverbank in the photograph. I can feel the grass brushing my bare arms. The heat of the sun beating down on my closed eyelids, and the knowledge of your shadow above, altering the quality of the light.

My stomach lurches with nausea, and all at once I'm thinking of the flowers in the bathroom, and of the music that Francis was playing yesterday when I came back here. For months I have sidestepped these kinds of reminders; these unassuming little trip wires that would have meaning only for me and you. Now they are crowding me so much that I can hardly think. I don't understand how they fit together, and why they're coming at me now, in this unfamiliar place. This house was meant to be an escape—a step out of my life. But this feels less like a step out than a step back in, into a place I don't want to remember.

I don't want to be here. The thought hits without warning, irrational but strong.

"Caro?" Francis is pulling back from my arms, alert to some change in my breathing. "Are you all right?"

I stare at him, and I can't work out if his expression is knowing or naïve. At the corner of my vision, the picture hangs. I can't understand how I haven't noticed it before. "Yes," I say slowly, fighting past the tightness in my throat. "Yes, I'm fine."

HOME

Francis, March 2013

Every day starts the same way. Being wrenched from what passes for sleep and glancing at the glowing orange numbers on the bedside clock, registering that they read 04:00. Give or take a few minutes either way. The air is thick with other people's sleep and the echoes of my own troubled dreams.

There is a pounding in my head, spreading down to my chest. At first it's wordless; a gut instinct, animal and fierce. Then it thins and clarifies. It's the same thing every time. A creeping, nebulous sense that something terrible is about to happen—or maybe that it has already happened, and I just don't know it. Every morning I wake up braced against this blow. It hasn't fallen yet. But it's just a matter of time. I lie there in the dark for a couple of minutes, collecting these thoughts and trying to press them down, but they spring up eagerly again and again, as if suspended on tightly coiled wires.

On this particular morning I drag myself out from under the covers and go to the living room to switch on the computer. I cycle through a few daytime TV programs, not really caring which I choose. I try to concentrate, because it's the only way to switch those thoughts off, but it's incredibly hard. Every line of speech seems to be delivered in some mysterious coded language that takes a conscious effort to interpret and decipher, so that by the time the meaning has filtered through to my brain I'm already playing catch-up and the action on-screen has moved on.

Every now and then I look at the time in the corner of the screen. 04:46. 04:59. 05:23. 06:32. That last hour went fast. I might have fallen asleep, but it's difficult to say. The boundaries are blurred, and getting blurrier. When I was a child I often used to sleepwalk. I remember the strange, fogged feeling of sensing a room around me as I moved, tracing the outlines of familiar objects without quite seeing them. Before the past few months, I hadn't thought about that for years, but now it's on my mind a lot. The memory is chemical. Muscular. I feel it seeping through my bones every day.

My temples feel tight and stretched, and there's a light film of sweat collecting damply at the base of my neck. When I reach out my hand to wipe it, my fingers are shaking. It would be easy to stop it. But I've got a patient today at 11 a.m., so I need to think straight. Just have to ride it out. It's past seven now and getting light, and through the wall I can hear Eddie making the funny little bursts of wordless song he often does around this time. I think about going in to get him up—get as far as stretching out my hand and pressing the pause button on the computer screen. But then I hear the bedroom door opening and Caroline's footsteps moving quickly down the hallway. So there's nothing left to do but sink deeper into my seat and wait. I hear them, the two of them, my wife and my son, getting ready in the rooms around me. They're only a few feet away, but they might as well be on the other side of the world.

Just before she comes in I get up and look in the mirror that hangs over the mantelpiece. I don't know who I'm expecting to see inside it. Not this man with the graying puffy skin and the grooves of worry sunk deep into the corners of his eyes, his face familiar yet strange, like a surreal caricature of myself. For a brief moment, I imagine tapping on the glass. Reaching in to pull him out and hold him up to the light, work out who he is. I see him the same way others seem to see him. Friends with baffled faces, trying to put their fingers on exactly when I stopped giving a shit. *You all right, mate? Seems like it's been a while . . .* My fellow therapists at the clinic, lightly sidestepping into corridors to avoid the kind of idle chitchat they apparently used to live for. My brother Greg, the last time he visited. *Francis, I barely even recognize you. What have you done with my brother?* Glancing out of the window every so often at his banker-wanker Porsche gleaming smugly on the pavement, as if he were worried someone was going to key it. Riffling through his overstuffed wallet, fanning out his platinum credit cards like a conjurer. *How's business?*

The anger flares and fades, a tired old torch I can barely be bothered with anymore. I'm sitting back down and the door is being flung open. Caroline heads across the room and stands in the spot I have just left, checking her makeup and straightening her tailored dress. Her skirt is tight and comes halfway up her thighs. I watch the fabric move and stretch across her skin, and there's a brief pointless stirring of desire.

"I'm off in a minute," she says, her reflection looking at mine in the mirror. It seems that a lot of our conversations are conducted this way, these days. We're staring at each other, but she isn't even facing my way. "I'm dropping Eddie off. I'll pick him up and bring him back for dinner, and then I'm going out again, yeah?"

"Where are you going again?" I ask, but I don't really care what the answer is, and five minutes later I can't remember it.

~

At twenty past ten I step out of the house into the frostbitten air and think about going inside to find a warmer jumper or coat, but it feels like too much effort and before I've decided either way I find that I'm walking down the street toward the station. Everything is too bright. The sharpness of the trees against the skyline sets my teeth on edge and there's a sickly clarity to the piled-up buildings around me. I can almost taste it, bitter and metallic. On days like this the die already seems cast. Just have to get through.

The train journey usually takes only ten minutes but there's some problem on the line and it crawls along, lurching to an abrupt standstill every so often. Opposite me, a young woman wearing furry headphones mouths along to whatever song is blasting into her ears. Her mouth is red and sticky with lip gloss. There's something disgusting about it. Once or twice she glances up, appraises me warily through shuttered eyes. I know I'm not smiling. I could diffuse the tension, look away, or at least soften the frown that I can feel creasing my forehead, but I can't be bothered. No room for social niceties today.

At the stop before mine she collects her bag and sweeps out of the carriage, muttering something under her breath. The old biddy on the next bank of seats gives her a quick look of sympathy, then stares at me pointedly for a few seconds before settling back into her seat. More and more these days I notice that the tide of public opinion is turned against me without me even speaking a word. In a way, it's funny. It's certainly not something I'm about to fight. In fact, sometimes I find myself playing up to it.

I remember hearing once about a celebrity, Madonna I think it was, who could apparently switch the ability of passersby to recognize her on and off at will when walking down the street—one minute blending into the crowd, the next radiating some indefinable superstardom that made people sit up and take notice. It's like that with me, only what I'm radiating isn't stardom but a kind of oppressive, prickly dissatisfaction with the world that pulls uncomfortably on people's coattails and makes them draw back for a second look. Right now, that aura is switched on at full blast.

"Morning, Francis," Sara singsongs as I come in, barely looking up from her notes. She's one of the other therapists who regularly uses this center, and sometimes I look at her sharp, ferrety eyes and the keenness of her gaze and wonder how much she sees through the mask I prop up every time I come in here. I prefer not to think about it.

"Morning," I throw back over my shoulder as I head to my consultation room. I find my own notes, try to think about what I'm about to do. It's a new patient, a man in his early forties. The notes from his assessment are dancing in front of my eyes and I can't hold on to the words. Giving up, I push them aside. I'll start fresh. Better that way.

My hands are trembling again and I pour myself a glass of water, cursing as it splashes over the table beside my armchair. Time to get it together. I can do this as easily as breathing. Used to love it. It makes less sense now than it used to. Now that I've cut down my commitments so much, Caroline's salary outstrips mine by three or four times. By comparison my payslips are hardly worth the paper they're written on.

These thoughts are like little needles, jabbing uncomfortably at my skin. Only one way to blunt them, and I can't do that yet. Focus.

He's lingering awkwardly at the door, a small unassuming man with a thinning hairline and round amber-rimmed spectacles. Nice enough face, but I can see from ten paces that it's been metaphorically stamped all over by some woman's stilettos. I'm rising from my chair, approaching with an outstretched hand. "Mark? Come in." My voice is measured, authoritative. I've had enough practice to know how to sound right when I need to.

A first session is often about little more than listening and prompting; this is no exception. It's a relief to absorb myself in it, to switch everything else off. He's a reluctant talker, often stopping mid-sentence or scratching the side of his face in embarrassment, but once he's under way the words come pouring out fast, a half-whispered torrent of dissatisfaction. It's standard stuff mostly—an underwhelming job, a lack of social activity, unfulfilling relationships with family members. He doesn't mention his wife until thirty minutes in, despite twirling the wedding ring on his finger 'round and 'round every few seconds while he speaks. When he does, it's hesitantly at first, talking 'round the houses, qualifying everything he says with caveats and assumptions.

"She doesn't seem to want to spend time with me." His eyes behind the glasses blink fast and erratically, as if the thought is giving him a minor electric shock. "I mean, I don't know. She has a stressful job, works late a lot. It's understandable, I suppose, if she just wants to relax. But sometimes I wonder if there's something more to it. Another factor. I'm probably wrong."

It takes another ten minutes for the truth to emerge: the late-night text messages that he hears arriving on her phone, the new clothes he's seen in the wardrobe that never seem to be worn at home, the sudden lack of interest in sex or intimacy. Each new detail seems to drag him deeper down into a pit he doesn't want to enter, but they keep coming. It's as if he's assembling the evidence, waiting for a verdict. At last he spreads his hands helplessly wide out, palms up, showing that he has finished. The tips of his fingers are very soft and pink, like a child's. "I don't know," he says. "Do you think she's having an affair?"

The answer is as easy as falling off a cliff. But it's not my place to say it, and instead I say, "Do you?" and watch as he measures his own inward certainty against the reality that it will become if he says it out loud.

"Yes," he says at last. He doesn't seem to want to say anything more.

I could interject at this point, try to force the issue. But sometimes silence is what works, and besides my head is buzzing, my own personal thoughts trying to surface. I'm thinking of Caroline at the mirror this morning, twisting this way and that, evaluating her own reflection in her short, tight dress. I'm thinking how strange it is that I can analyze the relationships of other people with such acumen, even now, and yet when it comes to my own I keep so much boxed up and out of sight that I can't even acknowledge the things I know to be true.

Physician, heal thyself. I wouldn't even know where to start.

"I suppose I've known it for a long time," he says after a couple more minutes, "but I didn't really want to admit it. Now I have to do something, and I don't know what the right thing to do is."

I nod and our eyes meet; a strange little moment of connection that cuts through the construct that keeps me sitting in this armchair and keeps him paying me for my presence. "Well," I say mildly. "Sometimes it can be useful not to do anything for a while."

"That's what I thought," he says eagerly, grasping the lifeline. I can already tell the way this is going to go. There'll be five to ten sessions of angst and repeatedly kindled suspicion that he tries to dampen down with hope and denial, then some revelation or climax that will force him to accept the reality of the situation, and then we'll have to start all over again. Sometimes it's better to turn a blind eye and save your sanity.

"I love her," he says as he stands up to go. "I really do." There is something proud, almost defiant in his tone. I want to tell him that there's nothing noble about loving someone. It's there, or it isn't. It happens, or it doesn't. And trying to talk yourself in or out of it is usually as futile as pissing in the wind. But instead I give a solemn, respectful kind of nod and tell him that I'll see him next week.

When he's gone I stand at the window for a few moments and Caroline comes into my mind again. This time it's as I saw her last night when I lay on the sofa half asleep: struggling to unzip her boots, steadying herself against the wall as she peeled them off. Afterward she stood in bare feet and looked at me for a moment in the dim light. I could tell she was trying to decide whether to wake me. I thought at first she would come over, but then she just folded her arms and leaned back against the wall for a few seconds, her head tipped up intently as if she were listening for something, and then left the room so quietly that in the semidark through my closing eyes I couldn't even be sure she had gone until I felt the coldness and the stillness of the room without her. And when I slept, I dreamed of our wedding day. Her face clear and shining against the summer sky, her eyes looking into mine and the crack in her voice as she said she loved me. It was real, but it wasn't. So little difference between dreams and memories.

These thoughts are rising up again and I don't want them here. Time to go home.

~

Caroline comes back with Eddie at a quarter to six and makes his dinner, then sits down with him at the table to watch him eat it. Every now and then she darts out of the room, then returns subtly changed. New nail varnish, a cloud of perfume. She thinks I don't notice these things about her, but I do. I always do.

"Better get going," she says, looking at her watch. "Get him to bed on time, OK? I've got my phone so call me straightaway if there's any problem."

"Where you going again?" It's difficult to get the words out. The fog is already starting to descend and my thoughts are gently squashed up against each other like cotton wool.

She wheels 'round, frowning. "I'm meeting up with Jess," she says. "You know that."

"Oh, yeah," I say. "That's right."

"I've told you loads of times," she says, and there's something about the way she's looking at me that makes me want to hurt her, the anger rising up again from its readily tapped well.

"Yeah," I say again thoughtfully. "Well, I don't listen to you that much. I guess a lot of what you say just isn't that—" I think carefully about the next word. *Important. Interesting.* "Worthwhile," I finish, and I can't help but feel a little smug at the instant reaction she gives, the little wince that tells me the word has hit home.

"Right," she says, "thanks. Well, I'll be off then." She lingers a few moments longer, biting her lip, trying to work out if there is anything more to say. It's strange looking at her, wondering what exactly she means to me. Sometimes I think she's so precious that tears come to my eyes, make me want to protect her from the world and never let anyone hurt her. Other times I can't actually imagine giving *that* much of a shit if she died.

She drops her gaze, shrugs, and crosses the room quickly to kiss Eddie good night, and waves vaguely in my direction before hurrying out. A few moments later I hear the front door slam.

"Just the two of us," I say to Eddie in the silence. He looks up at me, alert and half smiling, unsure of my tone. I get him into his pajamas and open his book to where we left off last night. "'The prince drew his magic sword and made the castle sparkle,'" I read.

"Sparkly," Eddie says softly, correctively.

I look at the page again. "'Sparkly,'" I say. "That's right." The brightly colored pictures and crudely formed words are blurring in front of my eyes and all at once I really need to sleep.

I stumble through a few more pages and then wrench myself up from the sofa and take him through to the nursery, get him to lie down, and push his favorite toy into his arms. "Good night," I say, and I bend down to kiss his forehead. He makes some little noise of acquiescence and curls himself tightly into a ball. It's going to be easy tonight, thank God. I uncurl his fingers from where they have crept around my hand and as I do so I feel a rush of love rising up from somewhere deep inside, and it doesn't feel great. It feels fucking painful and I don't want to think about why.

Back in the living room I turn the main light off and sit back down on the sofa, reach for the pill packet. Just one more tonight. The foil creases and splits under my fingernail—a tiny, almost inaudible sound that never fails to calm me. I ease the small blue pill out from its casing and hold it between the tips of my fingers for a moment. Somewhere in the back of my mind, the thought flickers that perhaps I don't need this. Perhaps I can cut down, maybe cut them out altogether. But the fuzziness from earlier is already wearing off and there is a faint sharp-edged nausea bubbling beneath the surface fighting to erupt, and before I know it I'm throwing the pill down my throat and swallowing hard without water, and following it with another, and then another. And that's it until tomorrow. Over and out.

Caroline's laptop is red and shiny, covered with fire engine stickers stuck on at awkward angles, presumably by her son. She keeps it in a drawer by her bed, and she's helpfully written down the password in the back of the appointments diary she uses for even more mundane thoughts than the ones in the notebook I burned yesterday. I fire it up. There's nothing much on the desktop, barring a few close-up photos of herself tucked away in an unnamed folder. I look at that inscrutable face for a while—her eyelids smudged with shadow the color of gunmetal, her lips dark pink and slightly parted. I don't think these are for the husband. Actually, I think they're for her.

I have better luck online. Caroline clearly doesn't bother to vary her passwords much; I can't open her email, but her Facebook page unfurls eagerly when I enter the same login details that I used for the laptop. I go through her private messages, reading each one carefully. Everything before the past twelve months has been deleted, but there's a little gold mine in the form of the messages between her and her best friend, Jess. From these I learn that Francis is—for the most part— sticking to his promises, that things are much improved between them, that nonetheless she isn't completely sure they have done the right thing. I learn that she still has trouble sleeping, and that sometimes she has dreams that drag her back to a place she hasn't been able to forget.

There are even a couple of references to what happened on July 9th, 2013. Nothing explicit, of course. She isn't a fool, and she knows that you can't really trust anyone. But all the same, it's enough to tell me that she's desperate to talk. Against her better judgment, she's half hoping that someone will have the ability to crack her open and pour her secrets out. She wants them out of her head. She wants them gone.

Before I log out, I decide to make a change to her profile picture. Currently it's a safe, soft-focus shot of her and her son walking hand in hand along a sunny seafront. It takes me a few minutes' searching to find the kind of picture I want, but eventually I stumble on one that is just right. I save it onto her desktop, then upload it. I wonder how long it will take for people to start noticing, commenting, speculating. What's this all about, Caroline? Are you OK? From what I can see, she doesn't let the mask slip much. She preserves her image for the people around her, because she's scared. She needs some help to rip the scales from their eyes and show them who she really is.

AWAY

Caroline, May 2015

It's not easy to make this place cozy, but we collect together all the cushions we can find in the house and dump them on the sofa, light some candles, and put some background music on the stereo. I step back and consider the room, realizing that it does make a difference. These small changes alter the atmosphere of the house, robbing it of some of its faceless unease. They make it easier to shrug off the strange thoughts and reminders that have been oppressing me. If only Eddie were here, it would almost feel like a normal family evening.

I glance at the photo my mother has sent me earlier in the day: Eddie smiling broadly at the camera, pointing to the "Good work!" sticker on his coat. For a moment, I wish I were there, but I push the thought aside, determined to enjoy the evening ahead.

Francis has cooked a curry, explaining in painstaking detail exactly what he has put into the spice mix and why. It's a bit too hot for my liking but I eat it anyway, gulping down vats of water in between mouthfuls even though he warns me it won't help. After dinner we clear the plates away and decide to play one of the games we brought down with us in the car. Predictably Francis chooses Scrabble and we settle down around the pristine glass coffee table.

"Better not scratch it," he warns. "It's probably rigged up on a hotline to the police station. They'll have us done for vandalism before you know it."

"Oooh," I say, biting my lip and feigning trepidation. "Better get our gloves on."

Francis touches the tabletop with a fingertip, widening his eyes before snatching it back in mock alarm. We're stringing out the joke, but it's the first evening since we arrived that everything feels so natural. It isn't easy, right now, to connect this man with the one I was faced with little more than a month ago, the one who surfaces every so often with savage, unpredictable frequency. The telltale swings between mania and lethargy, the sick regressive pull toward what he still can't quite consign to the past. But they're getting fewer, or at least I think so, and although it feels wrong, part of me knows that they throw the good times into sharper relief, make them more exhilarating and precious.

We begin to play, and sure enough within five minutes it's evident that I'm not going to win. I'm an averagely good player, but Francis has an annoying knack with this kind of game, despite claiming to have played it no more often than I have.

"Hey," I object, seeing the glint in his eye as he slides an X onto a triple-scoring tile, "X U, that's not even a word. It's just two random letters."

"Oh, right!" Francis draws back in pretend deference, squinting at the board. "I'm so sorry . . . although actually, Caroline, you're wrong, because I think you'll find that the xu is a well-known monetary unit in Vietnam."

"As any fool knows," I say sarcastically, shaking my head.

"It's a hundredth of a dong," Francis replies patiently, as if to a small child.

"A what?" I can't help laughing, despite my growing frustration, as I lamely add an S to the end of a word. "Oh, no, now that's just ridiculous—" He has slipped an I neatly in next to an O. "Io?! What the hell is that?"

"A cry," Francis says smugly. "Often of triumph, which is something you'd better get used to hearing, because if I'm not mistaken, I'm smashing this."

"You think you're so clever," I mutter, shooting him a glance across the table, "don't you . . ."

He holds my gaze for a few moments. The candlelight brings out the angles of his cheekbones and darkens the hollows under his green eyes. A little frisson of surprise runs through me; an awareness that this is my husband and that slowly but surely over the past two years he has been merging back into the man I used to lie next to and watch sleeping for hours, unable to look away.

"Your move," he says eventually.

I lean forward across the coffee table and kiss him, softly at first, feeling my breathing quicken as his hands reach out and pull my face toward him, his fingers running through my hair. The pressure of his lips on mine hardens, and I shift away from my seat and climb swiftly onto his lap, wrapping my arms around his neck and arching my back to let his hand slide warmly up underneath the fabric of my shirt. We have done these things thousands of times, randomly punctuating the past fifteen years, and, like anything you've done thousands of times, we're good at them. So good that it's easy to do them without thinking. My mind is clear and blank, white noise fizzing in my head. He's undoing the clasp of my bra and I reach down and wrench down the zip of his jeans and then my own, wanting it quickly and without ceremony, but suddenly he's pulling away and staring somewhere over my shoulder, his face intent and alert.

"Did you hear that?" he asks.

"What?" I shake my head, confused. "I didn't hear anything," I say. "It doesn't matter."

I start to kiss him again, but a second later I hear it, too—a little patter of knocks on the front door, tentative and soft. I glance at the clock on the wall; it's almost ten at night. "Fucking hell," I mutter. "What's that about?"

Francis is getting to his feet, doing up his jeans, and heading for the front door. "Hold that thought," he instructs, throwing me a brief glance through narrowed eyes as he leaves the room. "I'll see who it is and get rid of them."

I sigh and lean back against the armchair, my body humming with frustration, an itch irritated and unscratched. I glance across at myself in the mirror—my shirt half undone, my trousers rucked around my thighs. A thought flickers darkly across the back of my mind: your hands on me, pushing the fabric down. I suppress it instantly, but it's enough to send the moment slipping through my fingers like mercury.

I hear the front door opening and Francis's quizzical hello, then a female voice, low and charmingly apologetic. I can't catch the words, but I recognize the voice. Starting to my feet, I straighten and do up my clothes, then hurry out into the hall. Sure enough, Amber is standing on the doorstep, dressed in a short black skirt and a military-style coat buttoned up to the neck, her long fair hair falling smoothly over her shoulders. She's smiling up at Francis, using the same kind of easy charm that I felt radiating from her in the café. When I appear in the hallway, she glances across and the smile brightens dazzlingly. She gives a little wave, half greeting, half apology.

"Caroline," she says, "good to see you. I hope you don't mind me popping 'round. I was just sitting around at home with nothing to do, and I thought why not come say hello? I hope I'm not interrupting anything."

"No . . . ." I say automatically, seeing that Francis is standing to the side and gesticulating for her to come in.

"Great," she says. "I realized after we'd said goodbye yesterday that I hadn't really arranged to meet up again, and I thought it would be a real shame if you left and I hadn't seen you. You're still here for another few days, right?"

"Yes," I agree, "until the weekend." There would be nothing too odd about this conversation, I realize, if it were being conducted at three in the afternoon rather than ten at night. Amber is making her way efficiently through the hallway and pushing open the door to the lounge, scanning the room with a quick flash of her gaze.

"Not too late, is it?" she asks, as if she has read my mind.

"No, no," I say, overcompensating with my eagerness. Behind Amber, Francis makes a who-is-this-madwoman face, but I can't help noticing the way he looks at her as she sinks down onto the sofa, her skirt riding up her long slim legs for an instant. She's dressed for an evening out at a bar, not a casual neighborly visit. Sexual jealousy prickles over me. It's been a long time since I felt the slightest hint of this about my husband and another woman, and perversely I find that I like it.

"I'll get you something to drink," Francis says, disappearing to the kitchen. I sit down next to Amber on the sofa, and as I do so I catch sight of us both in the mirror and feel another jolt of that odd self-recognition that came to me as I walked away from her the day before. In the flattering candlelight the similarity between us seems accentuated. I can't help wondering if she sees it, too.

She leans in slightly, her voice low and intimate. "Your husband seems nice," she says.

"Oh. Yes—thanks," I say stupidly. There's something disarming about her frankness. "He is." I'm not sure if what I'm saying is true. *Nice* isn't a word I have ever associated with Francis. Unpredictable, mercurial, confusing, charming, infuriating, unknown. All of these, the hierarchy shifting from day to day.

"I miss male company," Amber admits, shooting me another glance from beneath her eyelashes. "My boyfriend works away from home a lot. Partly why I'm at such a loose end this week, you know."

I nod, making a vague noise of sympathy. The news that she has a boyfriend surprises me, despite her obvious attractions. She strikes me as compellingly self-contained, able to keep others at arm's length and study them. She's watching me, her pupils dark and liquid in the soft light. I have the feeling that she knows what I'm thinking, and it unsettles me.

"Here you go," Francis announces, sweeping back into the room with a glass of wine which he presents to her with a flourish. "Cheers. Nice to meet you. Caroline told me about your chat in the café yesterday." His gaze hardens for a moment as he waits for Amber's acknowledgment, and when it comes his face relaxes instantly. He was still not sure, I realize with a jolt of sadness, that I had been telling the truth about where I had been the previous morning.

"Yes. Sorry about that—it was a bit impromptu. You must think I'm stealing her away from you," Amber says, "and on your holiday, too."

"Not at all," says Francis smoothly, settling down opposite us.

Amber lifts her glass to her lips and swallows down half its contents in an easy gulp, not seeming to notice that she is doing so. "The thing is," she says, a confidential note creeping into her voice, "I'm just interested in people. A bit too interested, maybe. It's got me into trouble sometimes." She glances across at me and smiles. "I never learn."

Her face clouds for an instant and then she laughs, knocking back the rest of her wine and wiping her hand delicately across her mouth. Her red painted fingernails sparkle in the lamplight.

Francis leaps onto the topic she has opened up, going off on a tangentially relevant monologue about social media and its impact on how open we all are with our lives, albeit at a safe distance. It's a subject about which both he and Amber seem to have a lot to say, and I let them talk, the conversation washing over me. I'm thinking about the fact that she is sketching herself as an open book, and yet whatever she says seems to have some kind of sub-text shimmering beneath it that I can't quite catch. I can't read her, I realize, because I don't really know her at all.

Slowly I become aware that the interchange is winding down and that Francis is covertly looking at me, sending me a signal to intervene. "So," I say randomly, "is this house much like yours, Amber? They all look pretty similar from the outside." I cringe inwardly at my own inanity, but Amber seems surprisingly ani-mated, taken by the question.

"Actually," she says, getting to her feet and glancing out into the hallway, "it is pretty similar, in layout anyway. Mine is a lot messier. But yes, the basic structure." She stops for a moment, as if ponder-ing something. "I'm going to go to the bathroom if that's all right," she says abruptly. And before I can say another word, she has gone.

Francis and I sit in silence for a minute, listening to the sound of her footsteps retreating up the stairs, then the creak of floor-boards above. The footsteps are sporadic and spaced out, as if she's pacing the length of the first floor and back again.

"She's not going to the bathroom," I whisper. "Not straight

there, anyway." I smile uncertainly, wanting this to be funny, but my limbs have automatically tensed, and I realize that I am holding my breath.

Francis is quiet, listening. For a few moments there is silence, then the creak of a door, softly pushed ajar and released. Before I know it I'm starting to my feet, moving quietly toward the foot of the stairs. I'll go up there, see what she's doing for myself. But somehow, when I reach the staircase and peer up—the smoothly polished wood, the darkness of the hallway above—childish fear grips me and I can't do it. There is something in the cool anonymity of this place that reminds me of the set of a horror film.

All at once I hear the footsteps again, quicker and more decisive this time, heading for the top of the staircase, and I dive back into the lounge where Francis is waiting. In another moment Amber reappears in the doorway, smiling radiantly. Her handbag is back on her shoulder, her coat rebuttoned.

"I'll leave you two to it," she says. "Thanks so much. Caroline, we'll see each other again, yes? Perhaps another coffee or something before you go."

"Yes—of course," I say weakly. She has barely been in the house twenty minutes, and her departure is oddly abrupt, but it seems to have gained its own momentum and I find I'm following her obediently through the hallway and holding open the front door, waving her off into the night.

I close the front door and lean back against it, raising my eyebrows. Francis shrugs his shoulders and heads for the stairs. "People are strange," he says dismissively, but I can see he's unsettled.

"Some more than most." I think back over the past few minutes, and I can't catch on to anything especially incriminating; just a vague sense that Amber has not behaved as most people would have, that there's something about her that feels off-kilter.

I glance back at the table, still set with the Scrabble board. "We're not going to finish the game?" I call after Francis.

His voice drifts down to me from the landing. "Let's give it a miss," he says. "Got better things to do . . ."

With an effort, I remember what we were doing before the doorbell rang. I fumble to recapture the desire I had felt. I can't quite hold on to it, but I know from experience that it will come back if I let it, and I follow him up the stairs. By the time I get to the bedroom he's already half undressed, lying on the bed and lazily undoing the buckle of his jeans. "Coming?" he says.

I nod and start to pull off my own clothes, standing in front of the bed and looking around the room. I have the odd sensation of something being somehow out of place or disturbed. I look carefully in all directions, trying to pinpoint the source of the feeling, but nothing concrete emerges; just a vague sense of difference and unease.

~

In the same way that you can search your mind for a long-forgotten name for hours and then wake up with it instantly clear and present, I notice what it is that is different about the bedroom the instant I open my eyes the next morning. The little dark-purple umbrella that hung over a hook on the bedroom wall next to the mirror has disappeared. I glance 'round the room, in case I have moved it for some reason without remembering, but it isn't there. I think about the footsteps above our heads as we sat downstairs the evening before, and I try to imagine Amber coming in here, swiftly scanning it for anything of interest. Despite the austere minimalism of the room, I can see several items of clearly higher value at a glance. It makes no sense that she would have taken the umbrella.

"So maybe she's some sort of klepto," Francis shouts over the noise of the shower when I go into the bathroom to tell him. He shrugs, energetically shampooing his hair. "There doesn't have to be a reason, does there?"

"I suppose not." For a therapist, Francis is often surprisingly dismissive of human behavior. "Bit bizarre, though," I add, but he has already turned 'round, tipping his head up to the shower and lost to the roar of the water.

I stand there for a few more moments, then quietly leave the room and go downstairs to the kitchen. Once again I'm struck by its unnatural perfection: the spotless surfaces, the regimented rows of crockery and accessories. A shaft of sunlight is slanting through the window, hitting the surface of the worktop like a carefully placed spotlight. The only thing out of place is me.

I try to recapture the easy relaxation I had felt the previous evening, before Amber's visit, but it's gone. My whole body feels tight and strained, as if I am waiting for a blow. I fill the electric kettle with water, flick the switch, and stare at it. I can barely see what is right in front of my eyes.

My head is unexpectedly flooded with pictures, memories. They are flicking through me so fast that it makes me dizzy. I open the cupboard and take out the jar of instant coffee and a mug. I go to the fridge and get the milk. I pour the boiling water out, the thin stream of sound hissing into the silent air.

My body is going through the motions but I'm not here. I'm walking down a dark street toward your car and the air is warm and scented and your hand is in mine and I'm looking up at your smiling face and saying, *I want to remember this, I want this to be a night we don't forget.*

"No," I say aloud.

The sound of my own voice jolts me back and I say it again, louder. My heart is racing and the palms of my hands are slippery.

A shudder passes down the length of my back, bristling my skin. I close my eyes and count. I have not had to do this for months— had thought I would not have to do it again. The effort of blocking these thoughts out is immense.

At last I open my eyes again, and fear rips through me, sudden and fierce. It's coming here that has done this. The flowers, the music, the photograph in the hall . . . all these little sparks of memory fusing and starting a fire that I now have to smother. It doesn't feel like coincidence, no matter what I have told myself. I stare around at this stranger's kitchen, and I find myself breaking away, walking fast through the rooms, trying to find some chink in their anonymity. It's a show home, a shell. I'm opening cupboards, riffling through the limited possessions. They tell me nothing.

I begin looking deeper, excavating. Running my hands underneath the sideboards and sofas, checking behind curtains. I'm in the bedroom, kneeling by the side of the bed, when my hand closes around something hard and smooth pushed against the wall behind the headboard. I pull it out and stare at the small glass bottle in my hand. It's aftershave, and as soon as I see the slashed black logo on the front I recognize it. I bring it to my nose and the smell of it hits me, sends an instant rush of nostalgia right to my heart.

My mouth is dry and crazy thoughts are whirling inside me and I have to do something, something to get them to stop. I'm thinking about the meaningless little messages I exchanged on the house-swap site. I can't even remember what we said. They were functional, formal. Trading details.

S. Kennedy. It's just a name. It might not even be real.

Abruptly, I snatch up my mobile and tap the web address for the house-swap site into the taskbar. I know my login details, can read those messages again. But the site won't come up, my phone freezing, refusing to load.

Fighting for breath, I try to think. I open the available wireless connections and find a new entry in the list, but it's locked. Suddenly the strange little note that was waiting for me on the pillow pops into my head. *Information in kitchen folder.* I run downstairs again and immediately see a navy wallet file leaning against the microwave. I haven't bothered to open it before, but maybe the wi-fi details will be here. I cross the room quickly and snatch it up. I flick to the contents page and scan it. *Wireless Information, p4.* The paper creases and scrunches under my fingers, and my hands are shaking as I smooth out the page I want, and then I'm staring at the little printed words and something has exploded in my head and everything is clear and quiet and still.

Password for wireless internet: silverbirches

The words are in soft focus, blurring in front of my eyes, and I can't push it away anymore—the knowledge of what they mean, that night when I last saw these letters arranged in this precise formation and everything changed. I'm reaching for my phone and typing, connecting to the internet. I open my email and I enter the address I was told to use if there was any problem. There is nothing in my head, no space for thought. I type in the only words that I can bring to the front of my mind.

Are you there?

Then I hit send.

HOME

Caroline, April 2013

The mood in the office on a Tuesday morning is always low-key; the weekend glow faded, and a long stretch ahead until the next one. People chain-drink cups of coffee, hunch themselves over laptops and telephones, mutter to one another unenthusiastically. From his manager's office, Steven shouts out bon mots and questions at intervals through the open door, trying to inject some life into the atmosphere, but it's a losing battle. If offices could talk, ours on a Tuesday morning would say that it didn't want to be here.

It's different for me. My weekends at home are more to be endured than celebrated these days; a grim cycle of hope, frustration, disappointment, and despair. Coming to the office is an exhilarating relief. Although I try to contain myself, being here floods me with energy. It's like being drunk, except that nothing is blurred or out of focus—if anything, the world around me is startlingly bright and clear. I can't focus on my work for more than minutes at a time, and yet I'm getting it done faster and more efficiently than I've done in years. It's a distraction, and the quicker I can clear the decks, the more time I will have to think about Carl.

The instant messenger icon at the base of my screen is flashing. I open the window, glancing 'round first to make sure that no one is watching. **Pretty slow day, eh. Still, only twenty minutes until . . .**

Clock-watching? I write back. For an instant, I let my eyes slide across the room. He's reclining in his chair, staring at his computer with an expression of studied boredom as he stretches out and lazily taps a few words. I glance at my screen. **Too right,** the message says, **and don't tell me you're not.** As I look up, he does the same, and our eyes meet for a couple of seconds. The electricity of it makes me shiver, and I can barely believe that everything around us is carrying on as normal, sullen and oblivious. Impatience rockets through me. I push my chair back and walk quickly over to his desk, clutching my notebook to my chest.

"Do you mind if we go through those accounts now?" I ask lightly. "I know we said midday, but I want to get to the post office at lunch and I'd be better off going earlier."

He stares up at me, expressionless. "Sure," he says. "Just give me five minutes, yeah?"

I grit my teeth. "Of course," I say sweetly. I walk back to my desk and sit down, flipping open the notebook and bending my head over it with an air of studied concentration. Picking up a pencil, I color in between the lines, shading a pattern. My fingers are slippery with sweat. Out of the corner of my eye, I see that the messenger icon is flashing again, but I ignore it, seemingly intent on my task. I know he's watching, and sure enough it's barely two minutes before he gets up and comes over, albeit at a maddeningly slow pace.

"You know what," he says, "I think I'm ready now." He's holding his laptop under his arm, his other hand stuffed casually into his pocket. I stand up and walk beside him through the office, toward the turning that leads to the meeting room. It's the closest we've been all morning. He's wearing the aftershave I like best, and the scent of it collects in the air between us, making my head swim.

I follow him into the room and close the door, shutting the rest of the office out. He puts the laptop down on the desk, plugs it in carefully, and brings the presentation we have planned to discuss up on the screen. Then he turns to me and grins.

"Give me five minutes," I say, "you—" but I don't have time to say anything more because he's crossing the room fast and pinning me back against the wall next to the door, thrusting his body up onto mine and knocking the breath from me as he kisses me. His hands are holding me tightly in place and I push back against them. *No*, he says under his breath, increasing the pressure. My stomach clenches with desire and my fingers tighten in his hair, and I'm completely lost in this, wanting him to wrench my clothes away from my body and throw me down onto the floor. He kisses me again, harder. Time shifts and changes. I have no idea how long we've been doing this. I don't want it ever to stop.

At last his body relaxes and I feel the tension inside me unwind. He holds me more gently, brushes the hair back behind my ears. His smile starts at the same time as my own, and before I know it we're laughing quietly together, still loosely intertwined. We kiss for a few more minutes, slowly now, his lips barely grazing mine. "You know," he says after a while, "you'd think this would get old."

I nod, because I've thought the same myself. It's been almost eight weeks now—snatched half hours in this room or on the occasional lunch break, rationed to avoid suspicion; the odd precious evening out. We spend our time sitting around staring at each other like teenagers, talking and joking and kissing. Nothing else. It's a physical and mental boundary that I don't dare to cross while we are spending eight hours a day in each other's company.

He smooths the crumpled collar of my shirt, his long fingers stroking my shoulder. "Steven talked to me again yesterday, about the transfer," he says, as if he's read my mind. "Looks like it's all going ahead. Couple of weeks and I'll be working out of the Bishopsgate office. So, you know. No longer colleagues." His voice is a strange mixture of regret and anticipation.

"A bit of space to think. I guess it could have its advantages," I murmur.

"It could." He tightens his grip on me again, just slightly, but it makes me push myself up against his chest, wrapping my arms around him. "Only if you want it to," he says, his lips against my neck, "and if we decide it's a good idea."

"We'll have to see how it goes." It's the closest we come to talking about the future. When I am on my own, I spend hours turning it over—trying to understand what on earth we are doing, what the point of it is, what we want, where it is going. Somehow, when we are actually together, these thoughts crumble into nothing.

His hands are snaking up underneath my skirt, running slowly up my thighs and stopping just at the place where my skin meets the thin fabric of my knickers. I know he won't go any farther, not here—not anywhere, until I say. Sometimes it seems that his capacity for self-control is far greater than mine. I am constantly battling the impulse to move his hands exactly where I want them, show him that I don't want to wait anymore. His fingers are stroking lightly across my skin and I lean my head back against the wall, hearing my breath come hard and fast as his mouth finds mine again. He bites down on my lower lip, gently at first, then so hard that I gasp and scratch my fingers across his back, pulling him into me.

He draws back a little, his dark eyes thoughtful and appraising. "You really like this," he says, "don't you." His voice is low, sending a shiver rushing through me. Silently, I nod. We stand motionless for a few moments, regulating the rhythm of our breathing together. I dip my head down to his chest, feeling the warmth of him against me.

"We'd better go back," I say after a while.

"Yeah." He shifts against me and sighs. "You'd better go first. Give me a couple of minutes to calm down, you know."

"OK." I disentangle myself from his arms, slipping out and away. I glance back for a second, my hand on the door handle.

He smiles at me, his eyes creasing at the corners. "Go put your lipstick back on."

I nod, and it hits me again—the bizarre ease that there is between us, the lack of gameplaying or confrontation, the happiness. I know it when I feel it, even after all this time. The trust we had built as friends has moved unexpectedly and fluently into this new context, and it feels natural and right, despite the fact that we both know that it should be wrong. The truth is I don't care. All I know is that I need it, and I'm not about to stop.

~

At six o'clock I'm turning into our road and walking toward home, counting the houses and looking for the light burning in the lounge window. It's cold for April, too cold for the short skirt that I'm wearing, but that isn't why my legs are shaking. I'm replaying the telephone conversation I had with Francis on my lunch break, trying to remember how he sounded. There isn't a lot to remember, because he barely spoke at all. These days my husband only has two modes of expression: long, rambling monologues he rattles off so fast that they veer toward mania, and veiled, monosyllabic utterances that feel more like crossword clues than conversation.

As I turn the key in the lock, nausea flutters and tightens inside me, making me catch my breath. It's insane, to feel this level of trepidation at entering my own home. Gritting my teeth, I stride through the hallway and into the lounge. Eddie is sitting in front of the television, rapt before a Disney video; when he hears me, he waves and calls out a greeting, then returns his attention to the screen.

"Hello!" Francis is smiling, but my heart sinks. His eyes are too bright, his movements sudden and exaggerated. He's overcompensating, trying to make me think that he's fine. The disappointment roots me to the spot and I stand unmoving as he springs up from the sofa and embraces me. "Look," he calls to Eddie, too loudly, "Mummy's back."

"Not for long," I say, slipping out of his arms. "I'm going to give Eddie his bath and put him to bed, and then I'm going out again, remember?"

"Yes, yes, I know," Francis says hurriedly, though his eyes cloud with momentary uncertainty.

I glance at the sofa, trying to see the little white envelope that I've been checking almost every day since I first found the pills. They disappear at an alarming rate, and then they're miraculously and inexplicably restored—dividing and replenishing like cancerous cells.

"You don't seem yourself," I say, realizing as I do so that I have no real idea anymore if this is true. I have no sense of who this self really is. "Look, Francis—" I take a breath, knowing I have to continue. "I know you're taking the pills again. I think you need to—"

"What are you talking about?" he interrupts, his face creased in confusion.

"You're denying it?" My eyes flick toward the sofa again, and I know he sees me look, but he nods.

"Yes!" he declares, eyes forced wide and unblinking in an effort to convince me. "You're being silly. I'm fine!"

I open my mouth, then close it again. I know he's lying, but there's something so powerful and so grimly familiar about this outright denial, this impenetrable brick wall, that I can't think of anything to say.

"Fine," he says again. His hand is pulling at his shirt collar, fidgeting and scraping. I know this state: the strange hyperactivity that so often spirals into agitation, paranoia, and confusion. He lunges forward, tries to kiss me on the cheek, and I find myself shrinking back instinctively, barely able to believe how what I once wanted so much now almost repels me.

His face briefly twists with hurt, but a second later he wheels away from me and scoops Eddie up from the floor, throwing him into the air and roaring. Eddie loves him in this mood, of course, and as I watch him giggling and shrieking it strikes me that it's because he understands it, or thinks he does. The way Francis behaves at these times is like a child, with no adult thoughts or inhibitions.

I take Eddie quickly from his arms. "I'm going to run his bath," I say under my breath, avoiding Francis's eyes.

"Oh dear!" Francis shouts after me, waving his arms extravagantly. "I've done the wrong thing again!" His tone is shifting, turning subtly nasty, but I shut the bathroom door behind me and block it out.

I run the water and bathe my son, scooping up handfuls of bubbles and smoothing them over his skin. He's content, chatting away in a nonsensical stream of consciousness about the video he has been watching. *The boy went to the wood and there was a bright light and I saw the monster but its eyes were blue and I didn't remember . . .*

"That sounds good, sweetheart," I say, stroking my hands over his wet hair. The feel of him calms and grounds me a little.

I dry him and get him into his pajamas, then we snuggle together on his bed and I read him a story. "'And the mermaids swam in the silvery sea, and sang their beautiful song,'" I recite. I try to concentrate, but I can't help thinking of Carl and the things we did just hours ago, the things he said to me and the feel of his hands on my bare skin. It feels strange to be having these thoughts now, with my son curled up beside me, but they're my talismans, keeping me safe from the other thoughts I could be having.

"Night night, Mummy," Eddie whispers when I've finished. His gray eyes are large and solemn as I tuck him in, shining in the semi-dark. I gaze into them, and guilt stings my skin—the knowledge that there is so much he doesn't know, so much that is taking me away from living with him in the here and now, so much time when I want to be somewhere else.

Tears are threatening and I lean down and kiss his forehead, breathing in the scent of his freshly washed hair. "Good night," I whisper. "Love you." He smiles faintly and rolls onto his side, reaching for his favorite stuffed rabbit and burying his face into its neck.

I watch him for a moment, and unease ripples through me, too familiar to need voicing to myself. I remind myself that he will be asleep in minutes, and that he always sleeps through the night; that I always have my mobile switched on; that I have friends no more than five minutes' drive away if they are needed. That Francis is his father, and that he loves him.

Softly, I stand up and cross the room, slipping out of the nursery. I realize that I haven't even taken off my shoes since I came back. I hadn't realized how much I wanted a quick getaway.

"I'm going now," I begin, but Francis is slumped on the sofa, his energy burned out as fast as it came, eyes closed and head lolling to one side. It's impossible to tell if he is asleep or if he just doesn't want to acknowledge me. Either way it comes to the same thing.

I stand there looking at him for a full minute, maybe two;

searching for the man I fell for so hard that when we were apart I used to do little but sit around and dream of him, feeling his absence like a missing limb. These days, it's when he's right there next to me that I feel that absence the most. When he isn't there, I can remember him as he used to be. But when we're together, there's no hiding from it—the knowledge that whatever was once there has gone, and that I'm stuck in limbo, inextricably and unhappily intertwined with someone I can't fix.

In repose his face is almost serene. *I've been unfaithful to you*, I say silently. *I'm cheating on you.* These words have been running through my head for weeks with monotonous regularity. Maybe I'm hoping that at some point they'll unlock something inside me, that they'll find their force and hit home. So far it hasn't happened. I turn away and leave him alone, not bothering to switch off the light.

~

I have dinner with Jess in a little pizza restaurant where the smell of oregano and wood-fired dough curls enticingly through the air, then go on for drinks in a hot, packed bar, the tables glinting with colored candles. We chat about work, our children, things we've seen on television. A couple of times she asks after Francis. The first time I shrug and say he's fine, but when she asks again later I can't help saying that things are no better. She knows more than my other friends do about the way things are between us—has plenty of reasons to believe that our marriage is on shaky ground. All the same, I have never mentioned the pills. I drop hints sometimes, half wanting her to read between the lines, but whenever she begins to I paper over the cracks as swiftly as they opened up.

"Sorry to hear that," she says now, her face creased with concern. "Is there anything you can do, do you think? Is he still cutting down on things at work?"

I nod. "I'm not even sure how much he is working these days. I mean, he goes out sometimes, but I don't really know where he's going." I've long since stopped seeing the proceeds, in any case. They disappear into a black hole as soon as they've arrived.

Jess looks caught off balance, struggling to understand. I don't blame her. Before the past couple of years, Francis and I were the most open couple we knew. We spent so much time together that there was never any question that we wouldn't know all there was to know about where the other one was and what they were doing. "That doesn't sound good," she says.

"It's not." I pause, wondering how much to say. "To be honest," I admit, "sometimes I can't see how things are ever going to get better."

Jess blinks, her expression shifting with surprise. "God," she says. "I didn't realize . . ."

"I'm just feeling down about it," I interrupt, suddenly conscious that I don't want to talk about Francis anymore. "You know how it is. It'll probably pass."

"Right," she says slowly. She's picking wax off the candle between us, her red fingernails flashing in the light. "And, um, dare I ask how things are with Carl?" she asks, her voice carefully neutral. "Is anything resolved there?"

Even the sound of his name lifts me. I want to talk about him all the time, even if it has to be couched in angst and uncertainty. "Not really," I admit. "I mean, it can't last forever, obviously, but it's not easy ending it either, when we're seeing each other every day. I guess we'll have to call it off sooner or later." I know the truth of what I'm saying, but my mind is entirely closed off from it, wrapping itself up in a neat little cocoon away from reality.

Jess nods, pursing her lips in consideration. "How do you really feel about him?" she asks. "I mean, are you—"

"No," I say quickly, because I know what she's about to ask and it isn't something I want to think about. "I mean, we get on so well. Incredibly well. We just click. But he's so much younger than me, and looking at it logically, it would never work in reality, would it . . . I can't explain it," I finish lamely. What I want to tell her, I realize, is that it is fun. I want to tell her in minute detail about what we did that morning, giggle and blush over it like a young girl in the throes of a new romance. But that's exactly what I can't do. In my situation, fun is indecent; mental torture and self-flagellation are the expected norm.

She sighs and nods again. "I hope you sort it all out," she says. "I think it's really sad, you know. It's just so sad." She speaks without agenda or condemnation—simply, honestly—and I can't bear it, because it only takes a few words like these to twitch the veil aside and show me that she's right, and I can't let this sadness overwhelm me. Twisting around in my seat, I drain the last of my drink and reach for my coat.

At the station I hug Jess goodbye and see her onto her train, then pass back through the barriers and pull my mobile from my pocket. **Nightcap?** I text. I am only a few minutes' walk from where Carl lives, and although I had told myself I wouldn't see him tonight, now that the moment has come I can't resist. I imagine him lying on the bed I have never seen, hands clasped behind his head, thinking about me in the same way I'm thinking about him. It's too seductive to pass up.

The answer comes back almost instantly. **Where are you? X Outside the station,** I text back. **So cold and lonely! ;-) X Say no more. I'll be there in ten. X**

I pace up and down on the street, shivering in the cold night air, nerves and anticipation coiling in my stomach. When I see him walking toward me, I feel my face split into a smile, and without thinking I'm running to meet him and almost jumping into his arms, wrapping my own tightly around his neck. He kisses me. His mouth tastes of toothpaste and he's wearing a different shirt from the one he had on in the office earlier today. He's dressed up, made an effort. For me. The thought is giddying and delightful.

"Hello," I squeak, hugging him tightly.

"Are you a bit pissed?" he asks, laughing. He draws back to evaluate, his eyes teasing me.

"Maybe a bit." My head is swimming lightly and I feel a little unsteady on my feet, as if I'm walking on air. "Come on," I say, tugging at his sleeve, "let's go and have a drink in that bar." I gesture toward the place that Jess and I have just left, and he agrees readily, slipping his hand into mine as we cross the road.

"Back again?" the doorman asks as we enter. I think I see a spark of knowing recognition in his eyes: an awareness that a woman who leaves a bar with a friend at eleven at night and comes back ten minutes later with a man in tow is with someone she shouldn't be. Before I have the chance to consider, I give him a wink as I pass. It should feel sordid, this conspiracy of silence between strangers, but it excites me.

The next hour is a haze of mutual appreciation—neglected drinks, jokey conversation punctuated by kisses and caresses. I find myself touching him again and again, unable to keep my hands away. His hair is ruffled and I reach up to smooth it down, then slip my fingers up underneath his shirt and pull him toward me. It feels as if I have never done these things before. Through the haze of alcohol, I have the dizzying sense of everything falling into place—the strange, magical sensation of wanting exactly what

I have right now. I notice that he can't stop smiling at me, and it reminds me surreally of how I used to think of him, back in the days when we were no more than friends. Attractive, but a little detached and reserved, despite his banter—a little closed off. I feel as if I've discovered something incredibly precious. More than discovered: I feel as if I've created it. I've made him happy in a way that I can't seem to make my own husband no matter how hard I try.

On cue, my mobile buzzes in my bag, and I reach absently down to find it. Francis has woken up. **Not on your way back yet? Let me know when you are. Would have been nice if you'd have let me know you were staying out late, but I suppose given what a bitch you were before you left it's not much of a surprise.** I read it over a couple of times, momentarily lost.

"Something wrong?" Carl asks. I shrug, and on a sudden impulse I flip the screen toward him, showing him the message before stuffing the phone back in my bag.

"Hmm," he says, frowning. "Well. Don't quite know what to say to that. He must know a different Caro from the one I do."

The words are casual, but something in them drives to the heart of me and rocks me to the core. It's true, I realize. What is happening here is far more than the sum of its parts. It's a transformation. There is someone inside me who has been fighting to get out for years, and he's ripping open the doors and swinging them wide, dragging her and all her dangerous new desires and compulsions out into the light.

At first it was difficult sleeping in Caroline's bed—even though the sheets were freshly laundered, I couldn't help thinking about her lying there, a ghostly presence beside me. Last night, though, exhaustion overtook me swiftly and deeply. I didn't wake until ten, and when I did, it felt as if I were surfacing from something much greater than sleep. Like coming back to life.

I lie there for a while staring at the chaos I still haven't cleared up in her room, the debris of clothes and papers that mark my investigation. It's another half hour before I drag myself out of bed, get washed and dressed, then pick up my mobile to scroll through my emails. When I see her name at the top of the inbox, I feel something inside readjusting, calibrating—a soft internal blow to the heart. Are you there? It's not that I didn't expect it. I wasn't sure how long it would take, or which one of the subtle clues I left scattered around the house would tip her over the edge, but I knew she'd fall eventually. All the same, there's something about the message that gets me: its directness, its neediness, the acres of blank space packed with invisible meaning around the words.

I leave it unanswered for hours, knowing that she'll be compulsively *checking for a reply. Of all the lessons I could teach her, one of the most valuable would be that the world doesn't always spin to her rhythm. Not everything has to be adjusted to her needs, reconfigured around what is best for her. She isn't the exact center of anything but her own life. She isn't exempt from judgment or tragedy, any more than those who she sees as circling in her orbit.*

What Caroline wants isn't always what she gets. All the same, when I do reply, I find myself falling in line with her. I keep it short and simple, although it's twice as long as her own message.

If you want me to be.

AWAY

Caroline, May 2015

The tube is packed and too hot, even at eleven in the morning on a weekday. We've been standing for more than fifteen minutes now, and every time the train pulls into a station it lurches and almost knocks me off my feet. I keep trying to remind myself to hold on to the rail, but the message doesn't seem to be making it through. I can't focus on anything for more than a few seconds. The strangers around me are fuzzy, sliding off the edges of my vision and seeping away into bright blurs of nothing. Next to me, Francis fiddles unconcernedly with his headphones, turning the music up.

At least underground I can't check my email for a few minutes. I'd forgotten how it felt—the sick compulsive need to look at my phone every five seconds, a needle scratching over and over again in the same groove. I've already convinced myself several times that I've imagined the whole thing. But then I think about that folder, and the password printed inside it, and I'm right back there in the kitchen holding it tightly in my shaking hands and feeling as if I'm falling a thousand feet, with no way of stopping. I can't prove it, but I know the person who created that password is you.

And if that's true, then you're in my house. Looking at my things, touching them. Sleeping in my bed. You've put yourself back in my life.

The thought brings a complex surge of emotion. Confusion, sick excitement, even fear. I don't understand why you would do it this way. I can't reconcile it with the you I knew—unapologetically frank, direct to the point of bluntness. If you wanted to see me, why wouldn't you just send a text? An email? Even as the thought lands, something about it doesn't feel quite right, and I realize that you're *not* seeing me; quite the opposite. You're seeing the way I live, without me there. But why would you want to do that?

"Come on." Francis nudges me, indicating the sliding doors ahead. I push my way automatically through the crowds of people and tumble out onto the platform. We must be at South Kensington already.

I try to gather my thoughts, concentrate on the day ahead. We'd agreed last night to take a trip to the Science Museum, a half ironic nostalgia mission. I glance at Francis, smiling amiably at nothing as he wanders up the platform beside me, and a shiver passes up the length of my spine. I love him, I remind myself. Things are very different between us now from the way they were two years ago. If I really believe what I'm thinking, then even by typing that one question into an email, I've crossed a line that is unacceptable. I owe it to both of us to push it aside, for now at least.

Without realizing it, I've walked the length of the tunnel that leads from the tube station to the museum entrances. Glancing back at the way I've come, I feel a stab of uncertainty at the thought of those lost minutes. I remember this, too. The way that I used to lose time to you when you weren't even there, so sucked up in my thoughts that reality might as well have disappeared into a black hole. I don't like it. It's like my hands are being taken smoothly and firmly from the controls by some unseen force.

"Where do you want to go first?" Francis asks when we enter the museum. He is already striding ahead into the dimly lit ground-floor hall. Above our heads, lights whizz and swoop through colored tubes. There's a faint humming in the air, like static electricity.

"I don't mind," I say distractedly, staring at the maze of corridors around us. Francis has come to a halt in front of what looks like a huge replica of part of the solar system: starred spotlights dotted on three-dimensional models of planets and craters, lines and patterns etched redly into their surface. I stare at it. I have no real idea what I'm looking at.

"Read that," Francis says, pointing at the small dark plaque next to the display. "That's amazing, isn't it?" His face is rapt and engaged, shining with enthusiasm. It's something I always associated with him in the early days, this ability to find genuine interest in almost every aspect of the world, and yet for a long time I thought I'd never see it again.

"Yes. Amazing," I echo. The plaque says something about the formation of stars. Molecular clouds. Regional collapse. I can't wholly take it in, but I can't help but be touched by his eagerness. Reaching out for his hand, I link his fingers through mine. The contact is warm and solid, and my fingers curl automatically tighter. "Is there anything you specially want to see?" I ask.

"Well, there's a gallery on the second floor," he says. "I think it's about maths and stuff."

"OK . . ." I make a doubtful face, and he laughs and rolls his eyes.

"It's interesting," he says, "trust me." The words fall easily from his lips and he's smiling at me, and for a moment I feel my heart lift, as if it believes that maybe it can be this easy and we can live in this little bubble together and I can pretend that the message I sent you means nothing.

I follow him up to a secluded wing surrounded by walls of curved reflective blue glass. The floor is smoothly polished, glinting in the colored light—the muted sound of my footsteps across it echoing like falling rain.

We wander toward what looks like a huge, elaborately carved clock face hanging on the far wall. "It's an astrolabe. It was used to help astronomers measure the position of the stars and planets in the sky," Francis recites learnedly, shooting me a sly look to make sure I'm paying attention.

I nod. "Kind of like a sundial."

"Well, yes . . ." He half nods. "Except, you know. At night."

A beat, and then for some reason we're both laughing—quietly, complicit. We swing away from the astrolabe and move toward the next display, and I'm not even really thinking about it as my hand goes reflexively to my pocket and I pull out my phone again and check the screen. But this time there's a little envelope flashing at the top. A new email.

I swipe across and it's there. S. Kennedy. Six words.

The room lurches and even though I have never fainted before in my life I am filled with absolute certainty that I will do so now unless I sit down. I lean back against one of the cool glass walls and slide down against it, bending my head to the floor and listening to the sound of blood rushing through my head.

"Caroline? Caro, are you all right? What's wrong?" Francis is kneeling down beside me, his hand on my arm, trying to see into my face. "Do you feel sick or something?"

I shake my head, although I am briefly flooded with nausea. I press my curled fists to my eyes, pressing in hard so that when I release them the blue light around me explodes in bursts of color, making me dizzy again. I try to breathe in deeply, but my chest is so constricted that I can barely take in the air. My phone feels hard and heavy in my pocket. I want to look at the email again. I want never to have seen it.

Suddenly I realize that I'm alone. People are wandering up and down the hall, occasionally shooting me covert looks of concern, but Francis has gone. I leap to my feet, ignoring the whirling in my head, and stare wildly around the gallery. He's nowhere to be seen. The back of my top is slick with sweat, my pulse pounding through my veins.

At last I spot him, weaving his way laboriously back toward me, but I don't feel relief—just an inexplicable swell of anger and panic. "Where did you go?" I ask tightly when he is close enough to hear. "What were you doing?"

Concern ripples his face. He holds up a bottle of water. "I was just getting you this," he says, "from the café. I thought you might need it, if you were feeling faint."

"Thanks," I force out, taking the water. "I'm OK."

Francis steps forward, his face still creased with anxiety. "You don't look OK," he says. "You look very pale, and you're shaking, maybe you should sit down again . . ."

His hands are on my shoulders, gently pushing me downward, and all at once I can't bear it, this closeness, this solicitousness— it's too much, it's suffocating me. "Don't," I snap. "Don't touch me." I can hear how it sounds, but I can't take it back.

"What?" Francis says, his eyes wide and uncomprehending, hands still hovering lightly on my shoulders. I bite my lip, trying to resist the urge to twitch them off. "I'm just trying to help."

I know I should apologize, but your words are still pounding in my head. I glance at Francis, and guilt stabs at me unpleasantly— we're meant to be on holiday together—and I can't bear that either. "I don't want any help," I burst out, knowing I sound angry and ungrateful. "I don't want anything from you."

There's a moment's pause, and then his expression changes. "Well, fuck this," he bites back. "I can't win. I thought this week would be fun. But honestly? So far, you've been a bloody nightmare most of the time. Nice and affectionate one minute, on another planet the next. I don't know what's going on in your head, Caro, but I'm starting to think that whatever I do it'll never be enough. Christ knows I've tried." His voice is rising and people are starting to hesitate in their tracks and look in our direction. I motion for him to be quiet, but he ignores me. "I've tried to make up for the past few years," he says, "because I know I needed to, but you know what? Sometimes, it really fucking sticks in my throat that I'm the one who needs to make all the effort, when *I* wasn't the one who . . ."

He is abruptly silent. We are standing inches apart and my whole body is hot and trembling, waiting for his next words. "When you weren't the one who what?" I say quietly when he doesn't continue. "Go on, then."

He looks directly into my eyes. The contact jolts me, makes me feel more present in this room with him than I have felt all day. "When I wasn't the one," he says, deliberately spacing out the words for emphasis, "who dealt with our problems by lying on my back and fucking someone else."

For an instant the air between us lightens, the tension exploded— but what it leaves behind it is a sadness I can't look at head-on, something too raw and intimate to handle. He's wheeling around and away, stuffing his hands into his pockets and walking head down, elbowing his way through the crowd. In the old days, I would have run after him—grabbed on to his coat sleeve, begged him to come back, made a public scene to no avail. But my legs are weak and shaking and the strange blue light is still making me feel dizzy and unsure, and in this moment I want to be alone as much as he does. So I just stand still and watch him until he's disappeared.

~

I walk 'round the museum for another fifteen minutes or so, staring at smooth curved metal structures, twinkling maps of the galaxy. I remember the first time I came to this place, I was struck by a powerful feeling of being on the edge of something huge and unreachable—the minuteness of my own life in the face of the universal. This time it's the exact opposite. I can't see beyond what is happening right here and now. My own concerns have blown up to the size of the world.

Once I'm back at Waterloo, the next train twenty minutes away, I sit down on a cold bench in the station concourse and read the email again. **If you want me to be.** *If you want me to be.* You were always like this: batting my questions back, twisting them into self-reflection, saying that you only wanted to do what was best for me. Your own feelings were slippery, like mercury. I would seize on anything that gave me a clue as to what was going on inside your head, only to find that I was holding on to nothing, no wiser than I was before.

I press the reply button. **I don't understand,** I tap out, painfully aware of how inadequate these words are. **Why are you doing this? Why now? What do you want?** Too many questions. I can't think of what else to say. Somewhere in the back of my mind I've always clung to a little private fantasy, that if I ever had any contact with you again it would be tinted with tenderness and nostalgia—not this strange adversarial game of cat and mouse. For a moment, I can see you as clearly as if you were standing next to me and I badly want you to be there, to throw my arms around you and ask you to tell me it's OK, that there's some explanation for why you're doing this and that it all makes sense.

I put a C at the end of the message, then a kiss. I stare at the kiss, then delete it. Hit send. Already I'm counting the seconds, waiting for a reply. I can't stand it. Regret is surging through me— I'm not sure enough that this was the right thing to do—but it's too late to unsend it and now I've set myself up to wait for God knows how long, my nerves as scratchy and strained as barbed wire.

On the train back I press my forehead against the windowpane and watch the lines of trees and houses rushing by, trying to drive out these thoughts. There's nothing to replace them with. Only the image of Francis's face, and that painful mixture of anger, hurt, and regret in his eyes. It's been awhile since we fought like this. In the early days after I told him about you, exchanging this kind of vitriol felt too dangerous—as if every harsh word could be the one to tip the balance and break us apart.

I would have thought that it would feel safer now, but it doesn't. What we have remains precarious. We've fought hard to keep it against the odds, and the idea of losing it now is bleakly depressing. All this effort and sacrifice, and still no lifetime guarantee. Now I'm stepping off the train and walking quickly through the station and swinging out left toward Everdene Avenue, and suddenly I'm thinking of our wedding night . . . lying awake in the early hours and looking across the dark room at him sleeping next to me, and that powerful sense of tenderness, of knowing that I was where I was meant to be. How frighteningly easily certainty can crumble. How little it takes.

My hands are shaking as I unlock the front door and listen for signs of life inside. As soon as I step into the hall I know the house is empty, but I search in every room anyway, just in case he's there. Nothing. I call his mobile, but it's switched off. I've got no way of knowing where he is and what he's doing. I should know how to deal with it by now, but if anything it feels worse than ever before. Even without the drugs, Francis is impulsive. I can't predict what he might do.

I go to the kitchen and pour myself a glass of water, gulp it down in seconds. The coldness numbs and clears my head, and for a few moments I just stand there looking blankly at the glass. It's tall and curved, etched with a greenish line around the rim. It's the sort of thing I might have chosen. And then the realization hits me, long overdue—that if you're in my house, then I'm in yours.

The thought brings a rush of adrenaline, and I find myself pacing through the rooms again, searching for clues. Everything is so frustratingly anonymized. Bare wooden furniture, no photographs, almost nothing in the cupboards. I remember laughing with Francis when we arrived, wondering who might live in such a strangely minimal place. Now I realize that no one lives this way unless they want to hide something. You didn't want me to know straightaway. You wanted to drip-feed me with information, until the point it took hold and had an effect.

Sinister. The word pops into my head without warning. It makes me stop, arrested in the act of opening the hallway cupboard.

I've spent the past two years believing that you cut yourself off from me because you cared; because it was impossible to do otherwise and because however brutal it might have seemed, it was the sacrifice that had to be made to wipe the slate. I can't imagine what could be strong enough to overturn everything that happened the last time I saw you. Why have you changed your mind?

Something is rising in the back of my mind. Shadows stirring darkly at the end of a long road. Your voice, rising out of nowhere. I press my hands to the sides of my head, willing the image back down. I won't think about it. Not now. Not ever.

I hear the sound of sobbing and I realize that I'm crying, tears streaming down my cheeks and trickling onto my top. Blindly, I move to the front door and fling it open, step outside. There's nowhere to go, but I can't stay here. I see the rows of houses through my tears, with their neat, featureless windows and their prettily kept gardens. Across the street, a middle-aged man is carrying recycling bins out, setting them onto the front lawn. He's watching me through narrowed eyes, frowning, evaluating.

"Caroline?" It's Amber's voice, and I jump. She's appeared out of nowhere, just behind me, stretching out her hand tentatively to touch my shoulder. "Are you OK?"

I wipe my sleeve across my eyes, burning with sudden embarrassment and fighting to compose myself, but it's useless. Mutely, I shake my head. She is staring at me, her lips marginally parted and her smooth forehead creased. Her eyes are wide and unblinking, like painted glass. For an instant the thought flicks through my head that this isn't normal; the intensity of it, the tight focus of her concentration. And yet I can't help but respond to it. When you're at the center of that focus, I realize, it's hard to ignore.

"I've had a message," I hear myself say. The enormity of it all is swirling in my head, but I have to get rid of at least a fraction of it. "From an ex," I manage to say.

Amber nods slowly; her eyes are asking me to continue.

"I'm not . . ." Speaking is an effort. "I'm not sure what it means." Abruptly, the tears dry up. I sit down numbly on the low garden wall. Out of the corner of my eye I see the man opposite straighten up to dust off his hands, give me one last look, and then disappear slowly back toward his house.

Amber sees me looking. "Don't worry about him." She raises her voice, just loud enough that it might carry on the wind. "It's your business, not everyone else's." The man's back stiffens, and he slams the front door behind him without looking back.

Amber turns back, crouching down beside me. "Listen," she says, "is this ex someone you want back in your life, or not?"

"No," I say quickly. The word feels treacherous and unreliable in my mouth. "No."

"Then you ignore the message," she says, shrugging. "It's simple." All of a sudden the concern has dropped away from her face and she's smiling radiantly, as if she has solved a complex conundrum, the final piece slotting into place to illuminate the whole.

I nod, because there seems to be nothing else to do. There's no way of explaining that it's already too late to ignore you. And besides, the question she has asked me is redundant. You can't come back into somebody's life when you're already in it. What happened to us isn't something that can be brushed away or undone. Even after all this time, it's still under my skin.

HOME

Caroline, May 2013

It's Saturday morning and as soon as we get up everything is clear and sweet and simple. The night has passed uninterrupted, free of the erratic noises and movements that so often characterize Francis's wakeful hours before dawn. He's slept in our bed all night; opening my eyes to see him beside me feels gleefully novel, as if we're a young couple waking up together for the first time.

Eddie has slept well, too, and prattles through his breakfast, a barely comprehensible stream of consciousness that could be conversation or the aftermath of some half-remembered dream.

"Come on," I tell him, bringing him his clothes, "arms up," and he obediently stretches, his fingers splayed and grasping for the skies.

"You want to go to the playground," he says, his voice muffled as I pull his T-shirt over his head. It's a strange little quirk that always makes me smile, this inability to differentiate between the first and second person, as if we're two indistinguishable halves of the same whole.

"OK," I say. "We can do that. I'm not sure about Daddy . . ." I glance at Francis, expecting him to make some excuse, but he smiles.

"Why not," he says. "Nice day for it. We could go down to that one near the river?"

"There you go, Eddie." I nudge him gently in the ribs. "Mummy and Daddy will both come. Does that sound good?"

"Yes!" He beams and throws himself between us on the sofa, arms stretched haphazardly in an attempted cuddle. You could take a snapshot of us now, I find myself thinking, and we'd look like a happy family. And although I know that pictures lie and moments are transitory, it's a comfort nonetheless to think that even for an instant the pieces have clicked into place and are fitting together the way they were always meant to.

"We could leave now," I suggest tentatively. A little thought is flickering at the back of my mind—I don't think he has taken anything this morning, and if I can get us out of the house . . . His eyes narrow as he weighs up my proposal. For an instant the air between us sharpens and tightens as I wait. Then he nods, and I'm rushing Eddie into his shoes and jacket, pulling on my own clothes, and getting the buggy ready, filled with a crazy, stupid sense of elation.

We take the bus to the playground, and all the way Eddie sings loudly, tracing patterns in the air with his hands as if he's conducting the passengers. Sometimes strangers can be unfriendly, but today it's all indulgent looks and doting smiles. "He's lovely," an elderly woman comments to us as she hobbles off the bus. It feels like an award, a seal of approval. We've done something right. Francis brushes my hand with his fingertips and for an instant my eyes fill up with tears.

At the playground Eddie runs ahead and launches himself straight onto the climbing wall, struggling to get a grip in his canvas shoes. I buy a carton of juice from the café and stand watching him, laughing as he grudgingly accepts an offer of help from an older boy, then follows him minutes later to the sandpit and stands shyly, waiting to be invited to play.

On the bench behind me, Francis laughs, too, and it strikes me that I haven't heard this sound in a while. I twist 'round and look at him, trying to see him through fresh eyes. So many times in the past few months I've been ambushed by the sharp, unpleasant thought that he's little more than a ruin of who he once was—the pale bloated face, the glazed eyes. But today, with the brightness of the early summer sun streaming across his face and the happiness he radiates as he watches Eddie, he looks almost well.

He catches me staring and gets up, hands in his pockets as he strolls toward me. "He's enjoying it," he comments. A beat, and then he slips his arm around my waist. "I am, too," he says.

I nod, suddenly not trusting myself to speak.

"Listen," he says quietly, bending his head closer toward mine, "I'm sorry. I know I've been rubbish lately. I'm going to change things, you know."

It's the first time for months that he has said these words, and it feels as if some tension has snapped and released. The warmth of the sun is on our faces and we're watching our child playing and even though I've heard it all before, in this moment it feels like there's nothing wrong and nothing in the way.

The words I've held back for weeks are forcing themselves to the surface. "The pills . . . ," I say. "I know you say you aren't, but I know you're taking them again." I hesitate. "Too much," I force myself to say.

For a moment his eyes cloud and I think he will shrug and retreat into another distant denial. Then he gives a brisk, decisive nod. "Yes," he says. "It's stupid. I don't know why."

"I know," I say quietly, and I do believe this. At first I used to search for a reason. I tried to unpick it, rationalize it, trace it back to those first few weeks when a bout of stress at work and a few lingering family tensions had first driven me to suggest that he should get some help. It has taken me a long time to realize that, try as I might, this won't fall into the neat little boxes of cause and effect that I want it to. It's bigger than that. Senseless, irrational, powerful.

"They did help at first, you know," Francis says. "Too well. When you're so used to being wound so tight, and then that gets released, it's a relief. More than that. And of course you want that feeling again and again. It's not just the big stuff—it makes everything easier. But that's the trouble with those pills. The more you take, the more . . ." He breaks off, frowns in half surprise. "The more you need," he says finally, and his face is briefly flooded with almost childlike revelation.

"I understand," I say. I've heard these things before, but there's something different about his tone. Despite the sun, I'm shivering slightly. I have the feeling of walking a tightrope, delicately balanced, not wanting to move too fast. I bite my tongue, watching him as he looks out across the playground at Eddie in the sandpit, his hair fluttering in the wind as he bends his head in concentration.

"I'll stop for good this time," he says at last, his tone heavy with decision. "I don't even want them anymore. When I woke up this morning, it was really good to feel clean. They're just fucking up my head." He pauses, then gives a quick ripple of his shoulders, somewhere between a twitch and a shudder, throwing the thought off. "I feel really good," he repeats. His gaze is steady and for an instant his green eyes widen and look straight into mine.

We stare at each other for a good ten seconds. It has to be nine more than I've spent looking into his eyes in months. The thought comes strong and unbidden. *It's going to be all right.*

Across the playground, Eddie is shouting something. I glance toward him and see him scrambling out of the sandpit and gesticulating toward the seesaw, demanding to be put on. "Hold on," I say and start to move away, but Francis stops me.

"No, I'll go," he says. I watch him heading toward Eddie, lifting him high into the air and placing him gently onto the seesaw, then striding across to sit on the other end. My heart is beating fast. For a moment, an image of Carl comes into my mind. I'm sitting on his lap in the bar we went to last week, my arms laced 'round his neck and his hands holding the small of my back as we whisper to each other. He's listening to me and his face is lit up with eagerness and affection.

I can't quite connect it with reality. A strange sense of division: two lives played out in parallel and sliding smoothly past each other without touching. Rarely, if ever, have I told myself that sooner or later I will have to choose one. But in this moment the truth of it comes to me sadly and strongly, and it's suddenly clear which life it should be.

Eddie is sliding off the seesaw and running toward me, his little legs doggedly pistoning up and down, a smile splitting his face open. Francis powers behind him in his wake. The sunlight is behind them and they're cast in its glow, and my eyes are smarting again because I could so easily lose this and I don't want to, I don't want to.

"Good running!" I cry as Eddie reaches me and I kneel down so that he can hug me. I dip my face to his hair, drawing in the scent of mint shampoo and cut grass. I'll text Carl when I get home. I'll cancel our meeting tonight. The thought gives me a pang of loss, but I push it down. It'll give me some time and space to think, and Francis and I can spend the evening together. A film, maybe a takeaway. Normal things. It's amazing what a powerful rush this idea is.

We stay another twenty minutes, then wander back toward the bus stop. When we're on our way back home I can barely keep my eyes open. It's as if the tension of the past few months has dissolved into nothing and every muscle in my body has relaxed. I find myself slipping luxuriously in and out of sleep, resting my head against the warm glass of the window, Francis's arm slung loosely 'round my shoulders.

"Caro." Hazily, I realize that he is nudging me, trying to rouse me. "He's fussing. Not sure what the matter is."

With an effort, I raise my head and look at Eddie strapped into the buggy in front of us. Sure enough, he's grizzling for no clear reason, his earlier good temper forgotten. Still half asleep, I lean forward and reach for his hand, trying to calm him, but I move too clumsily and knock the rice cake he's holding out of his fist, sending it skidding across the bus floor. He stares at his empty hand, then squeezes his eyes tight shut and screams. Across the aisle, I see people flinch and whisper.

"It's OK," I say uselessly, stroking his forehead. "I'm sorry, that was an accident. I'll get you another." I'm scrabbling around in my handbag, looking for the packet of rice cakes, but when my fingers close on it it's empty. "All right," I say, feeling the first tiny flickers of panic start to lick, "sorry, I don't have any more, but when we get home we'll get you another treat, OK?" He ignores me, turning up the volume of his screams so that his face turns bright red. The noise jars through me, wiping out any trace of relaxation. I can feel myself begin to shake. I can't stand this. I know what he's like when he gets into this state, and there's no way to calm him down. He needs to burn it out, and we're trapped on this bus, still fifteen minutes from home.

Out of the corner of my eye I see Francis looking at us intently but blankly, the kind of expression he adopts to watch a news report of mild interest. "For God's sake," I snap without thinking, "can't you help?"

He looks taken aback, then shrugs, retreating into some private space. "I'm not sure what I'd do that you're not doing."

"Well, Jesus," I fire back, "that's useful. Thanks for nothing." As soon as I've said it, I bite my lip. The intimacy of the morning pops and dissolves. Francis leans back in his seat, eyelids hooded darkly, and turns to stare out of the window. "I'm sorry," I start to say, but I don't know how to continue and Eddie is still yelling, drumming his fists on the side of the buggy for emphasis, and the words are drowned and suppressed.

By the time we get off the bus Eddie's tantrum has died down into the occasional hiccupping sob. We walk down the road toward the house in silence. The sky has clouded over and my muscles are tight and clenched. I force myself to smile at Francis shuffling next to me. "That was stressful," I say lightly once we're inside. "Sorry. Let's just have some lunch, yeah?"

"Yeah, sure," Francis says distantly, reappearing from the lounge. "I'm just going to pop up the road to get some juice, OK?"

"Don't go." The words leap to my lips so swiftly that I don't have the chance to consider them. "Please."

He looks at me, frowning, arms folded across his chest. A beat of silence, the tension stretched between us. "So I can't even go up the road now? You want to police me twenty-four seven?"

"No . . ." I search for something else to say, but nothing comes.

"It's fine," he says, but there's a coldness in his tone that wasn't there before.

I watch him walking slowly away from the house, head down. My mental timer clicks on. If he's less than fifteen minutes, it'll probably be all right. On autopilot, I make Eddie a sandwich and then settle him down for a nap.

Twenty minutes. Twenty-five. Half an hour.

It's almost two hours before he returns and when he does he

stumbles straight to the bedroom, drags the curtains across the window, and collapses on the bed. There's no point shouting but I do it anyway. I stand in the darkened room with tears streaming down my face and call him every name under the sun and none of them makes the slightest bit of difference at all.

~

The bell outside Carl's flat doesn't work, so I stand outside and text him. **I'm here. X** Seconds later I hear the sound of a door opening inside, then footsteps coming quickly down the hall. He pulls me into the dimly lit hallway and kisses me hello, kicking the front door shut with his foot.

"Evening." Already I'm relaxing, unable to stop smiling as the trauma of the day fades away into nothing. He never says he's pleased to see me, but he doesn't need to, and it's infectious. He's wearing a faded red shirt and a pair of black jeans. I think about telling him he looks sexy, but perhaps I don't need to either. These days it seems we can read each other's minds, probably because we're usually thinking the same thing.

"Come in," he says, taking my hand and leading me back into the flat. "Do you want the guided tour? Not really." He answers himself, grinning. I have time to take in polished wood floors, sparse pale furnishings, bare walls. Then I'm in his bedroom and the door has shut tight behind us. In here, there's not much to see. If I walked in here as a stranger, I wouldn't be able to pick up too much about the person who lived here, and perhaps that's the way he wants it. He's private, watchful. I've often seen the way he looks at people, as if he's coolly sizing them up and drawing his own secret conclusions. He doesn't look at anyone else the way he looks at me.

"I can't believe it's only one more week until you go," I say.

We're standing very close together in the center of the room, his hands on my waist. "I'm going to miss having you in the office."

"I'll miss you, too." He narrows his dark eyes, passing a hand over the side of his face, considering. "But it's not like we won't see each other."

"Of course." The truth is that we haven't spoken at all about what will happen when he leaves, beyond the vaguest of references to us having to wind things down eventually. I say it, but I'm not sure I mean it yet. It's easy to believe that these encounters exist in a little pocket of space and time outside judgment and reality. I can't imagine them ending. I can't imagine any other option. The future is blank space, closed off. The thought gives me a brief trickle of dread and I put my arms around his neck to ground myself.

"We should speak about it," he says, understanding my silence, "but maybe not yet, hey."

"Right."

I don't want to talk any more just now, not about anything, and he picks up on it straightaway. Instead he kisses me again, pressing himself up against me, sliding his hands up my body, taking the material of my dress with them and unpeeling it over my head in one swift movement. His hands are warm on my skin and I hear myself gasp as his lips trail over the path they have taken, making me shiver. My fingers are working at the buttons of his shirt, fumbling impatiently with them one by one. He puts his hand over mine, stilling me. *Say please.* His mouth moves almost silently and I whisper the echo back.

Slowly, he moves his hand away, and I'm finishing what I started, running my hands over the muscles of his chest and pushing the shirt off his shoulders as he unclips my bra and then takes me up in his arms without warning, throwing me hard down onto the bed. He stands over me for a moment, looking down.

"Come here," I say, "please," and he lies down on his side beside me, propping his head up on his hand.

"Dangerous times," he says, his breath hot against my neck. His hand is sliding down my body again, hooking into the side of my knickers and pulling them slowly over my thighs, pushing them away. He doesn't take his eyes off me and in this moment I want him so much that the rules I have made about us not crossing this boundary yet crumble into dust. I reach for the buckle of his jeans, tugging at the belt. He stops me again, shaking his head. "Oh, no," he says quietly, "I don't think so. You wanted to wait, didn't you? So we're going to wait."

I bite my lip hard, saying nothing. We're kissing again and I'm pushing myself into the heat and hardness of his body, wrapping my legs around his waist and scratching my nails across his back. I know he likes it but he pushes my hands away, shaking his head again. He reaches down to the side of the bed, scoops up a scarf that is lying there, and then before I know it he's forcing my arms up above my head and tying my wrists together quickly and efficiently, smiling as I gasp. "There," he says when he has finished. "Got you where I want you now."

We stare at each other and for a moment it feels like it's too much to bear, too intimate, like a crushing weight on my heart that knocks the breath from my body. His hand is between my legs and he's stroking me softly at first, then harder, slipping his fingers inside me, and I don't care if the neighbors hear the noise that I'm making because there's no control here, not anymore, and I'm raising my hips off the bed and he forces them down with the flat of his free hand. It hurts and I can't tell if I like it or not, but it barely even matters and for a few burning hot moments there's nothing in my head and I'm looking into his eyes and I've completely forgotten who I am.

Later we get dressed and go out into the dark and sit drinking for a while in a crowded red-lit bar. We speak about work, about our plans for the rest of the weekend. There's no effort and no restraint, and despite everything I can't resist the delight that is sweeping its way through me. It's too easy, too seductive. It wants me, and every cell in my body wants it back.

At the station we stand at the back entrance against the low brick wall and hold each other tightly for a few moments, my face pressed against the side of his neck. *God*, he says quietly, *I want to fuck you*, and the word sends surprise jolting electrically through me—as if my body is remembering that it can be used for something other than an insult, a means of telling me to get lost and leave someone alone. Excitement pulses through me. I lace my fingers through his, gripping on to his hand. I can't speak but I know he understands.

"It isn't just that, though." He pulls back slightly. "You know that, right? I really—" He stops, half frowns in confusion, takes a short breath. "I really care about you," he says, and for all the dampened-down restraint of the word he has used, there's something behind it that makes my heart constrict.

We stand there a few more moments, watching each other. His eyes are kind and liquid, drinking me in. We kiss goodbye, and as we do there's a sudden weird lift of vertigo . . . the brief, queasy realization that I'm in way over my head. I'm no longer sure what is happening here or if I can contain it, and if there was a moment when I could have reined it in, then I guess I didn't know it when I saw it. And now it's too late.

*S*ometimes these days I find myself in the mood for destruction and there's nothing I can do about it. If there's one thing I've learned over the past couple of years, it's that most possessions mean nothing. It doesn't matter if you break them or tear them or burn them. They're replaceable. Most of the time, I don't bother replacing them, which shows how much I cared about them in the first place.

There's a real power in that moment when you hold something in your hands and you know you can do what you want with it. There's so much in life that comes on you hard and without warning. If you can carve out a little space of your own agency, and if that stops you from going insane, surely that's a good thing. So I don't beat myself up about it.

Today the urge arrives and I go to Caroline's wardrobe and fling open the doors, pulling all the skirts and dresses from their hangers onto the floor. It's a production line, with a workforce of one. I use the large metal kitchen scissors, and their sparkling silver blades flash satisfyingly and methodically in my hands. It doesn't take long to build up a rhythm. Cut and slice, back and forth. Material distorting and multiplying, until all that's left is a heaped-up multicolored pile *of useless fabric. Acrylic and polyester, silk and velvet. The cheap and the precious, all mixed up together and reduced to the same level.*

The buzzing in my head dies down when it's done and the tightness across my temples relaxes, but it still doesn't feel as satisfying as it should. Perhaps it's because no matter what I do, none of it seems to get me any closer to her. I can't get to the heart of her. I'm living in her house, inside her life, but still the greatest connection I feel is when I see her words flashing on a screen, sent from miles away. I get to my feet and dust off my hands. Time to write another message.

AWAY

Caroline, May 2015

I **suppose I wanted to see where you lived,** the message reads, **but not to see you. Hope that doesn't sound rude, or frightening. There are things that have been on my mind for a while. I know this is strange. I don't want you to worry too much. You have to do what you have to do.**

I read it several times, finding it more frustrating every time. Each sentence builds a new layer and I can see the links that loop from one to the next, but at the same time they're bizarrely unconnected. A series of thoughts with all the important parts left out, and little hooks designed to snag and confuse. What things? How much worry is too much? What has to be done, and who has to do it? I could stare at these words all day and continue to tie myself up in knots.

This was always the way it was with you. You prided yourself on being so straightforward and simple, but the real meaning of what you said was buried maddeningly deep. I used to think that if I listened hard enough, concentrated for long enough, then out it would pop in a flurry of stars, like a white rabbit from an inverted conjurer's hat. But I never found the mental flourish that would produce it, and it seems I still haven't.

I want to reply straightaway, but I force myself to put the phone aside and carry on with my makeup. I smooth foundation up and over my cheeks, working it into the corners of my eyes. In the unforgiving stream of sunlight that falls across the mirror, I look tired and older than I am. Forty-five, not thirty-five. I reach for the eye shadow, smoothing the brush across my lids, first covering them in pale gray, then highlighting the sweep above my eyelashes with a darker shade. My face seems composed of sections. I'm painting by numbers, coloring it in. I draw a black line of eyeliner and stroke mascara across my lashes, then fill in my lips with pale pink lipstick. I'm unpleasantly reminded of the way I used to stand in front of the bathroom mirror, back when things were at their worst, assembling this precarious house of cards.

Things are different now, I remind myself. Francis came back at just after nine last night, subdued and monosyllabic, but still himself. It shocked me, the level of relief I felt—the ease with which I had plunged back into expecting the worst. All evening, the words my counselor once said to me had circled 'round my head. *It's a long road. And that uncertainty will always be there. This is the reality of it, when you live with any kind of addict. It will be up and down, and when it's up, you will never be entirely sure that it will be this way forever. Some people can cope with this, and some people can't.* Sometimes it seems that I've spent the past two years waiting for the answer to the unasked question behind these words. *Can you cope with it, Caroline?* I still don't know, and I'm starting to think that I'll be dead before I find out—and then I'll have answered the question by default, through limbo rather than decision.

I snatch up my hairbrush and brush my hair methodically, dragging the brush through the tangles. My thoughts are working overtime, buzzing insistently in my head. Part of me is wondering if I should walk out of this house and take the first train back home. I imagine walking in through my own front door and finding you there, looking you in the eye. Even the thought gives me a rush of longing and terror. I can't do it. Shouldn't want to.

I look back at the message. Once again, I have the sense that something doesn't feel right. I still can't think of any reason that you would want to be in my house without me there. Although, of course, it isn't only mine. With a sudden throb of disquiet, I wonder if this is the closest you can get to my life with Francis, with Eddie. Because, of course, when we were together, it was entirely sealed off. You rarely asked about it, and I had always thought that it suited you to pretend that we existed independently, in a hot little bubble of excitement and desire. Just as it did me. But perhaps you feel differently now . . . perhaps you have turned into someone else.

As the thought flashes across my mind, I can't help testing it, prodding it, wondering if this might be right. It's been a long time, and so much has happened since that terrible night when I last saw you. I picture you again, and now I'm imagining you riffling through my husband's things, trying to get beneath his skin. Picking up his clothes, looking through his papers. Trying to understand our marriage, trying to understand why I'm still there. Trying to work out how happy we are, and wondering if I deserve it, after what I put you through.

I could talk to Francis. The thought rises up, fresh and tantalizing. But when I think about it, it feels as crazy and undoable as placing an atom bomb at his feet. If a couple of emails can rock my equilibrium so much that it could lead to the scene in the museum yesterday and the silent watchful night we've just experienced, lying side by side, not speaking as night became day, then there is no way that I can go to him and inform him that I think you are currently living in our house. I've worked too hard. I haven't come this far to fuck it up. And for the first time I feel a surge of anger race through me—at you, and at myself and the fallibility of my own defenses.

Riding the wave, I pick up my phone again and tap out a response to the email. **I don't know what you expect me to think. It's been almost two years. I have no idea why you're really doing this or why you even want to be in touch with me at all after what happened. I don't understand it. I want you** – and before I can finish the sentence my thumb has skidded impatiently across the screen and the message has sent. Staring at it in horror, I swallow. *I want you to leave me alone.* That's what I meant to say. What I wanted to say. I hit reply again, but now I find I can't do it. By itself, it looks too stark, too certain. I can't be sure it's how I really feel.

That sentence wasn't finished, I write. **Just in case you were getting ideas above your station.** Reading that last line over, I wince. No. That sounds light and flirtatious, the opposite of how I'm feeling. I delete it. **It doesn't matter,** I write instead. Hit send again. The message is useless. Ridiculous.

Throwing the phone down, I put my face into my cupped palms and breathe inward, then shakily out again, trying to steady myself. Relax. Calm down. But of course the only one who had ever really relaxed me was you.

As I raise my head, the bedroom door swings open and Francis puts his head cautiously 'round, edging inside when he sees me sitting at the dressing table.

"Hi," he says, leaning back against the wall. He looks tired, too, but not hostile. "Look, we should talk. I'm sorry I disappeared yesterday. I knew it would worry you, but I needed to get away and think. I knew if I stayed it would just end up in a bigger fight and I didn't want either of us to say anything else we didn't mean."

He pauses, as if to allow me the chance to point out some of these things, but my mind is still spinning and I can't remember anything I might have said. He sighs, leaning forward away from the wall and coming to perch on the edge of the dressing table.

"I shouldn't have said what I did," he says, "about you and Carl." The name falls like a stone between us, making me blink in shock. I can't remember the last time he said it. It must have been months ago. "I really don't think about it that much," he says quietly, "anymore."

I remember the hurt that twisted his face as he said those words to me yesterday—the speed and alacrity with which they seemed to come, as if wrenched up from some private and carefully cultivated well of resentment. I have no doubt that there are many more, patiently living out their time in the recesses of his mind, awaiting their turn in the spotlight. But his words are all I need right now to be grateful, and I lean my head against his side, closing my eyes as he rests the flat of his hand on my hair. "That's OK," I say into his shirt. "I'm sorry, too. Let's try to forget about it, shall we? Move on."

"That's what I thought." He puts a hand underneath my chin, moving my face up to look into his. "I thought maybe we could drive down to the coast today, if you don't mind an idea from left field. It looks really nice outside. I looked it up and we could be in Brighton or somewhere like that in an hour, maybe ninety minutes. What do you say?"

"I say yes." The idea of getting outside the M25 fills me with unexpected relief. Maybe this is what I need. A chance to be somewhere with no memories attached—clear my head, get some sea air. Putting my arms 'round Francis's neck, I straighten up to give him a hug. "Just give me ten minutes," I say, "and I'll be down, OK?"

"You got it." Francis quits while he's ahead, disappearing from the room swiftly, humming a jauntily triumphant tune as he goes back downstairs.

Guilt twists inside me as I watch him go. I shouldn't even be replying to these messages. In the mirror, I stare myself out. I have my own life. You're not part of it. *And that's what you wanted.* The words are forming themselves silently on my lips, my reflection mouthing them earnestly back at me.

Suddenly my phone beeps and jars on the table next to me, making me start. It's a text from a number I don't recognize, and for a second my heart leaps into my mouth before I read it. **Hi Caroline. Hope you don't mind me texting you, but I was a bit worried about you yesterday. Maybe you'd like to come over to mine for a coffee or something? Amber x.**

Frowning, I try to work out how she could have got my number. I'm not even sure I've ever told her my last name. I think my details are still listed on the website I set up a couple of years ago, when I was thinking about going freelance, and I seem to remember mentioning that brief career dalliance in the course of our chat in the café, but still, it would have taken some pretty rigorous searching to turn that up. I picture Amber hunched over the keyboard in concentration, trying various clutches of search terms, the light from the screen illuminating her face. It's very easy to imagine her this way, and once again I'm conscious that her interest in me seems a little more than normal.

I lay the phone aside. I won't reply just yet. I'm not sure I want to see her, and besides, the less I let the past trickle out into the world, the more I can suppress it. It's a rule I've lived by for years now. If something is alive only in my head, then it's barely real at all.

~

It's seventy degrees by the time we arrive in Brighton and for a midweek afternoon the seafront is busy, small crowds of locals and holidaymakers lured out by the promise of some early sun. We wander along the promenade and back again for ages with no real plan, content to be aimless until something catches our eye. As I had hoped, the clarity of the sea air soothes me. I feel drained but somehow pure, limbs faintly aching as if I've burned out the last stretches of a long illness.

Francis nudges me, indicating some girls in their early twenties striding along the seafront in cutoff shorts and bikini tops. "Bit optimistic. It's not exactly roasting yet, is it?"

As we draw closer I see that they are all wearing glitter on their faces, and that the tallest and most scantily clad of the group has a satin sash looped around her body. "Hen do," I murmur. The girls are laughing uproariously, swigging from bottles of alcopop and flashing their eyes challengingly at anyone who meanders into their path. "Got to get into the spirit."

"Yours wasn't quite like that, was it," Francis comments as they pass.

I struggle to remember. Eight years ago. A relatively sober and restrained affair in a central London bar and restaurant with a dozen friends, followed by a few hastily organized activities. "Things were different then," I say, but whether I mean they were different when it came to social norms, to expectations, or to me, I'm not sure.

"I remember you being pretty pissed when you came back, mind you," Francis says. "Didn't you fall over the coat stand?" He carries on talking, reminiscing, but I'm still watching the girls as they stride toward us and his voice fades away.

I'm looking at one of the more subdued members of the group, wandering along toward the rear. Her hair is long and dark, blown behind her shoulders in the light breeze, and she's wearing a chiffon scarf draped around her neck. There's something in the way she looks, something in the way she's walking, that makes me shiver. All at once it hits me—the start of that black cloud descending, the weight of memories that are too dangerous to be faced pressing down on me.

I turn to Francis and grab on to his hand. "Come on," I say, "let's walk out onto the pier," and I hold on to him tightly as I steer us away from the hen party and toward the horizon's blaze of white light.

I won't think about this. I can't. The words echo in my head with every step I take, and with each repetition I feel these thoughts being driven out. I ride it out until it's over.

"We could do it again," Francis says after a while, when we are wandering toward the arcades. I look at him blankly. "Not the hen night," he clarifies. "You know. Renew our vows or whatever." His tone is light, as if he hasn't really thought about what he is saying.

I can't work out if it's a joke or not. Renewing vows is something I connect with couples in their twilight years, casting around for some entertainment to give them some focus and purpose—or with those eager to pull the wool over their own eyes, convince themselves that their love is still worth celebrating despite the mess they've made of their lives.

"Don't look so worried," Francis says. "I wasn't being serious. Well . . ." He waves a hand, letting the thought drift off half formed.

"Yeah," I say nonetheless. We have wandered along the left-hand side of the pier and I lean onto the railings, looking out at the gently rocking water, curls of foam carved out and smoothed over by the wind, the smell of sea spray sharp and salty on the air. Seagulls are swooping and crying above our heads, wheeling in wide-winged circles. One settles on the railings inches from me, cocking its head inquisitorially in our direction, black glassy eyes surveying us beadily. I smile. "Sorry," I tell it. "No food here."

"He's not the only one who wants food," Francis says, taking my hand. "Let's walk a bit farther and then go back and get some fish and chips. Could eat them on the beach, if you like?"

We waste a few pounds on the arcade games, feeding coppers into the brightly flashing machines with no hope or expectation of return. Francis wins a small stuffed dolphin toy by a lucky throw knocking over some stacked-up aluminum cans, and presents it to me.

"There you go," he says. "Don't say I never give you anything."

"Thanks, but I think Eddie might appreciate it more." Looking down at the small purple dolphin, I imagine his hands grasping out eagerly to snatch it, and there's a pang of sudden sadness. It seems odd that he isn't here with us, galloping up the promenade, pestering for candyfloss and ice cream.

"You could give him a call," Francis suggests, noticing my silence.

"Yeah, I think I will." As we retrace our steps and wander toward the fish-and-chips place we spied earlier, I dial my mother's number. There's a scrambling at the end of the line when it's picked up, and a muffled "Go on, then" in the background, but Eddie doesn't speak. I listen to the sound of his breathing, heavy and intent down the line, waiting.

"Hello!" I sing out. "I'm just here at the seaside with Daddy. He's won you a toy."

"A toy?" His voice comes loud and clear now, piqued with interest. "What toy?"

"A dolphin," I say, not sure if he will understand. "Like a fish, you know . . . but bigger. We can give it to you when we get back. Are you having a nice time?"

". . . Yes," he says thoughtfully. "We went to the playground. I miss you."

His voice is even and untroubled, but all the same my eyes

smart briefly with tears. "I miss you, too, sweetheart." I want to say more, but Eddie's breathing is already growing more distant, and I hear the clunk of the phone being laid down. He's too young to concentrate on the phone for long, and it comes to me now how much of our bond relies on simply being there, in the same place at the same time.

Another scuffle, and my mother comes on the line. "Having fun?" she asks.

"Yes," I say, slowly. "But it's hard. Being away from him, and . . ." Something shifts nebulously in the back of my mind, a half expressed, suppressed thought; the image of you, nearer my child than I am.

"Come on now," my mother says briskly. "Eddie's fine. You're meant to be relaxing." I know she means well, but there's a brittle edge to her tone that makes me wonder if she's getting exasperated. It's as if there's an unspoken question there: *What more do you want?* I'm not even sure what the answer is.

As I hesitate, I see Francis coming out of the fish-and-chips shop, holding two bulging paper bags and a bottle of wine, his eyebrows raised inquiringly. "I'd better go," I say. "Just about to have something to eat."

"All OK?" Francis asks when I have hung up, and I nod.

We pick our way across the pebbles to find a flat spot to sit, and as we settle down I feel my muscles untensing again, seduced by the sea air. I pop a chip into my mouth, feeling heat and salt spread sharply on my tongue. The pebbles we're sitting on are faintly glistening, slicked with spray.

"We could move here," I say suddenly.

Sprawled next to me with his face turned upward to the sun, Francis squints. "What? But . . . we only moved to Leeds about eight months ago. Don't you like it?"

"It's not that." Leeds still doesn't feel like home, but I wouldn't fully expect it to, not yet. As I struggle to articulate what I mean, I realize that it's stupid. I want this sense of being outside my own life, all the time. I want a holiday every day of the week. I put aside my crumpled newspaper of fish and chips half eaten, staring out to sea. "Forget it," I say. "Just an idle thought."

Francis nods in acquiescence, draining the wine from his plastic cup. I glance at the almost empty bottle beside him. "Hadn't you better stop?" I ask. "You've got to drive, remember."

Francis looks across at me, and I have a small, uneasy premonition of what he is about to say. "I probably have had a bit too much," he says. "Couple of glasses. Maybe you should drive back."

I shake my head. A sudden gust of wind blows across our picnic spot, bristling the hairs on my arms. "No," I say. "I've been drinking, too, remember."

"You've had half a glass," he insists, "at the most. Come on, Caro. It makes sense."

With a lurch of nausea, I realize that he is serious. "No," I repeat. A pulse is starting to beat in my head, coloring the scenery around me in a tremulous pale blue haze. I can barely remember the feeling of my hands on the steering wheel, the way the engine flared up and sputtered when I turned the key in the ignition. It comes to me now in flashes—evil little glimpses peeking through the blackness. The long narrow road I last drove up. The gleam of headlights scattering light onto the asphalt; you sitting beside me, your hand resting at the edge of the skirt rucked up to my thighs; the last few minutes beautifully free of what was to come.

The sky darkens, and I lie down, closing my eyes. I'm shivering, suddenly lightheaded.

I can feel Francis watching me, and after a while he speaks again. "You know," he says, "there's really no reason not to."

It's unfair, but I feel rage pushing its way to the surface. He knows nothing. Doesn't understand. I remind myself that I can't expect him to. It's like trying to turn a juggernaut, forcing the anger back into its box and packing it safely away, out of reach.

Another minute's pause, and then he sighs. I hear the sound of scuffling as he settles back down. "Fine," he says. "We'll stay another couple of hours then. Wait for it to wear off."

Silently, I nod. I don't open my eyes.

HOME

Francis, May 2013

The trains are fucked again. As soon as I get to the station I see
the departures board striped in pale blue: delayed, canceled,
status unknown. Down on the platform dozens of people are mill-
ing restlessly and muttering to themselves like maniacs, jabbing at
phones and swigging coffees.

A bored announcement filters through the hum of noise every
so often. *Trains to London Waterloo are subject to delays and last-
minute cancellations. This is due to a fatality on the line. We apologize
for any disruption this will cause to your journey.* Some clever dick
has thrown himself under a train. Of all the ways to go, it's one of
the hardest to imagine. Cinematic, comedic almost—a high-speed
impact and an extravagant gush of red. I read once they sometimes
find limbs miles away from the site of the crash. Nasty. All the
same, there's something about the idea I like. Inconveniencing a
few hundred fat cats on their way to work isn't a bad by-product of
self-obliteration and normally I'd be all for it, only of course this
time it affects me, too.

The announcement is looping 'round again. *We* apologize *for the
disruption.* The apology is aggressively stressed. We've said sorry,

so fuck off. I leave it ten more minutes and then walk back home and take the car. Usually I avoid driving in because there's hardly anywhere to park near the clinic and the roads can be snarled at this time of day, but there doesn't seem to be much choice. Strangely, I'm in quite a good mood. I turn the radio up and concentrate on the road. My hands are shaking and there's a familiar pulse aching in my head, but that's minor stuff. No pills this morning. Maybe not until the evening. I'm singing along as loud as I can and my head is white noise.

The drive is quicker than usual but I spend more than ten minutes crawling around the roads by the clinic waiting for a space. Nothing's doing and in the end I give up and park on the double yellow. These days this sort of rule feels even pettier than it did before and the idea that there are people who make it their life's work to prowl around the pavements looking for somewhere to slap their little tickets seems so irrelevant and inane that it isn't worth bothering about. Besides, if I don't get inside soon I'm going to have to go straight into the session without even having a coffee and I can't face that.

As I duck across the road a bright red Range Rover comes bombing around the corner and the arsehole up front slams on the brakes, blaring his horn as if he's the one with the right of way. I give him the finger and stare him down for an instant through the windscreen before carrying on to the other side. Life is chock-full of these lovely little interactions. Warms the cockles of your heart, doesn't it? That said, it's the closest I get to human contact these days, if you take out the hours in the counseling room and the odd ships-in-the-night moments with the woman I think I'm still married to, only she's barely said a word to me in weeks and I can't remember the last time we slept together. In fact I can't remember the last time we slept in the same bed. Nighttime is something of an artificial construct for me at the moment. When you spend half the daylight hours asleep and half the dark ones awake, the days blur into one and it's harder with each rotation to tell where one ends and the next begins.

By the time I'm in reception pouring myself a coffee and checking my notes, what passed for a good mood is already hanging by a thread and it snaps entirely when I clock who it is I'm seeing. Going in blind isn't something I used to do but it's getting harder to plan ahead and so far it seems to have worked out all right. In this case, though, forewarned might have been forearmed. It's a couples session—Mark and Kirsten, a pair of fortysomethings who've been dipping in and out of counseling for almost three years. He's an alcoholic and she doesn't like it. He keeps saying he'll knock it on the head and she believes him, then gets uptight when lo and behold he decides he might as well just stick to the status quo.

Sometimes my job leads far too easily to self-reflection. There might as well be a neon sign hanging from above the clients' chairs, flashing in capital letters: REMIND YOU OF ANYTHING? No one understands—Caroline least of all—that it isn't awareness that is the problem. We all have our sickening moments of clarity, our hours of bleak revelation in the graying dawn. But in the background life is grinding on and sooner or later the machine takes over and we're swept along in its wake, and getting off that treadmill seems like a pipe dream in the face of the inexorable progress of habits and compulsions that have been hardwired for years.

Mark and Kirsten are hovering in the waiting room, making subservient little coughs and rustlings designed to make me realize that it's almost ten minutes past.

I usher them into the room. "Get yourselves settled." They both look bloody awful, like they haven't slept in weeks and have spent their days screaming at each other with the occasional break for cigarettes and hard drugs. Having said that, they're looking at me as if they're thinking the same thing. I didn't look in the mirror before I left this morning. Haven't done for a while. I can do without the disconnect.

"So," I say when I've sat down, "tell me about the past few weeks. How have things been?"

Mark just shrugs and stares at his feet. Early on, I remember we had frequent moments of awkward but genuine connection, he and I—it was relatively easy to crack the shell and get to what was inside. I can already tell that's over. He's gone into lockdown, where the no-man's-land outside his fortress stretches so far that everyone else is just mist and shadows.

Kirsten is talking, a relentless barrage of words. "Nothing's changing. I just keep hearing the same promises and things get better for a short while, and then we just go 'round again. It's like it washes over him. In one ear and out the other." Her fingernails are bitten down, streaked by remnants of hot pink nail polish. She hasn't washed her hair in a while and the roots are faintly glistening with grease. From what I remember, she used to keep herself in pretty good condition. I wonder if it's a tactic, an attempt to show Mark how he's grinding her down. If so, I know from experience that it won't work.

I suggest that Mark respond to what she's said, but he shrugs again and mumbles something about doing his best. We go back and forth for another twenty or thirty minutes this way—a bizarre counterpoint between trying to get blood out of a stone and battling to hold back a tsunami. Kirsten's had enough. They're finished. It would have more force if it wasn't the hundredth time she'd said something similar, and it's clearly lost all its power on him, if it ever had any at all. I don't think he's drunk right now. Just in the fog. It comes to much the same thing.

"You know something," Kirsten says at last, when she's exhausted the litany of Mark's wrongs. "I was watching telly the other day and that old clip came up of Princess Diana talking about her marriage. You know, when she says there were three people in it so it got a bit crowded." She's crying now, although none of us is acknowledging it and she doesn't reach for a tissue or make any attempt to wipe away the tears. "And I thought, bloody hell, I'd rather that than what I've got right now. There's only *one* person in this marriage. It's the *opposite* of crowded. It's—empty."

The last words are jerky, half drowned by the uneven rhythm of her tears. Mark glances over at her and I think I see a flicker of something in his eyes, the first stirrings of some kind of understanding or compassion. I know I should pounce on it and push at that door. But something in her words has set something off in me and all at once my moorings are lost and I've forgotten who I am and why I'm here . . . and all I can think is that they're doing one better than we are because I'm not sure there's anyone left in my marriage at all.

We push on through the next ten minutes but the bleakness in my head is unfurling, suffocating everything else. I'm watching their mouths move and responding on autopilot, barely even sure of what I'm saying. A glass partition has risen between us. Thick, impenetrable. The pale yellow walls of the counseling room are fuzzing and shimmering like static on a screen.

I get them out and when they've gone I go to the desk drawer and pull out the envelope from the back. I said nothing until this evening but trying to hold back this tide is impossible and all I want is for this spreading numbness to stop and check out for a while. I shake a few pills out and swallow them. I used to keep track of my daily consumption, set it to a certain number of milligrams and not take more, but these days I have no idea what the limits are and I stopped counting long ago. Besides, like I said, days don't have much meaning anymore. Some are longer than others, and something tells me this is going to be a fucking record breaker. Better be prepared.

～

I'm not sure how long I stay in the clinic before I remember the parked car and the double yellow line. When I do, I heave myself out of the armchair and lurch out of the room and down the stairs onto the street. Fresh air. It shakes me out of my head and all of a sudden I wonder if I should be driving right now. Just like this morning, though, there doesn't seem much option. Can't leave the car there forever. I'm walking down the road toward it and as I do I'm thinking about the fact that choices seem to be things that happen to me rather than things I make for myself, and I'm on the verge of some thought that feels significant but it slips out of my grasp. I feel it a lot, this trembling sense of being on the edge of something important that never comes.

There's no ticket on the windscreen—it's a petty victory but I flip the bird to whoever should have caught me out. I sling myself into the car and turn the key in the ignition, steer it carefully out onto the main road. Only two or three minutes in I realize I've made a mistake. The road is blurring in front of my eyes and my hands on the wheel feel like they've been slicked in oil. Signs and streetlamps rush up on me at the speed of light, then veer away and disappear. It's a computer game, a virtual nightmare.

Slow the pace. The arrow on the speedometer tells me I'm crawling along but from the rushing in my head and my ears it's hard to be sure. I fix my eyes on the center of the road. I know this route so damn well I could do it with them shut. Might be easier. Cars are flashing and beeping as they overtake me. It must be only ten minutes until home—maybe fifteen. Not long but my heart is pounding and all at once I'm staring down the barrel of a gun and I'm more scared than I would have thought someone who didn't have much left to lose would be. I'm swallowing down panic. Clenching my hands on the wheel. And then it comes out of nowhere—a car cutting up from the right at the roundabout—and I realize too late that I should have given way, and I'm dragging the car blindly to the left and shooting forward with no idea of what I'm doing or if it's safe, the horn blaring in my ears and an ache spreading across my shoulders, somehow miraculously still alive.

I pull into the next layby and get out of the car. There are tears on my face. The air is sweet and clean. I lock up and walk the rest of the way home. I'm chillingly sober. It's like the pills drained out of my system the instant I swerved the car. Words are falling like rain in my head and I'm telling myself—enough now. Can't do this anymore. Scaring myself. Time to get clean. So many times I've said these things only for them to fall down like dominoes the instant a breath of trouble touches them. Not this time. Not this time.

I stumble through the front door and into the lounge. Caroline is on the sofa, knees drawn up to her chest, her face intent on the lit screen of her mobile. I'd forgotten she had a day off. She's texting and she doesn't see me at first. When she does, the color drains out of her face and she stuffs the phone into her pocket and glares at me hard, like she's not sure who I am. She's texting him. That Carl guy, from her work. I'm not an idiot and I worked it out long ago, but I've found it increasingly hard to give a shit about anything much lately and the sum total of my thoughts on it so far has been that it's hardly a fucking big surprise. Easier to write her off as a faithless slut than think about it properly, but right now all I want is to move forward into her arms and feel her cheek warm against mine and have her tell me it's all right.

"Caro," I say, and the instant I open my mouth I realize I'm not sober at all, far from it. My head has tricked me again and now the words won't come out.

She's looking at me with disgust written all over her face. "You didn't even go to work, did you," she says.

"No," I say. I mean that she's wrong, but it doesn't sound right. The room is dipping and spinning around us. I'm trying to remember how many pills I took in the clinic and why this feels so different and so strange.

"You bastard," she's saying, her voice thick with tears already because they're only seconds from the surface these days no matter where we are and what we're doing. She's run out of things to say as well but that doesn't stop her. She just says the same ones over and over again, and I want to tell her that I understand and that I'm finally on the same page, but I can't decide how to say it. My thoughts are swelling and popping in the air like bubbles.

"We should talk," I tell her, but for some reason it enrages her and she swipes at me with a half-closed fist, yelling something that I can't catch and bursting out of the room, slamming the door before I even have a chance to take in what's happening. I hear her in the hallway scrabbling for her shoes, sobbing and banging her fists on the wall, shouting like she's gone insane. It sounds crazy but I envy her. She can burn it out. She's so fucking good at being angry and all I can do is stand here and wonder how the hell it all went so wrong so fast.

The front door slams and I'm alone in the house. My hands are shaking and it isn't just the pills. I'm replaying that instant on the road in my head, the way the car jerked out of control. Still can't believe I'm alive. And now I'm wishing I'd taken my hands off the wheel and closed my eyes and I can't understand why I didn't. I'm moving uselessly forward into the room and I can see that

Caroline's left her handbag slung next to the sofa, and before I know it I'm opening her wallet. I don't have much left this month. I'm going to need it. I pull out the two ten-pound notes I find there. Stuff them into my pocket. And fuck yes I feel like a bastard. But there's no change there and all it does is dig the writing on the wall in a little harder and deeper—and at times like this it's like it's written in blood, carved right into my own skin.

I've taken to sitting in the window seat in Caroline's lounge. It's a vantage point onto the main road, three floors below, and although the view is pretty industrial and bleak there's a strange sort of relaxation in watching the cycling rhythm of cars and passersby. It's midafternoon and I'm not sure how long I've been here. I've been thinking about how to reply to her latest message, not getting too far. I thought I'd enjoy seeing her suffer, but the reality isn't what I expected. It's like trapping a butterfly under glass, and only seeing once it's up close that maybe it wasn't as beautiful as you thought anyway, and now that it's where you want it the point of it has almost gone.

I'm staring down onto the street, barely seeing, when I dimly register something strange—a point of stillness in the churning procession below. The scene snaps into focus and I see that a woman and a young child are standing at the foot of the building. The child is pointing upward toward the window I'm sitting at, his mouth moving with words I can't read. He's wearing a blue school blazer and gray trousers, and his fair hair is neatly parted in the middle. There's something in the heart-shaped curve of his face that keeps me looking, and suddenly I'm going to the photographs in the hall and examining them closely, pressing my face close to the glass and trying to match up what I'm seeing with the mental picture of what I've just seen. It's him. Eddie.

The urge is strong and primal, blanking out thought. I drag my shoes on, snatch up the key, and run down the three flights of stairs toward the front entrance. By the time I'm there they've turned away and they're walking slowly down the road. The woman—Caroline's mother, it must be—is clutching tightly to the child's hand and the sight of them brings a rush of something so complex and undefinable that it brings tears smarting to my eyes.

I follow them down the road to the bus stop, hanging back out of sight. They wait there for a few minutes. Eddie's sitting on the red plastic bench, kicking his legs back against the glass and singing some loud rambling song of his own invention. When the bus arrives, the woman takes his hand again. They climb onboard and settle down into their seats, and as the bus pulls off I could swear that Eddie looks straight at me for an instant, his eyes wide and clear. And although I know it means nothing to him, it feels like something has changed for good. I've moved into his orbit. He's seen me. My image is locked away for good in the crevices and caves of his memory, and no one will ever be able to pull it out.

AWAY

Caroline, May 2015

I'm listening to Eddie down the telephone line, trying to piece together the funny breathless narrative of what he's been doing today. I can visualize the way he's sitting on the staircase, one leg draped through the banister, and balancing the phone awkwardly in the crook of his neck, muffling his words.

"I miss you," I say. His voice is at once distant and near and the scent of the peppermint shampoo I use on his hair is suddenly in my nostrils and I want him here with me.

"I miss you," he parrots back in his clear, uncomplicated lilt. I clutch the phone to my ear, listening to the sound of his breathing down the line, trying to work out what he is thinking. "Are you and Daddy coming back soon?" he asks.

"Three days," I say. "Not long at all." This is not how a holiday is meant to be. Living on countdown—ticking off the days until you can return home.

"Nanny's got biscuits," says Eddie distractedly. "They're chocolate ones. Do you think I should have one? Would you like one, Mummy?"

"Well, I'd like one," I answer, "but I can't really have one, can I, because—" As I speak I realize that Eddie has cast down the phone and made off in search of the biscuits. His footsteps echo down the corridor, fading into silence. I hear him laughing, protesting in response to my mother's half-hearted chastisement. I strain my ears to hear their conversation for a few more moments, and then I give up and hang up. A minute or so later a text comes through. **Sorry! Lure of chocolate digestives too strong. Give us another call later or tomorrow if you like. All fine. Mum x**

I imagine them settling down together in front of the television or a board game, and how it would be if I could step out of this room and into theirs—into the warm orange light of the living room with my mother and my child, the strong and simple bonds between us. Closing my eyes, I'm almost there. And then I'm thinking about how it would be to walk into my own home . . . unlocking the front door and entering the hallway, and seeing you by the window turning 'round to greet me, and moving forward into your arms to be kissed. The feel of your stubble roughly on my face, and the tight grip of your hands around my waist, pulling me smoothly into your body to fit me there like a key clicking into a lock.

The picture jolts and sparks, blacking out. I've had these thoughts about you at times over the years—haven't been able to avoid it, whether or not I wanted them. But I've never felt this complex mixture of emotions; desire and fear muddled up together. There's a part of me that still can't help but be excited at the idea that you're back in my life, even in such a bizarre fashion. But another part—a growing part—is telling me that this isn't the way it should be, and that there's something wrong, dangerous even, in what's happening here, something that I still don't fully understand.

I glance at my phone again. You still haven't replied to my last message. Last night when we got home from Brighton I drank too much, setting myself up for a restless night, and at three in the morning I was prowling 'round this kitchen, sitting at the table in the dark and typing thoughts to you that I never sent.

As I think of it, a horrible doubt grips me and quickly I scroll through my emails, exhaling in relief when I see that the message remains in my drafts. I don't recognize my own words. **Why haven't you replied? Why are you doing it like this? Do you know how long I've been waiting for you to write?? You have no idea how much I missed you back then, how much I needed you—I thought it was going to kill me. And now you're back but I didn't think it would be like this and I don't know why**

The message cuts off, an unspooling thread suddenly and brutally cut. Staring at it in horror, I wince. I must have been more drunk than I realized.

I can't help thinking of what Francis said to me last year, in the early days when he was just starting to wake up and understand, about how recovery can only be taken day by day. At the time I found it depressing. *But that means I'll never relax*, I remember saying. *If every day is the first day for you, then there's no progression.* But now I'm thinking that it's only taken forty-eight hours for my own addiction to feel like it's spiraling out of control, taking me with it. And almost two years has counted for nothing at all.

Day one, I think. Start again.

"You all right?" The shock of Francis's voice makes me spin back 'round. He has appeared in the doorway, scanning me warily. Things have been strained again since the drive back from Brighton, which we made in near silence; him in the driver's seat, steering the car calmly and efficiently through the falling dusk. Me staring out of the window and watching the scenery flashing by, barely knowing where we were, and too afraid to close my eyes because of what I might see.

Making an effort, I drag myself back. "Yeah, I'm fine."

"Have you thought about today?" he asks. There's the faintest hint of challenge in his tone. So far this week he's been in the driver's seat in more ways than one. Our movements have all been orchestrated by him. He's called the shots, and now he's wondering if I've got any loaded, and if I care enough to fire them.

I consider throwing out one of the ideas I've toyed with: a trip to the Aquarium, an exhibition at the British Museum that I thought he might appreciate, a visit to the cinema. I can't seem to settle on a thought. "Well, I was thinking of going to a meeting this morning," he says after a pause. "There's a local one at ten."

"Here?" I ask stupidly.

"Yes," he says mildly. "Believe it or not, they have addicts in Chiswick, too."

"Right. Yes, of course." Francis has been attending Narcotics Anonymous with varying degrees of frequency for the past two years and it shouldn't surprise me that he wants to go to a meeting. When I think about it, once I get past the unease that he needs this even when we're supposed to be on holiday, I find it reassuring.

"We could do something in the afternoon," he volunteers. "If you want."

"Yes," I answer quickly, "I'd like that."

"Would you," he says, his green eyes raking me with sudden coolness. There is no questioning lift in his voice. It's drier than that, a faint echo of skepticism and suspicion.

"Yes," I repeat, softening my voice. I can tell that he's searching for some clue that will tell him if I mean it, but it must be hard to find, because after a few moments he just shrugs and turns away.

~

After he's gone I make myself a coffee and try to relax in front of the television. I can't concentrate on the unfamiliar daytime soaps and talk shows and after a while I switch it off, but when I do I'm unsettled by the sudden silence and the faint noises that break it: the occasional creak of floorboards or the rattling of pipes. It's as if the house is breathing, shifting minutely around me. I catch a movement out of the corner of my eye and my whole body tenses before I realize that it's my own reflection in the mirror across the room. I take in my appearance; hunched in the corner of the armchair, my face pinched with concern. Abruptly, I get up and go to the kitchen, but it's no better. Everything is too still—the carved clawlike drawer handles, the open mouth of the sink gaping in a fixed, sightless smile.

All at once the sound of the doorbell shatters the silence, shrilling through the air. It makes me jump and I start to my feet, but I'm grateful. Right now, I don't want to be alone here.

I push open the front door to see Amber standing on the doorstep. She's wearing a red cotton shift dress, another deceptively simple outfit that is harder to carry off than she makes it look. Her hair is swept back behind her ears, revealing small diamond studs.

"I thought it would be easier just to come 'round," she says, and belatedly I realize that I never replied to her text the day before, the one suggesting coffee.

"Sorry," I say, although I don't know why I'm apologizing; surely arriving to chase up a tardy reply in person is extreme. "I've been a bit busy," I add feebly.

"No worries," Amber says graciously. "Do you fancy that coffee now, though?"

Thinking of the half-drunk cup in the lounge behind me, I half nod. "Maybe a tea . . ." As ever, there's something about her manner that brooks no denial, but as I pull on my shoes I acknowledge to myself that I'd follow pretty much anyone out of this house right now. Besides, it's been a long time since someone sought out my company so intensely, and part of me can't help but respond to it.

I catch a breath of her perfume as I stand up, and with a little start I realize that it's one I used to wear myself a few years ago, or something very similar. I used to love its powerful scent of rose and spice, and the smell of it now makes me think of darkly lit bars and the kind of recklessness I have long since left behind. I threw it out after I came back from the Silver Birches, along with much else, but breathing in that scent now I feel that pull again, those elusive reminders of myself in this woman that are hard to ignore.

I follow her across the street, noticing again how her front garden breaks the regimented repetition of the street. She has planted a sprawling wild rose at the edge of the lawn, and the ragged splashes of color of its dark orange blooms are a stark contrast to the prettily planted rows of pansies and peonies that neatly line each of the neighboring beds. The whitewashed walls of the house are scuffed in places with unidentifiable, patchy stains, like drifts of soot. On its own it would look unremarkable, but in this company it seems almost defiant.

We go into the house and she wanders through to the kitchen, where she's already set the mugs out waiting. "Have a biscuit if you want," she says lightly as she makes the tea. "I've eaten most of them but I think there are still a few left."

I glance at the packet of digestives lying on the arm of the kitchen chair, and think of her curled up lazily on it, eating her way through the packet. There's something unthinkably decadent about the image, and yet it's exactly the sort of way I would have spent an idle morning, before Eddie. "I'm all right," I say, and then take one anyway, on impulse.

"So," she says, as she sets down my mug with a clatter and slides into the chair opposite mine, "are you OK? The other day, you seemed—well . . . not OK. Not the way I'd expect someone on holiday with her husband to be."

She's watching me closely, unblinking. In her own way, I think, she's just as much of a curtain-twitcher as the people in this road that she speaks about with such derision, only the curtains she's twitching are the edges of my own feelings, and she's flicking and peeling at their corners in the hope that something will spill out.

"It's been a difficult few days," I say at last. "A difficult few years."

"For me, too," she says quickly, and for an instant I wonder if I'm wrong and her real purpose is to unload rather than to absorb, but she doesn't elaborate and raises her eyebrows slightly, waiting for me to continue.

I'm struck again by the strangeness of this situation, and by how little I know this woman who is asking me to turn myself out for inspection. I'm not sure I trust her, but at the same time there's something tempting about being with someone who behaves so unconventionally. It frees me up to do the same, and I'm tired of keeping all these thoughts trapped in my head.

"I love Francis," I tell her, "but our marriage is—complex." I hesitate.

"All marriages are," she says mildly, "aren't they?"

"Some more than others." I find that I want to explain. "He's a recovering addict and he doesn't really know himself how things will be from day to day. Sometimes, like this week, he's incredibly upbeat and positive, proactive, making an effort. Other times he's very distant. Not quite there. At times like that it's easy to feel that there's nothing much holding us together." Now that I've started, there is a kind of wild pleasure in saying these things aloud. I don't voice them with such frankness to anyone, not even my closest friends.

"I can understand that," Amber says carefully. "It's a hard thing to live with."

"Well, it's not only his fault." I pause again, but I already know I'm going to continue. "A couple of years ago I had an affair." I glance at her quickly, but her face betrays no emotion. "It lasted about six months," I say, "and even though I never left my husband for him, I really loved him. I haven't spoken to him for a long, long time. We agreed that we wouldn't be in touch ever again. It—it ended horribly. Not between us, not exactly, but . . ."

I take a breath. Up until this point the words have poured out as easily and swiftly as bloodletting from a vein. Now there's a tightness in my throat and my hands are shaking with what feels like delayed shock. Saying these things out loud has made them real, but it hasn't dispelled their power. If anything they feel more dangerous, and the weight of all that I haven't said is looming darkly behind them, pressing at the door and waiting for release.

Amber nods, swirling tea in her cup as if she's reading the leaves for the answer to my problems. "But he has been in touch," she comments. "You said that, the other day."

"Yes. I think so." I stare around the kitchen, suddenly lost. Pressing these thoughts back into their box is exhausting, leaving me drained and passive. I find myself looking at the piles of crockery on the buffet: dark blue china, rimmed with white.

"I can see why it's unsettling," I hear her say. With an effort, I drag myself back. "I imagine it's very tempting to fall back into contact with someone who helped you through a difficult time. But if you don't mind me saying so, Caroline, it doesn't seem to be making you very happy. It sounds like you have enough to cope with without him."

Silently, I nod. I'm thinking of those first few weeks afterward, when not having you on the end of the phone felt like agony. I needed you to talk to, to process what had happened, to make sense out of the senseless. It isn't like that now. But they say that often, amputees feel the presence of the missing limb, something at once ghostly and strangely real. There are still times when I feel you stirring invisibly next to me, and right now that presence is stronger than it's ever been.

"I do understand what you're saying about your marriage," Amber says. "Especially that feeling you mention of him not being quite there . . . I feel that with my boyfriend, all the time."

I look up sharply. "Really?"

She hesitates, as if examining her own words for accuracy. "Yes. Of course, in my case, a lot of the time he *isn't* there. He works in a satellite office a lot, and he's usually away for a week or so at a time."

"That can't be easy." Something clicks into place. Her words make sense of her aimlessness, the vague aura of expectancy and isolation that I sensed buzzing around her from the first time we met. "You end up feeling like you're just filling in time when you're not together," I add, and unavoidably I'm thinking of you again. The way I used to cling to you when we said goodbye, trying to imprint you on my body, and the way that the sensation always faded in minutes, impossible to hold on to.

"Exactly," Amber says. "So when he is around, it puts . . ."

"Puts pressure on?" I prompt.

She half nods, sips her tea again. "Puts a spotlight on things, I was going to say. Everything's—exaggerated. I find myself wanting to know exactly what he's thinking and feeling all the time, and it just makes him . . ." She brings her hands away from her mug in a sudden, violent movement, snapping them together. "Close up."

I look at her painted fingernails, digging into her own skin. There's a rawness to it that shocks me. "I see," I say.

She releases herself and leans back in her chair, tipping her head back to the ceiling. "Oh, well," she says flatly. "That's men for you. I blame his ex. That relationship hurt him a lot. He told me all about it, a while ago. I'm not sure he'll ever fully get over it. He sacrificed a lot for her, kept her secrets. I don't think she has any idea of the effect it had on him."

All at once I feel claustrophobic. The conversation is too intense, making me short of breath, and there's something prickling over my skin, some small wordless instinct that I don't quite understand. I push my chair back and take my mug to the sink, turning on the tap. "I'll wash this up," I say, but she doesn't seem to hear me. She's twisted 'round now with her arms locked across the back of the chair, her face angled toward mine.

"You know," she says, "funnily enough, her name was Caroline, too."

And I'm not sure what comes first, the hearing of the words or the flash of color and shapes that catches my eye as I turn from the sink and reach for the tea towel hanging from a hook on the side of the fridge. Just below the hook, there's a collage of photographs in small magnetic frames. Amber in a bikini and sunglasses, shading her eyes on a sandy beach. Amber smiling nose to nose with a small tabby cat. Amber dressed up for a party. And in the center, she's looping her arms around a man's neck and pressing her face close up against his and her eyes are half closed in bliss—and the man is you.

I say something, or think I do, but the words are strangled in my throat.

I can't drag my eyes away from the photograph. You're smiling, your eyes crinkled at the corners. You're wearing a shirt I've never seen and you're someone I don't know.

"Caroline," I hear her say, and when I force myself to turn 'round her face is so pale that I can see the veins translucent beneath her skin. We look at each other for a long moment. "It's you," she says at last.

We stand there motionless opposite each other, only a few feet apart. It's as if we're reading parts, and the scripts have dropped out of our hands and neither of us has any idea what to say.

She finds the words first, raising her chin, narrowing her eyes. "What the fuck is going on?"

I gasp, trying to sort my thoughts into some kind of coherence. I glance at the photograph again, and this time the narrowness of your eyes looks calculating. I have the strangest feeling that you're here in the room with us, watching this unfold. "I have no idea," I say shakily. "I'm not the one you should be asking."

"What?" she asks, louder now, folding her arms across her chest. "What do you mean?"

"Where is he?" I say. "What has he told you?"

"He's not—it's not something he's *told* me," she bites back. "It's something that's real. He's working away, just like he often does. I told you that. He's at the other office, in Cambridge, he's—"

"He's lying to you," I say swiftly, before I have even stopped to consider if I want to be saying this. "I don't think he's there at all. I think he's in my house."

"What?" she says again, shaking her head. "Caroline, that's insane. Do you expect me to believe that my boyfriend—"

"Carl," I interrupt again. "You can say his name, you know, I'm not going to fall to pieces if you say his name," but my voice is rising and I can hear the telltale shakiness in my own words. My eyes are filling with tears and I'm pressing my fists angrily against them, shutting her out until I can't see her anymore.

HOME

Caroline, June 2013

He's already waiting for me at the station by the time I've fought my way off the tube—wearing sunglasses and a short-sleeved shirt in response to the new heat wave, lounging back against the wall. I've seen him from way off but pretend I haven't, walking slowly and composedly, feeling the Lycra of my dress stretch and rub against my thighs. I know he's watching and it's only when I'm a few feet away that I let my eyes meet his and quicken my pace, almost running into his arms. He sweeps me up and holds me tightly, kissing me as I slip my hand briefly inside his shirt. His skin is warm and smooth against mine, and I feel a pang of desire twist in my gut.

"You look hot," he says simply, pulling back to examine the dress clinging to my body; the band of pink and red flowers running across the bodice that pushes my breasts out beneath it, the short black skirt molded to my curves. I found it in the back of my wardrobe this morning. It's been years since I wore it—probably not since I was his age. When I first tried it on and looked in the mirror, doubt rippled through me, but the longer I stood there the more I liked it: the brazenness of it, the way it shouts for men to turn their heads and stare. I had forgotten that I had this power, but now that I've rediscovered it, I find I only want him.

"Thanks. You too." His hands are running up and down my sides as if they have minds of their own. It wouldn't take much to peel this dress over my head and have me where he wants me, and for a crazy moment I wish he'd do it, right here in the station with the sun beating over our heads through the glass roof. "Let's go and get something to eat," I say instead. "I'm really hungry."

He takes my hand as we walk out onto the street and head for the covered market. I hardly ever come to this part of town and it's taken me the best part of an hour to get here, but that's its attraction. No one knows us here. We're just a couple, scanned idly by strangers, accepted and dismissed.

I lace my fingers through his more tightly, unable to stop the spread of happiness and excitement pulsing through me. This feels like a treat. It's the first time we've ever had a day off together, and although I need to pop back home and collect Eddie from nursery at five, I'll be back with him again by eight. I've earned this, I tell myself. I've been a good wife all week. Made Francis's dinner, cleaned up after him, listened to his ranting. Kept our son away from him when he's too out of it to see him. I think of these things, and a savage surge of entitlement steals my breath for an instant. I look at Carl, tipping his face up to the light as it glints off his sunglasses, relaxed and at ease. Right now, this is what I want. Just this. I won't think about anything else.

"So how is it in the new office?" I ask as we wander around the stalls, trying to decide what to buy. "New lease on life?"

He shrugs. "The work's the same, to be honest. No Steven spouting random crap all day, but beyond that it's not much different."

"And you said the people were friendly?" I probe. "Who are you sitting next to?"

He glances at me. "A girl." His expression is serious but the corners of his mouth are twitching. "She's very friendly, and quite ugly."

Laughing, I press myself up against him, the embarrassment at being rumbled outweighed by the pleasure that he can see through my unreasonable jealousy so easily. "You know me too well."

"Yes, I thought you might like that." He kisses the top of my head, pulling me closer. "Seriously, though, it's OK, but I can't say I'm getting a lot of work done. I probably shouldn't spend so much time messaging you, but it's hard to resist." He shoots me a quick smile as he draws back, but for an instant I think I see a kind of confusion in his eyes. I'm reminded of the strange queasy feeling I had when we said goodbye a couple of weeks ago, the sense of this having slipped out of my control. It's the first time that it has occurred to me that it's the same for him. There is no one steering this ship. In our different ways we're both wildly out of our depth.

"Well, like Steven always says, you can resist anything but temptation," I say lightly, trying to dispel my unease. "Though I'm not sure he said it first."

We eventually buy a couple of tacos from a Mexican stall and wander up to the nearby park to eat them, settling down in the full glare of the sun. Carl lies down on his back, pillowing his hands behind his head, and I lie next to him, feeling his heartbeat where my head rests on his chest. "This is nice," I say quietly after a while. "Nice not to have to rush off."

"I know." His chest rises and falls in a sigh. "Sometimes," he says, "I wish we could just stay in one evening and, I don't know, watch TV. Get a takeaway. Normal stuff."

"Well, we could do that." I know exactly what he means but even as I speak I know it probably won't happen. Our time alone is precious, too short. We spend most of it in bed, and it feels like the opposite of normal.

He doesn't answer, but strokes my hair, his hand running idly up and down its length and gently pulling, teasing his fingers through the strands. "There's a couple at the new office," he says at last. "They're in their twenties, I think they've only been going out for a few months. It's funny, they hardly ever talk to each other at work. Don't often go out for lunch together, even. It made me think there's no way I'd be able to stay away from you in that situation."

"You managed it OK," I say, "when we did work together."

"Well, not really," he points out, snorting briefly with laughter. "Not by the end. Anyway . . . it doesn't matter. I just couldn't help looking at them and thinking, you know. It wouldn't be like that for me."

I scratch my fingernails lightly down his abdomen, thinking about what he is saying. These days, more and more, I find myself trying to imagine what it would be like if we were a real couple. I think about the routine trips to the supermarket, the household chores, the aimless rainy days when there's nothing to do. "It wouldn't be like this either," I say. "You know that."

I feel him breathing deeply, thinking. "No," he says finally. "I've got no idea what it would be like. To be honest, I don't tend to second-guess stuff too much. I just take things as they come. You know—work, family, friends . . . my life's not so complicated really."

I angle my cheek inward, resting it against the warm rise and fall of his chest. "Apart from me."

He makes some vague noise of agreement. "Our situation, certainly. But anyway," he says, "there isn't much point going down that road, is there? Wondering about how we'd be together. As far as I'm concerned, you're married, so there's no decision to be made. That's just the way it is and I've always known that."

His tone is without malice and the words are rational, but all the same something in me rebels against the ease with which he seems to be able to shrug the thought off. I wonder, sometimes, if he even realizes how rare this dynamic between us is. He's barely out of his mid-twenties, and he's never had a serious relationship; a few months here and there with various girls, nothing that seems to have had a major impact on him. Unable to help myself, I sigh. "Well, that was easy."

"No," he says flatly. "It's not."

A cloud crosses the sun, and I press my face into his shirt, feeling suddenly cold. "Come on," I hear him say after a while. "Let's go for a walk."

We stroll around the park chatting until it's time for me to head back to the tube and pick Eddie up from nursery. Outside the entrance he presses me back against the station wall and kisses me hard, biting my lip and thrusting his hips against mine. Our conversations are forgotten and we're in the moment together, unable to see past it. "Three hours," he mutters. "Not sure I can wait that long."

"You're going to have to," I say, but the truth is that I'm not sure either, and all at once lust is pulsing through me so powerfully that I can barely speak. My hands are sliding up his back, exploring and teasing. I'm thinking about how it will be later, when we're alone.

"I want you so much," I tell him as I curl my fingers around the loops of his belt and pull him hard up against me, and saying it out loud gives me a dizzying sense of pleasure. I've never been this honest with anyone. It's shockingly addictive . . . so much so that as soon as he's released me and I'm walking away from him all I want to do is run back and say it again and again and again.

~

Eddie is out of sorts from the minute I pick him up from nursery—scowling mutinously at the ground when I ask how his day has been, fussing on the bus for no apparent reason, and dragging his feet all the way up the road. Five steps from the front door he trips and falls on his face, which sets him off into instant meltdown, screaming as if he's being flayed alive. Bundling him through the front door, I examine his face, but there's only the tiniest of red marks, barely visible.

"It's OK," I try to comfort him, "you're fine, it's all right," but it has no effect and he stomps off into the nursery, still wailing. Moments later I hear the thump of a toy being thrown against the wall, then a long high-pitched scream of frustration before he calls for me, over and over. I hurry into the room, but there's nothing to be done, and when I try to scoop him into my lap he almost growls, his little hands pushing me violently away. Breathing in sharply, I count to ten. My tolerance for these tantrums seems to be getting lower and lower, and my heart is thumping, warning me that I'm losing control.

Setting my teeth, I stride out of the nursery and into the lounge, seeking a few moments' quiet. Francis is in his customary position on the sofa, slumped in front of the laptop with his headphones plugged in, barely glancing at me when I come in. He's there, but he isn't. His eyes are glazed and unblinking, hooded darkly in the light of the screen.

"Good evening," I say sarcastically, though I know he can't hear me.

With an expression of infinite weariness, he reaches slowly up and plucks the headphones from his ears. "What?"

"That's a nice welcome." In seconds the relaxation of the

afternoon has disappeared. I glance around me at the state of the flat. There are toys everywhere, unwashed crockery piled up on the dining table, streaks of dust and dirt across the floor. I know Francis has had no appointments today. He's simply sat here, surveying the carnage. "I'm so glad I came back," I spit.

"No one asked you to," he points out, sighing as if the five words were an unwillingly bestowed gift.

"Yeah—because I'm sure you'd be coping really well with this situation if I wasn't here," I bite back, gesticulating toward the screams coming from the nursery.

He half turns his head, listening for an instant, his expression as vacant as if the noise were coming from another planet. "It's you," he comments. "You make it worse. You wind him up." And with that, he screws the headphones back in and directs his attention to the screen again, the frown between his brows deepening as his lips silently move to the music that must be so loud that it's shattering his eardrums.

"Fuck you," I hiss, "you useless tosser," and then I'm turning on my heel and leaving the room, shaking with the adrenaline of it—the way it happens so fast now, the split seconds it takes for any prospect of civility to vanish. My own ugly words are beating in my head, and behind them, the nasty little thought lurks—that maybe he's right. Maybe in some way it's my own stress that is seeping out and throwing everything out of kilter. I stare 'round at the chaos surrounding me and all at once I'm filled with hopelessness; the knowledge that the family we have tried to build is all distorted and wrong, and that I don't know how to fix it.

I calm Eddie down in the end and take him through the ritual of dinner, bath, and books, snuggle up with him on the sofa and read him a favorite story. He's docile and placid now, watching the pictures intently and cocking his head to soak up the words. It's as if Francis isn't in the room at all. With a little tremor of shock, I realize that Eddie's ignoring him; that on some level, he knows there is no point in trying to engage.

"Good night," I whisper as I tuck him into bed, switching on the blue night-light. I linger in the doorway for a few moments, watching as he rolls onto his side and his body heaves in a small sigh. One thing I have never doubted is Francis's love for him, but I know that the reason I always come back to put him to bed is not simply to see him. I don't fully trust his father with him on his own. I don't want to leave him here, not until he's safely tucked-up asleep. The realization is bleak and fathomless.

In the bathroom I have a quick shower, then sit in the bath and shave my legs carefully from top to bottom, rubbing in strawberry shower gel and stroking the razor over my skin. I've almost finished when he comes in. When he sees me, he just stands there for a few moments, arms folded, looking at what I am doing. His face is twisted with contempt and disgust. My eyes meet his, and for the first time it hits me that he knows exactly what is going on and exactly why I'm keeping myself smooth and scented. At the very least, he knows it isn't for him.

"I hope your friend Milly appreciates the effort," he says at last.

I want to say something in return, but I have no idea what, and after a few more beats of silence he turns and leaves the room. My hand is shaking, and when I pull the razor up the length of my leg the blade twists and grazes my skin. I stem the blood with my finger, my head lightly swimming. I need to get out.

Forty minutes later I'm running up Carl's road, my new silk underwear sliding beneath my clothes and my phone switched off. He opens the door to me and the sight of him works faster than any drug. I'm suddenly, crazily happy, throwing myself into his arms and winding myself around his body. He kisses me hard and

suddenly I know that tonight is the night. I've had enough of agonizing over whether or when it should happen. I want it now and
I draw in a breath to say so, but my eyes lock on his and I realize
that I don't need to.

He carries me through to the bedroom—pulling at my clothes
and throwing them to the floor, unbuckling his trousers and shrugging off his shirt until we're naked on the bed together, entangled
in a sudden hot mess of limbs and sweat—and his breath warm
against my neck as I open my legs and clasp them around his
waist. He's inside me in an instant and I barely have time to register the shock of its rightness, the sudden incredulity that we spent
so long not doing this. I'm clutching at him, gasping for breath as
we kiss, waves of heat breaking over my skin. He fucks me hard
and fast and I'm arching my back underneath him, almost screaming because I want this so much that even now when we're right
in the middle of it I'm thinking about wanting to do it again.

He's talking to me, whispering things that drive me over the
edge into someplace I've never been, and all at once we're staring
into each other's eyes and he's coming inside me, and the thought
hits brutally hard and without warning, for the first time—I love
you, I love you, I love you.

Afterward neither of us speaks for a while. We lie together on
the bed. He's stroking my hair again, in a soft soothing rhythm. I
could so easily fall asleep here, but I know I can't, and the thought
brings tears unexpectedly to my eyes and running down my face.

"Don't," he says, but when I look up I see that he's crying, too.

We lie there for a few more minutes. I watch his tears falling
and put out my hand to touch them with my fingertips, stemming
the flow. And in that moment I realize that he loves me, too, even
if he doesn't know it himself. I've never known anything so deeply.
I've never felt so sure.

"God," he says after a while. "This is cheerful." And despite it all we both smile.

We don't talk much more that night. When the clock hits eleven I get up and get dressed, and he comes with me to the front door to kiss me goodbye. Outside it's colder than I expected, and I'm shivering without a jacket as I walk to the station. I put one foot in front of the other, and with every step I'm thinking: I could leave. I could end my marriage. The idea is new and overwhelming. In all this time, I've never seriously considered it as an option. But now it's out of its box, and as I'm getting on the train and straightening my crumpled clothes, reapplying my smudged lipstick, it's flooding every inch of me and suddenly I'm filled with fierce certainty and I know that I could do it.

*S*he's found out about Amber and suddenly my inbox is full of her. *Her name repeats itself down the page, again and again. Some of the messages are brief and tragic, helplessly posing questions that I know she doesn't expect to get answers to.* **I've just been having coffee with your girlfriend. Is this some kind of sick joke?** *Others are longer, haphazardly designed to try to provoke some kind of reaction.* **If I ever meant anything to you at all, then you need to answer me and tell me what is going on here. I'm scared, and I don't know what to do. Please, you have to get in touch and explain this to me before I go completely insane** *. . . They ramble on and on in this vein. There are a couple of references to Amber herself and how pretty she is, thinly veiled pleas for reassurance. There's no control, no thought. Just the contents of her head splashed out messily onto the screen in the hope that I'll clear them up.*

When I read these messages I can't help but be angry. She's expressing all this doubt and confusion, but it's founded on beliefs and judgments she's made without even stopping to consider. She's so sure of how it is, so used to seeing the world through her own particular prism, that it doesn't even enter her head that things may not be as they appear.

I nurse this anger for a while until it threatens to explode, and then I take the long, sharp kitchen scissors again and go to the rows of photographs in the hallway. One by one, I take them down and pry the backs carefully away, lifting out the sheets of glass. My hands are trembling but this job needs precision, so I sit and wait until I'm steely and focused, my concentration narrowing to the small pocket of carpet before me with the photos laid out in rows. I take each one in turn and I cut carefully into them, digging the points of the scissors into the center of her face and then snipping outward until I've removed her from the picture.

At the end of it I lay the glass gently back on each one and replace them in their positions on the wall. Standing back, I see how it looks, and I like it. A series of small black ovals popping out from the frames, conspicuous only by their absence. She's gone. All that's left of her is the small mangled pile of photo print at my feet. I think about throwing it away. But then I remember what she's said, about how if someone cares about you at all then it's their duty to engage with you in some way, and in the end I just leave it there.

AWAY

Caroline, May 2015

I'm sitting on a bench at the edge of the playground, watching children scramble like ants over the blue metallic climbing frame. It's cold for the time of year and the sound of their shrieking and whooping is jarring, but I don't know this area and the only other place I could think of was the coffee shop I went to with Amber, where she might easily have appeared. No one without children comes here. Every now and then I notice the other mothers giving me funny sidelong looks, trying to pinpoint which child I'm attached to. A couple of them are clearly discussing me, sharp, beady eyes gleaming at the sight of a stranger in their midst. Usually it would make me feel uncomfortable, but today I don't care. My mind is still buzzing with shock and everything else is just background noise.

I read over the text Amber sent me a few hours ago. **Caroline, I'm sorry I asked you to leave yesterday. It was a shock for me as well as you. It just all seems too much of a coincidence. I still can't believe it, to be honest. Look, please call me back.** I picture her face as we stood in her kitchen—taut, disbelieving, coldly dismissive of my tears. She didn't ask me to leave; she told me to get out.

She's been ringing on and off ever since she sent the text. The sporadic bursts of noise coming from my phone are getting more frequent and shorter, only lasting a couple of rings before she realizes I'm still not going to answer and gives up.

I know I should call her back, that I'll have to talk to her eventually, but I can't do it yet. There's too much jumbled up in my head. I look again at that text, the word *coincidence* jumping out from the screen. She understands that it's not possible for this to be some bizarre quirk of fate, but she doesn't understand that I'm not the one who has brought it about. You've planned and engineered this, and you must have known that there was a chance that this would happen—that my path would cross with hers. I have no idea if you viewed it as a risk that you decided to take, or if it was what you wanted all along.

At the thought, I breathe in sharply, feeling pain sear through me. I don't know why you would want me to see her. Now that I have, there's no way I'll ever be able to unsee the images that are cycling through my head like reels of film. The way you might have lingered at your window, watching her move in across the street, sizing her up and liking what you saw. The carefully engineered meeting, the quick flirtatious glances of appraisal. *Just moved in? Let me know if you need anything . . .* The excitement of those first dates, the electricity of your first kiss. Fast-forwarding to the two of you draped comfortably over each other on your sofa, watching TV or chatting about your days. Sitting together at her kitchen table, sharing a meal over a glass of wine. Doing the chores on a Sunday morning, hanging up the washing or scrubbing the bathroom. All those cozy domestic things that we never did. And that's before I even get to the part that hurts most—your hands encircling her slim waist, your lips kissing the hollow of her neck, her legs wrapped around yours, and the sound of your voice whispering the things to her that you used to say to me. If I've let myself imagine you, in the past two years, it's always been alone. I've been unable to cope with the idea of putting someone else in that picture beside you.

I think of the letter I sent you a few days after I last saw you— the one I scrawled on yellow lined paper that I had torn from an office notebook, a ridiculous attempt to spark some nostalgia in you. I scribbled down all the memories and everything they had meant to me, and at the end I told you that I hoped you would be happy, and that I knew you wanted me to be happy, too. Now I'm not so sure, about either part. The thought of you being happy with her tightens my chest with almost unbearable sorrow, and it's increasingly clear you don't want me to be happy at all. This feels more like torture, as if you want me to be punished.

The idea sets something off inside me, a violent reverberation of unease. I can't help remembering the last time I saw you; the way I turned and left you standing there, the sight of you standing motionless by the side of the road when I looked back. I've never been able to widen out that picture, to let myself wholly remember. I walked away and didn't look back again. I pushed down the guilt and the pain, smothered it into submission out of sheer desperation. I know that you couldn't have done the same. You've had to live it, and I have no idea how it might have changed you.

It's half past two and I've been out for hours. Forcing myself to stand up, I start to make my way back across the park. I turn onto the road that leads back to the house, and hurry along, hugging my jacket to my body and shivering in the cold spring wind.

Lost in my thoughts, I am only vaguely conscious of the noise behind me—a rush of sound, a squeal of brakes. And then it's right there, in a split second of violent color. A car veering too close to the pavement—cutting so close to me that I feel a shudder of semicontact, my force field bristling in sudden shock, before it swings away again and zooms off up the street. I fling myself back against the hedge. The car is already out of sight, but my mind and body haven't quite caught up. It was close. Very close. And suddenly I'm bending down, my legs weak, and crouching at the side of the road, ducking my head between my knees and struggling to talk myself down.

It must be five minutes before I manage to straighten up and walk on. I tell myself not to be stupid. It was a moment in time, with no significance. It means nothing.

By the time I'm back at Everdene Avenue it has started to rain lightly and I put up the collar of my coat and duck my head down. If Amber is looking out of her window then she'll still recognize me at once. But there's no swinging front door, no plaintive call across the street, and I quickly unlock the door of number 21 and slip inside.

My heart lifts with relief when I see the note scrawled on white paper in the middle of the kitchen table. **Gone to supermarket to pick up some stuff and might swing by the cinema on the way back to see if there's anything on this evening that we might fancy seeing. Back by four. F.** At least I have another hour or so to collect my thoughts. But I can't seem to settle for long, and before I know it I'm prowling restlessly through the house once again, going from room to room and staring at the barely there possessions—searching for any clue as to how you live, what you're like, what you care about now.

The more I cycle through the faceless rooms the more my helplessness grows. This is pointless; I have already done this search, back when I found the aftershave bottle. There's only one place I failed to look: the little cabinet under the desk in the study room, which was locked. At the time I let it go, but now conviction grips me that I need to look inside. I go quickly to the study, cross to the empty desk, and drop to my knees beside it. I tug at the drawer, but of course it's still locked. I peer underneath, run my hands across the floor in search of a key; then I look around the rest of the room, meticulously combing every nook and cranny I can find. The key isn't there.

Frustrated, I kneel back down and pull again at the drawer. I can feel the resistance, but the mechanism is a cheap one, rattling against the strain. Frustration surges up inside me, and before I have time to check myself, I set the flat of one hand on the cabinet above the drawer and use the other to yank the handle hard, once, then again. The catch rips and breaks, and the drawer is sliding out fast and smooth on its rollers, opening up what's inside.

It's a single wallet folder, green and unlabeled. I reach in and pull it out, opening it and taking out the contents. Several sheets of paper, printed from the internet, with some scribbled, illegible annotations in dark pen. I glance at the first sheet, and my throat seizes up. It's a printout from 192.com of every household in the UK that is registered under Francis's and my surname, and picked out in yellow highlighter is our own Leeds address in full.

I can feel my heart hammering as I spread out the other sheets on the floor in front of me. A photograph from a property website of the block we live in, advertising one of the other flats for sale. The home page of the company where I now work, along with the team page where my own face smiles out blandly from the thumbnail photograph. A few screenshots of my social media profiles, locked down and basic as they are. It's all public information, but the collection of it, the fact that you've bothered to print it out . . . it feels quite odd. Invasive.

On the final sheet, I see the profile I set up months ago on the house-swap site: the photographs of the inside of our home, the chatty description of its location and the invitation to contact me. It had never occurred to me to wonder how you had found me on the house-swap site, but now I realize that you must have set up a Google alert or something similar on my name, my address. It's what anyone might do, if they wanted to keep abreast of something. But even as I try to rationalize it, I'm aware that there's a world of difference between something and someone, and especially the kind of someone I am to you. A world of difference between attention and obsession. My head reels and I'm pushing the papers shakily back into a pile, forcing them back into the folder and shoving it into the drawer again, as if in another moment I might be discovered. I lean back against the desk, thoughts buzzing.

Next to me, my phone is blinking, signaling a new email. I sent so many messages yesterday, caught up in disbelief and confusion, and you didn't reply to a single one. Until now.

The message is brief. **Don't worry. I've been keeping myself busy.** Scrolling down, I realize it's a reply to one of the angrier emails I sent. **What's the point of all this? How are you occupying yourself there, in my flat? What the fuck are you actually doing?** Your response is cryptic, brief, and anonymous. It seems hardly worth the effort of typing. And then I notice the attachment.

I open it, my breath coming suddenly fast and shallow. At first I don't understand. It's a picture of the hallway, taken in low light, from the far end by the kitchen. There's nothing distinctive about it, no signs of activity. Then I see the photographs. They're hung up just as I'd left them, but they've been altered somehow. Then I see. My own face has been cut out of them, leaving only black space.

The shock of it stuns me for a second, my head reeling with sudden lightness. There's something so systematic about it, the effort it would have taken. Sinister precision. I gaze at the photograph, trying to understand. Why would you do this? Something is troubling me about it, something beyond the obvious surrealism of the act. With a rush, it comes to me that it's the fact that it's *my* face that has been removed. Somewhere in the back of my mind, I've still been clinging to the thought that whatever is driving you to conduct this whole performance, it must be underpinned by love. I could have understood a symbolic removal of my husband, a desire to cut him out. But this isn't love; it's the opposite. You're telling me that you hate me.

HOME

Caroline, June 2013

Without really meaning to, Carl and I have established a kind of rhythm over the past few weeks. We message each other sporadically throughout the day, just to share the odd funny story or moan about our workload, and in the evening he usually texts me at about eight after Eddie is in bed, when we'll chat for half an hour or more. I find myself waiting on these texts, compulsively glancing at my phone throughout the business of making dinner and navigating Francis's unpredictable moods. When Carl gets in touch, I retreat to the bedroom and carry on the conversation there. Francis is generally passed out by the time it's under way in any case, and even if he wasn't, I'm rapidly growing to believe he wouldn't care. The invisible lifelines of connection between us are shriveling and draining. One by one, they're dying and dropping away, and I'm not even sure if he knows it or not.

I'm at my desk, working on autopilot, shuffling rows of data and organizing figures. It's brainless activity, leaving my mind free to wander. I flash back to the previous evening—Francis and me sharing the sofa, conversing amicably enough about the weekend ahead. These patches of normality, when we manage to get through a few hours of civility and he behaves in a way that passes for average, are few and far between now, and they don't have the effect on me they once had. I used to clutch at them like the last clumps of grass and earth grasped at by someone tumbling off a cliff. I know they won't last—that even as I hold them they're crumbling into nothing in my hands and, like it or not, I'm still falling.

The messenger icon flashes at the base of my screen, and I smile, knowing what the message will contain. Sure enough, Carl is confirming the plans for tonight, telling me he can't wait. Friday night is always reserved for the two of us these days and today is only Wednesday, but I've said that I need to work late, and he's coming to the office to meet me after hours. It's a risk, one we haven't taken before. Coupled with the knowledge that I'll be seeing him twice this week, it feels like a shift. I've been thinking more and more the way I felt the other week when I left his house, when I first tentatively started to consider the possibility of leaving Francis. I haven't said anything to him—won't, until I'm sure I know what I want—but I can feel these thoughts within me every time I'm with him, a secret growing and blossoming out of a tiny seed. I can't yet think about Eddie, or about sitting down in front of my husband and telling him that I intend to walk out on him exactly when it seems he needs me most. But he has never not needed me, and he doesn't seem to give a fuck about what I need myself. The thought gives me a surge of anger. I shake my head, and with a jolt I realize I've been calculating the figures on my screen wrong, not concentrating at all.

See you at half six then, I type back to Carl, pushing everything else out of my head. **I'll be waiting . . .**

You better be, he writes back.

My fingers hover over the keys, and I think about saying something dirty, spilling out a fraction of what always runs hectically through me in the lead-up to our meetings, but in the end I just type a kiss and close the window. I can't afford to get too distracted yet, if I'm going to finish everything on my plate on time. Ironically, it's he who has bred this self-control in me. He's good at holding me off, making sure that we get through the week balanced on this delicate trip wire of desire, never peaking too soon. At first it didn't come naturally to me: I wanted it all, as fast as I could have it. Now I understand the pleasure of delayed gratification, and I find myself doing the same.

At six o'clock, people start to peel away one by one, calling farewells around the office and packing up their stuff. Soon it's only Steven and me left. As the boss, he's often last to leave. He's frowning over a presentation, clearly practicing it to himself, lips moving soundlessly. Every so often I glance at him, wondering if I should text Carl and tell him to wait somewhere nearby.

"Should I lock up this evening, or are you staying late?" I ask him at last. With a start, he looks up, noticing the empty desks.

"Oh. No, I didn't mean to stay late," he says vaguely, and starts collecting paper into piles, pushing down the lid of his laptop. "You're not coming, then?"

"No, I'll stay on," I say quickly. "Got a bit to get through still."

"OK." He pulls on his jacket, then stands looking at me for a moment, bag slung over his shoulder. "Are you all right?" he asks.

"Yes!" I look up, smiling brightly, looking straight into his eyes. "I'm fine. Why?"

Steven scratches his chin. "I'm not sure. You just seem a little— I don't know. Nervous. Not yourself." The words fall awkwardly from his lips, and his face clouds in embarrassment. We don't have the sort of boss-to-employee relationship that generally covers personal observations, and when I think about it, I'm not sure that he knows who "myself" really is, not on any deep level.

"I'm fine," I repeat. "Just a bit tired and stressed, that's all."

"Right." Steven nods, then ducks out of the door, clearly relieved to be escaping this conversation. I sit alone in the office for a minute. My heart is pounding, and I'm suddenly hot, as if I might faint.

I get up and go to the cloakroom, swing the door open to stare into the little mirror hanging on the wall. My cheeks are flushed and vivid, my eyes shining darkly. Steven is right. I'm not myself. The woman in the mirror has a power and a presence that I haven't felt for years. I remember Jess last week, stopping to look at me when we met at the station with an expression of almost quizzical surprise. *I have to admit, this seems to suit you.* Combing my fingers through my hair, I stare at myself. These days I veer from misery to ecstasy with frightening speed and irregularity. If this is what suits me, I'm not sure what sort of a person that makes me.

The door opens behind me and I swing 'round to see Carl slipping inside, slamming it shut behind him. He runs his eyes quickly over my buttoned-up white blouse and my short black skirt, the bare legs in high heels. We're walking fast toward each other and as we collide he wraps his arms 'round me tightly and my whole body relaxes into him. We kiss slowly, deeply. We're standing in front of the long window, in full view of the offices opposite, but there's no one around.

"Do you want to take your coat off?" I murmur at last.

He laughs, glancing down. He hasn't even taken the bag off his shoulder. "Yeah," he says. "Sorry. Hello."

"No need to apologize." I unbutton the coat for him and slip it off, letting it fall to the floor. "Do you want a drink?"

He shakes his head, prowling 'round the empty desks, looking at the place where he used to sit. "It's weird being back here. You know, I almost bumped into Steven on the way in. Saw him coming down the road and had to duck down a side street until he'd gone. That would have been embarrassing. Oh, errrm, hi. I was just . . ."

". . . Just passing," I finish off, giggling. These near misses should concern me, but part of me can't help feeling excited at the thought of discovery. I want to broadcast it—want them to understand it, understand that it's real.

"Mmm," he says, watching the rise and fall of my chest. "You like that idea, don't you," and he's crossing the room and lifting me up into his arms. I wrap my legs around his waist as he carries me through into the meeting room and lays me down on the desk, his shadow blocking out the light as he bends over me. His hands are sliding up my thighs, stroking my skin. "No knickers," he murmurs, "naughty girl," and he's pinning my arms up above my head and keeping his hand locked hard around them, the other hand fumbling impatiently with his belt now that the waiting is over and he knows we both want the same thing. He's on me in an instant and the force of it drives me back onto the wood, the rhythm of our movements scraping and thudding against the small of my back—and it's going to hurt tomorrow but his breath is hot on my lips and I'm seeing stars as I close my eyes and I don't care at all.

~

We lie around in the office afterward for another hour or so half dressed, lounging on the makeshift bed we've created on the floor. The sun has dropped and it's warm and dark. I've switched on the television above the desk but the sound is turned down to an almost inaudible hum; I can see the images cycling out of the corner of my eye, a blur of shifting light. He's staring up at the ceiling, his hand threaded through my hair and tugging gently at its strands every so often, and I realize this, too, has become a routine of sorts. We've fallen into our own ways of being together, without even trying.

"Are you sure it's all right about the eighth?" he asks at last.

I roll onto my front, throwing my arm across his chest and looking up into his eyes. "Definitely." We're going away for the night together—a small hotel called the Silver Birches that he booked weeks ago as a stop-off in an anonymous town en route to his friend's thirtieth birthday celebrations the next day. When he first floated the idea that I might join him, I was equally attracted and terrified. Even now, despite Francis's apparent lack of interest in my movements, I can't imagine stepping this far out of my life without it being discovered. Whenever I think about it, though— no need to get up and get dressed at the end of the night and go out into the cold, and the intimacy of waking up with him there in reality and not only in my head—excitement beats a pulse through me and there's no way I'm going to back out now.

"Well, good," he says, "if you're sure. It's not that I don't want you to come. As you no doubt realize. It's just that I don't want you to do anything too risky."

"It'll be fine," I assure him. "I can't wait." As I speak I realize how often these words fall from my lips, and his. It seems we spend our lives in a permanent state of poised expectancy, and when it lifts, our time together is so temporary that I've blinked and it's gone, driven back to the same old state of anticipation as if I'd never left.

He sighs, shifting beneath me. "And, you know, after that," he says, "we're going to have to start scaling this down. Things can't go on like this forever, can they?"

"I know." It's automatic. We have been saying this for a long time, and July 8 has become a marker in the sand—a kind of last hurrah before we start to unpeel the bonds we've spent months making. Now, more than ever, it seems senseless. I think about saying so, to suggest the idea that things may not have to be this way, but the time doesn't seem right and something silences me. "I don't want to," I say instead.

"I know you don't," he says. "It's not going to be easy for me either. But there's not much choice, is there." It isn't a question. He's said this kind of thing before, several times. Last time, he went further. *I'll be thirty in a few years, and what have I got to show for it? I'm living in a flat share with no girlfriend and I'm seeing a married woman with a child. When this is over, you'll have him to focus on, but I've got nothing. I've got to live my own life. I need to get on with it, without you.* And I had recoiled in near shock and surprise, the hurt written across my face as clearly as if he had shouted it, and he had placed his hand over mine, apologizing silently, but not taking it back.

We lie there in silence for a while longer, and sadness filters through the room like smoke. It's seeping in more and more when we're together, this indefinable melancholy that colors every look and touch. We used to spend our time laughing like teenagers, entertaining each other effortlessly. It seems we've conducted everything on fast-forward. In six months we've aged ten years, already sensing the shadow of separation.

He turns onto his side to face me and moves my face toward his. Even as it's happening I'm thinking that I've never been kissed so carefully—with such attention, as if he's trying to imprint the way our lips fit together onto his memory. I know what it means. I don't want to lose this. The desire is primal and I push myself up against him wordlessly and hard, willing him to read what's in my head.

"We'd better get out of here," he says after a while. It's not what I wanted, but glancing at the time, I see he's right. I nod silently and reach for my clothes.

It's barely half an hour before I'm home but it's already getting dark, and I realize I've stayed out later than I thought, later than I would plausibly be working. I brace myself as I turn the key in the lock, but as soon as I enter the hallway I hear the sound of Francis's snoring coming from the lounge, uneven and jagged.

I check on Eddie first, finding him sleeping serenely, tucked up in bed. I stroke his hair softly, feeling guilt surging through me. It feels as if I've barely seen him this week. Tomorrow I'll come home early and spend some time with him, maybe take him to the playground. Quietly, I back out of the room, then close the door.

Tiptoeing into the lounge, I peer at Francis where he lies sprawled on the sofa. With a shock, I see that he's left a pill packet out, tossed next to him carelessly. I can't remember how many there were last time I looked, but the foil is torn all the way along now and there's nothing left. The sight of it lights a bright flare of anger inside me, white hot and hopeless. I reach out and shake him roughly by the shoulder, redoubling the pressure when he barely stirs. He makes a noise, something that might be a greeting or a command to leave him alone. His eyelids peel open for a fraction of a second, then droop closed again.

"For Christ's sake, Francis," I say, hearing the hysterical rise in my voice and knowing that I'm on the path to losing it. "What the hell are you doing to yourself? Do you even understand what's happening here? Have you got a fucking clue?"

His eyes open again, a slow painful movement, as if he's wrenching them up with pliers. There's little recognition in the glazed look he gives me, and even less acknowledgment of what I'm saying. I stand there in the middle of the room, my arms wrapped around myself, and I can still feel and smell Carl all over my body, and all at once my heart lurches sickeningly and I have no idea how we got here. Tears are pushing themselves out of my eyes, choking my throat. "I've had enough of this," I hear myself saying. "You're supposed to be looking after our child, for God's sake. What if he woke up and needed you? How can I trust that you wouldn't just ignore him?" It's my own hypocrisy as much as the fear that's driving the tears. I have no idea what trust means now, between my husband and me.

Francis struggles aimlessly in his seat, wiping a hand across his face and trying to collect himself. "I wouldn't do that," he says. "I know my responsibilities. I look after him." The words are placatory, but there's a bite behind them and his frown is thunderous. It's all I can see.

"Well, that's good to know," I spit back. "It's good to know that you'll do it for him, but—" I pause for a second, unsure if I really want to say the words that are trembling on my lips. "But not for me," I force out.

He frowns again, as if confused, thrown off base. Perhaps it's the emotion implicit behind what I have said—an emotion that seems to have no place between us these days. I don't even know myself why I care anymore. His mouth opens briefly, then snaps shut, and he leans his head back against the sofa cushions, closing his eyes again.

Anger is still burning through me, making it hard to breathe. "I don't want to do this," I say, loudly and clearly, spacing the words out. When there is no response, I grit my teeth, hug my arms tighter around myself. "I don't want to be married to you anymore," I say. "I think I'm done here."

His eyelids flicker minutely, but still there is no response. I stare at his dark eyelashes, the moldings of his face that remind me of Eddie's, the shadow of the bones that I once used to trace with my fingertips while he slept, trying to transmit my love for him secretly through his skin.

"I'm leaving you," I finish. The words are simple and strong but I can hear the tremor of uncertainty in my voice and I know that on some level he will hear and understand it, too. Now that I've said it, we both know that I don't quite mean it yet. But I will, I tell myself. Sometime soon, I will.

*T*hey're back. This time I'm ready for them—as soon as I see them pause outside the building, I'm pulling on my shoes and running down the staircase to the ground floor. I fumble with something in my coat pocket as I push my way out of the front doors, feigning self-absorption; then I let myself glance in their direction and do a double take, smiling in surprised recognition.

I address the little boy directly. "You're Eddie, aren't you?" He half smiles back, then puts a fist to his mouth and sucks on it, suddenly shy. His eyes slide up toward his grandmother, who is eyeing me with polite suspicion. "I'm house-sitting for Caroline and Francis," I explain. "Eddie's photos are all over the flat."

"Oh, I see." Caroline's mother sounds relieved to be presented with such a pat explanation. "We're not really lurking," she explains. "The flat's on our route back from school, and . . ."

"Paddy," says Eddie suddenly and clearly, his silence temporarily broken. His wide gray eyes are filled with expectancy. For a moment I have to stop and think, but then I remember the little silvery hamster that occasionally reminds me of its presence by scuttling around its wheel like a creature deranged. Caroline left painstakingly detailed *instructions on its care, but I've simply thrown a handful of food into the cage every so often and nothing catastrophic has occurred. Most things take less effort than you think to keep alive.*

"I'm sorry," Caroline's mother says gaily. "He's been talking about him a lot. We could have had him this week, only I'm allergic."

"Well," I find myself saying, "you must come up and see him. Would you like that, Eddie?" The child nods, his face brightening with anticipation. Even as he does so, I realize that I can't let them into the flat now. Not with the possessions slung haphazardly all over the floors, the mutilated photographs in the hallway. "I have to go out now," I add, "but maybe tomorrow, on your way back from school?"

Eddie jumps up and down, letting loose an excited volley of approval. Caroline's mother smiles, a little tightly. "Well, that's very kind of you," she says. "We'll see how we go tomorrow. Anyway, we won't keep you any longer. Nice to meet you, um . . ."

She pauses, expecting me to fill the gap, but I simply smile and head off down the street, giving a quick wave of farewell. My footsteps are echoing in my head like gunshots. I'm not sure what I've just done, but it's flooding me with sudden exhilaration and my head is light and giddy. I was stupid to think that the way to get close to someone was through the place they lived, the things they owned. It's the people they love that tell you the most about who they are.

AWAY

Caroline, May 2015

I'm lying wide awake in the darkened bedroom, watching the rise and fall of the duvet next to me as Francis sleeps soundly, the furnishings gradually emerging from blackness and taking shape as my eyes grow accustomed to the dark. There's a kind of unreality to being here at night. Anything seems possible, and as my thoughts churn I'm seized by restlessness. I want to get up, search the house yet again in hope of finding some new clue.

Looking 'round at the stark minimal lines of the bedroom, I know there's nothing more to find. But there's no way that this is the sum total of all you own. It can't be. The wardrobes and cupboards are practically empty, and you can't have taken an entire house's worth of stuff away with you this week. Even the display cabinets are the kind no one has in real life—hollow wooden cubes studded sparsely here and there with a candle or decorative sculpture. You were never messy, but I can't think of you as this stripped back. There must be more. So where is it? As I lie there a thought suddenly strikes me. Galvanized, I push the duvet quietly aside and slip out of bed, reaching for my phone and stepping out onto the darkened landing. A shiver racks me; part cold, part fear.

Looking up, I see the answer staring me in the face. There's a neat whitewashed square in the ceiling with a small hook embedded at one side, the entrance to a loft. Now that I see it, I remember noticing a long metal pole standing in the hallway cupboard, and quickly I go to fetch it, hooking it up to the ceiling panel. Sure enough, it swings open and I see that there is a ladder attached, one that unfolds as I tug on it. There's no light on in the loft, but as I peer up I think I can make out an array of shapes in the darkness below the crosshatched beams, faintly illuminated by the streetlights shining through the skylight window. The thought of climbing into the dark is terrifying, but I set my teeth, telling myself that there is nothing and no one up there. It's only my own thoughts that are scaring me.

Grasping the ladder with both hands, I climb carefully up, mindful not to make too much noise in case I wake Francis, my heart pumping with adrenaline. I scramble through the opening at the top, landing on my hands and knees on the loft's wooden floorboards. Shining the light from my phone across them, I can see they're heavy with grit, but when I squint across the darkened space I see that it has been recently disturbed. There are clear tracks in the dust, the kind that could have been made by dragging heavy objects across the floor. As I cautiously stand up, I notice a light switch on the nearby wall and flick it; a dim orange bulb glows nakedly in the center of the room and although it still strains my eyes I can now see that there are several large white bin bags piled up in the corner of the room, at least a dozen. Stacked beside them are a few cardboard boxes—they're brand-new, not even dusty.

I find that I am holding my breath, my throat tight, and automatically softening the sound of my footsteps as I approach. Wild pictures form in my head: bags full of mangled, severed limbs, leaking blood. I can't suppress a shiver as I reach for the first bag and rip open the string tied at the top.

A jumble of kitchenware, tea towels, and crockery, bundled together carelessly. The next few bags are similar: hastily assembled collections of utensils and ornaments that don't seem to have any personal value or significance. There's no reason to hide these things, none other than wanting to keep the mundanities of your life entirely secret and removed from me. I tear open bag after bag, finding nothing much of interest. A few of the boxes are stacked with books, and I linger for a while, sifting through the titles. Various classics, a few biographies, even some pop psychology that's hard to imagine you ever reading.

There are a few extra bags bundled behind the boxes, much lighter and softer than the others, and I feel a sudden surge of nausea when I realize they must be clothes. This feels more intimate. If I close my eyes I can still remember the way your clothes used to feel against my hands, and the scent of your aftershave that clung to them. My heart is beating a quick tattoo against my ribs as I open the nearest bag, but when I reach inside something feels instinctively wrong. I pull out a few items, studying them in the dim light. They're jumpers, in soft pastel colors. I reach farther down into the bag, shake its contents out onto the floor. These are all women's clothes, not yours at all. They're all in a size 10, and some of the brands are expensive. With another shiver, I realize they must belong to Amber. I sift through the other bags, and it's more of the same. It's as if practically her entire wardrobe has been transported up here.

My mind buzzing with confusion, I sit back. Why are there so many of these clothes, and why are they up here? I turn out the final bag, and amidst the soft slide of fabric something clatters, hard metal striking the floor. I snatch up the object. It's a pale pewter locket, and as I ease open the catch I feel something familiar yet unexpected grazing my fingertips. It's a lock of hair, frayed at the ends.

Instinctively, I draw my fingers away, dropping the locket. The hair is too dark to belong to Amber, unless her current shade is heavily dyed. Is it yours? I peer at it again and realize it's possible. It's a similar color, and I think a similar thickness. I stretch a fingertip out to it again and close my eyes, trying to remember the way your hair felt against my skin. I can't quite catch on to the memory, but something shifts inside me, and for an instant, the murky orange light blurs and fuzzes before my eyes and my head swims. I push the locket back into the bag along with Amber's clothes, feeling like an intruder.

Hunched on the attic floor in my vest and knickers, I'm shivering and thoughts are racing around my head, demanding attention. I force myself to slow them down, and sure enough something rises to the surface—something that's been nagging at the back of my mind for days. I'm remembering her that day in the coffee shop, the sudden reserve that swept over her face when I asked her if she knew who lived here. *Not really. You see people around, but that's about it.* Why would she lie? Did she suspect who I was even then, and want to hide the truth from me? But the more I turn over the possibility the less right it feels. She hasn't behaved like someone who wants to hide herself or her lover away; she's sought out my friendship, gone beyond the call of duty. And then I remember something else: the way she prowled around this house the evening she came 'round, the intentness of her expression. I know on some visceral level that it wasn't the way you would behave in a house you knew well. It was as if she wanted to soak it up—as if she didn't belong here at all.

A quick decisive shudder rocks my body, and I wrap myself up more tightly, clutching my knees to my chest, trying to think. Is it possible that Amber isn't your girlfriend at all? That she's developed some crazy obsession with you, is stalking you at close range from across the street? But then I remember the photograph on the fridge, and the women's clothes in front of me, and the idea slips through my fingers again and I'm no better off than I was before.

I press my fingers to my aching temples, my breath hissing with frustration. Impulsively, I snatch up my phone and tap out a text message. **I'm sorry I haven't answered your calls. I will soon, I promise. Just tell me, if you didn't know who I was, then why did you hide it from me that Carl lived here? Please. Just be straight with me and we can talk.**

As soon as I've pressed send I'm unsure if it was the right thing to do, but it's too late and I watch the screen, waiting tensely for a response. Some instinct tells me that she's as awake as I am, and sure enough it's barely a minute before the phone buzzes and the new message icon flashes.

Caroline, we need to talk about all this face to face. I haven't come over there, because I know this must be a difficult situation for you, and I don't want to involve Francis, but I'm not going to wait forever. The warning is lightly veiled, but tangible. There is nothing incongruous in the idea of Amber hammering on the front door in the middle of the night, demanding an immediate conference. I know she would do it, just as I would.

My fingers move slowly across the screen. **I'll come over. Five minutes.** Then I climb down the ladder and go softly back into the bedroom, reach for the clothes that I slung across the back of the armchair an hour or two earlier, and wriggle back into them. Combing my fingers roughly through my hair, I think about putting on some makeup, but I don't want to switch any lights on, and perhaps it doesn't matter what I look like now. I want her to see me as I am. Thirty-seven, with the evidence of the past few years written all over my face. Giving Francis a final glance, I slip out of the bedroom and tiptoe softly down the stairs, then ease open the front door and step out onto the street.

It's so still outside that I feel like the only moving point in a static world. The regimented rows of windows are dark and blank, flanked by the lines of carefully coiffured trees, tips pointing motionless to the sky. Streetlamps glow along the road at measured intervals, small beacons of muted orange light that cast their surroundings dimly in their aura. As I walk toward number 14, my shadow catches me out several times. I tell myself fiercely that there are few places safer than a suburban cul de sac. It would take only one burst of noise, one scream into the silence, for the windows to light up in a chain reaction like dominoes, and for the watchmen to appear from behind their curtains. The thought isn't as comforting as I'd hoped. Now, of all times, I need to stay quiet. I don't want to be seen.

I have barely raised my hand to the doorbell before I see her shadow through the frosted glass, reaching forward to let me in. There's a single lamplight burning in the back of the house, in the little room I now realize must be your study. She moves aside silently so that I can pass, her expression unreadable. When she's followed me into the back room, I can see that her face, too, is free of makeup; she has the look of a marble Madonna, stripped back and unsettlingly pure. Her blond hair is swept back and plastered against her scalp, as if with sweat.

"I don't really know what to say," she says at last. Neither of us has sat down; we're standing facing each other, a foot or so apart, our bodies mirroring each other's tension. We're the same height, the same build. More clearly than ever before, the thought flicks through me that I've been replaced. Replaced with a younger, prettier version of myself, without my sins and scars.

I open my mouth to reply, in search of some smooth social nicety that will carry us through the strangeness of this moment, but nothing comes out.

"How long have you been together?" I ask. It's a question pulled at random from all those swirling in my head, but as I speak I realize that it's the one I most need an answer to.

Amber thinks for a moment, wanting to get it right. "Eighteen months," she says eventually. I work it out. November 2013; four months after I last saw you. Too fast. Implausibly fast, for you. You used to tell me that no one had ever got to the heart of you like I had, that nothing had ever really seemed worth pursuing.

She's watching me, her head tilted slightly upward with what could be defiance. "We moved in together here after seven months," she says, and now there is a definite challenge in her tone. "It was quick, but when it's right, it's right, isn't it." She speaks with efficient, dispassionate fierceness, as if daring me to disagree.

"I suppose so," I find myself saying.

Now that she knows I'm not out to attack her, her posture softens slightly and she moves forward into the light, letting me see the shadows in her face, her pupils almost pinpricks in her dark green eyes. For a moment, I try to put myself in her position—me as the current occupant, threatened by a woman from the past—but I can't do it. She still doesn't feel quite real to me, not as your girlfriend. Her skin is luminous and the lamplight is shining through her blond hair, and under the thin fabric of her white T-shirt I can see the curve of her breasts, her nipples faintly outlined. A vision comes to me, a little mental ripple—you pushing the fabric up with your hands, over her head.

"Look," she says in a rush, "you must know how this seems. Be honest with me. Did you come here to see him?"

"Of course not," I tell her, trying to make my words brook no denial. I know I would have thought the same, in her place, but all the same I can't help but resent the implication.

"OK," Amber says slowly. I can't tell if she believes me or not. "But you said he had been in touch." She pauses, biting her bottom lip. "Outside," she says, "the other day. You told me your ex had messaged you. You meant Carl, right?"

The sound of your name on her lips, dropped with such easy, possessive familiarity, makes me not want to tell her anything. She's on your side, not mine. She'd dismiss it, painting me as a fantasist; she'd be straight on the phone to you, if she hasn't been already. At the idea, my heart jumps into my throat and I have to ask. "Have you told him?" I force out. "That I'm here?"

Amber shakes her head. "I don't want to upset him. There's no point in dragging up the past—unless I need to." I catch the glimmer of a threat. She's not sure, yet, what I plan to do.

"I see." I have to admire her reticence. In that way, she isn't like me at all. I couldn't have kept this secret for more than a few minutes . . . although as soon as the thought passes through my head I realize that I've been keeping it from Francis, for days now. I'm not sure what the difference is. Perhaps it's simply that I'm used to hiding things from him, to dividing our life together into little pockets and playing the complicated game of twisting some of them outward for public view, some of them inward for my own consumption.

Amber is staring at me expectantly, still waiting for the answer to her own question. "You told me he had gotten in touch with you," she says again. "And you told me you thought he was in your house. Why would you say those things?"

I open my mouth, on the brink of trying to explain, but I don't know where to begin. "I did get a message recently," I say slowly, and as I do so I realize that there is a way of telling the truth while hardly telling anything at all. "It wasn't from him, or at least it wasn't under his name. It mentioned my house, and . . . there was something about it that reminded me of him. I thought it was him. But I could be wrong."

She takes this in, frowning imperceptibly. As she does so, she sinks into a chair, gesturing for me to do the same. She leans forward, knotting her long fingers together, scratching her pale pink painted nails thoughtfully back and forth over her own skin. There's something hypnotic about the movement. "I think you are," she says at last. "I think you are wrong." Despite the qualifier, it doesn't sound like an opinion. She speaks with absolute confidence. "If you know Carl," she continues, "then you should know that he doesn't change his mind. It's almost a weakness, as far as he's concerned. And he made a very definite decision to leave your relationship behind." Only now does she meet my eyes, and the unblinking directness of her gaze is unnerving. "He's moved on," she says.

When the words first land they hurt, a well-aimed blow that makes me flinch. But the impact is glancing, fading into nothing almost as soon as it has come. What she says is hollow in the face of the evidence I have—not only the secrets I am keeping from her, but the simple, tangible force of how similar we look. "It's a strange way to move on," I say, gesturing into the space between us.

Amber's face flickers briefly with doubt as she catches on to my meaning, but she shrugs, brushing her hair behind her ears. "He has a type," she says. "A lot of people do."

I know it's more than that, but I let it go, letting her hear the echo of her own words in the silence. "How much has he told you?" I ask. "About me. About our relationship."

She seems on safer ground now, drawing herself up, and meeting my gaze again head-on. "Everything." Her face twists, as if she might say more, but she presses her lips together and half shakes her head, a little internal self-check.

Without wanting to, I'm giving that one word its context. Images are rising inside me, headed with increasing speed toward that final still point: the road outside the Silver Birches hotel, the place where I last saw you. I see Amber watching me, and I wonder how much of what I am fighting hard to suppress is written over my face, and if she really knows, if she really understands. For so long I have believed that our secrets have existed only between you and me, in a tight unhappy little club of two. It's an unspoken bond, stretching across the distance. It's kept me in your life, and you in my mine, whatever the facts might say. The thought that the circle might have expanded to include her disorients me.

"Look," her voice cuts into my thoughts. "That message you just sent me." With a shock, I remember the reason I texted her. "I don't really understand what you were asking. You're asking why I didn't tell you Carl lived here?"

"Yes," I say. "That first day we had coffee, when I asked you if you knew the person who owned the house I was staying in, you said no. Why didn't you tell me it was him?"

She frowns, clearly thrown off base. "Why would you think that?" she asks. "Carl lives *here*. Here. In this house, with me."

I blink, trying to take in what she is saying. It makes no sense, and yet it rings true. The crockery in her kitchen, the bright colored walls, the stark black-and-white prints in the hallway. These are your taste, not hers. I can imagine you in this house, in a way I've never been able to imagine you at number 21. The mental images of you here flood my brain with a certainty that tells me she isn't lying.

I'm wading through treacle, trying to catch up with a meaning that I can't quite grasp. Does number 21 belong to another of your girlfriends, someone who trusts you and lets you into her home and whose absence you've timed to coincide with my arrival? Have you posted her details on the house-swap website without her knowledge? Somehow enlisted her, obtained her keys, and intercepted mine? Or do you own both houses? But every idea that comes to me feels implausible.

"When is he coming back?" I ask at last. I need to drag the conversation back to firmer ground. The here and now is what we need to concern ourselves with; it's the only thing we can deal with right now.

"Tomorrow afternoon," she says, and she can't suppress the lift in her voice for an instant, her face momentarily illuminated by the private happiness that the thought is giving her.

I clench my hands into fists, digging my fingernails into my palms. I'm not due to return to Leeds for two more days, and although I still don't understand how, you must know that. You're choosing to return early. Why would you do that? Surely only because you want to see me?

"We need to decide what to do," Amber says bluntly. "I'll be honest, I don't think you should stay. I don't think it will do any good for you to see him. No good for you, or for him. Or for me," she adds—casually, but I know that this is what must be burning brightest in her mind.

My immediate reaction is to defy her, but I have the sense to keep my mouth shut and bite my tongue. "I'll think about it," I say at last. "I'll text you in the morning."

Amber nods, and I see her body sag in the armchair, as if drained by the intensity of our conversation. "OK." She rests her head back, half closing her eyes.

I stand to leave, but when my hand is on the door I can't help turning back and asking the question that has been nagging at me ever since I knew that she was the one person who could give me the answer. "How is he?" I ask simply.

She raises her head slowly, looks at me through narrowed eyes. "Good," she says. "Fine. Happy." Her voice is soft and noncombative, but each word has the feel of a muffled gunshot, killing off further questioning. I think about these words, turn them over in my head. They don't fit with what she said the other day, when she talked about your remoteness, the feeling she often had that you weren't quite there. But I don't have the energy to work out which I would prefer or which is more likely to be true, and I just nod and leave the house, closing the front door quietly behind me.

~

Somehow in the few hours I've been asleep since I returned from Amber's house I've managed to work my way across the bed toward Francis, so that when I wake my lips are pressed into the crook of his neck and his arms are wrapped loosely around me. He's still sleeping, his breath coming evenly and quietly, stirring the hair that falls across my face. Lying with the warmth of his body pressed up against mine, the surreal midnight encounter with Amber seems like a dream.

Francis is stirring, stretching and yawning. "Hello," he mumbles, tightening his arms around me in a hug. "It's good to have you here."

I push my face into his shoulder, my eyes suddenly stinging senselessly with tears. "Morning." His hand is resting lightly on the top of my head, then sliding to the back of my neck, applying a little pressure to encourage me to look up at him. I blink the tears back. "Did you sleep well?"

He frowns gently, his face angled down to study mine. "I slept all right," he says, "but when I woke up at one point in the night, you weren't there. Where did you go?"

"I couldn't sleep. I was just downstairs for a bit," I say quickly. Too late, I realize I have no idea if he went in search of me and found the house empty. My muscles tense, but he doesn't contradict me.

"You know," he says instead, at last, "I really am worried about you. I have been all week. I know we've had some tense moments, particularly the other day at the museum, and I'm sorry for my part in that, but it's not just that. You've just seemed . . . troubled. Jumpy." He pauses, as if searching for the definitive comment on my behavior. "Absent," he finishes.

The word sends a shiver through me. Absence, detachment, is a dangerous thing between us. I used to come home to a man who seemed not so much a husband as a robot put in his place; a hologram with Francis's face and nothing inside. At first I fought back with anger, pouring double the emotion into the empty space that his disappearance from the relationship had left. I'm not even sure when the anger turned to an indifference that numbed me to the bone and sucked up my love. But I know what hardened it and made it set in: you. And now, after all this time, you're starting to do it again.

I wrap my arms around his neck, trying to bring myself back. "I know," I whisper. "I'm sorry. I just . . ." I release him and roll over onto my back, staring up at the shadowed sunlight flickering warmly across the ceiling. "I'm not happy here," I say honestly. "I know we looked forward to coming away, but I feel strange. I miss Eddie, and the flat. I miss being at home." As I speak I feel the resolve strengthen inside me. Amber was right. I have the opportunity to cut this mess off before I'm tempted to have any further contact with you. "We could just go home today," I say.

Francis draws in a breath, confused. "Today?" he repeats. "But we're going back tomorrow evening anyway—what's the point of going now? Maybe you've forgotten, Caro, but there's someone staying in our house this week, too. They're not going to want to be turfed out a day early."

"I haven't forgotten," I say, the irony tasting bitter in my mouth, "but . . ." The words dry up. There is no way to explain to him that I know you have no intention of staying in our house until tomorrow night; that probably even now you're packing up your things and preparing to make the long drive back here. "I'm sure it would be OK," I finish lamely. "Or we could go somewhere else, drive back and stop off somewhere in the Midlands at a hotel for the night."

"Why would we do that?" Francis asks bluntly. "It's just unnecessary money. Look . . . I hear what you're saying. But I think we can turn this 'round. It hasn't been all bad, has it? And we could do something nice today. I admit I've kind of run out of touristy things to visit, but I'm sure we can think of something."

I open my mouth to argue back, but inspiration deserts me and I can't think of any reason to protest. He lifts my hand to his lips and kisses it encouragingly, taking my silence for consent. "OK," he says briskly, leaping out of bed. "I'm going to hop in the shower, and then we'll work out what to do today."

When he has disappeared into the bathroom I pull the bedclothes up around my neck, suddenly cold. Already I'm interrogating myself—wondering if I could have tried harder. I tell myself it will be fine. We'll go out all day, come back late. I'll walk straight up the path and into the house, not even glancing across the street. Being a few yards away from you is no different from being hundreds of miles away. There is no invisible aura that grows more powerful when you're closer. It makes no difference at all.

Even as I'm trying to convince myself I know it's useless. Despite everything, an insane part of me doesn't want to go, and doesn't want to keep away either. I want to see you.

I close my eyes briefly, hating myself. I don't even know who it is that I'm wanting. The you I knew wouldn't have done this at all, let alone sent that sinister photograph. At the thought of it, I turn to my phone and open up the email again, wanting to present myself with the evidence. The shock of it hits me afresh: the crudely doctored pictures, the ovals of blank space where my face has been removed. I keep looking, until I've been staring at it for so long that it's starting to blur before my eyes. And then all at once, my focus shifts and in the same way that you can look at an anagram and see the letters suddenly rearranging themselves into meaning out of nowhere, I see something else.

In the corner of the picture, the hallway mirror is hanging, almost out of shot. The light is dim, and the camera flash has hit the glass, but I can just about make out the figure in profile, holding the camera up to take the photograph. I can't see the face, but I can see the length of the hair, the slightness of the shoulders and the curve of the neck. The figure is a woman. It's not you.

HOME

Francis, July 2013

The only thing more frightening than the knowledge that you've hit rock bottom is the fear that you haven't. I've been there several times these past few months. A dark place, a prison with no clear exit—a windowless box filled with the smell of decay and destruction. And then the gears grind into action and the lift shudders down another floor, and I realize that wherever I've been, it was just a holding room. You can always go lower. That's the lesson I'm learning, over and over, every day.

Today is a first. It's almost 8 a.m. and the summer sun is shining through the wide-open French windows, and I've been awake all night. No patches of uneasy sleep, no drifting losses of consciousness at the computer screen that end with a violent jolt, as if I've been falling and am only just hitting the ground. I've been sitting here wired up for ten hours and my eyes are wide open. Not to say that I can remember much of it. When I cast back over the night in search of something to catch on to, it's like looking for driftwood in a constantly churning sea. The sunlight hurts my eyes and despite the heat I'm shivering.

There's noise in the rooms beyond. A child squawking and

shouting, wordless bursts of song. Eddie. His name feels blank and unfamiliar in my head. Love sits uneasily on me, a worn-out, too-big coat that doesn't mold itself to me in the way it once did. At some point it's going to fall apart just like everything else.

Caroline comes into the room. A woman in a sleeveless vest top and a black skirt with transparent pleats that shine through to a short silk layer beneath, and which fly out and settle again against her skin when she turns. Her hair looks soft and she smells of roses. We have nothing to do with each other. In fact, the idea that this woman used to look into my eyes and tell me with passionate impatience that she loved me, that she used to come for me as easily as breathing, is so strange that it makes me wonder if I've dreamed it all and woken up in a whole other life.

She's checking her appearance in the mirror, rolling lipstick slowly around her mouth. "We're leaving in a minute," she says.

"Where are you going?" I'm not sure why I bother to ask. Life happens and it doesn't have much to do with me, but some habits die harder than others and I still want to know where she goes and what she does, or at least what she tells me.

She stops, stares. "To my parents' house." The words are slow and spaced out, as if she's talking to a child. "I'm taking Eddie there for the weekend, remember."

"That's next weekend." I do remember this being talked about. A little pathetic flicker of pleasure, that something has filtered in. But it wasn't happening today, or at least I don't think so.

"Today is the eighth of July, Francis," Caroline says. "This was always the plan. We're leaving now, and we'll be back on Sunday morning. That's the day after tomorrow." I glance up sharply. That sounds like sarcasm, drip-feeding info to an idiot. But when I meet her gaze it's serious and straight. It's like she thinks I can't understand her.

"Yeah, I know," I say, shrugging it off. "See you, then. Have a good time. Call me."

She pulls her handbag onto her shoulder, spends some time adjusting and fiddling with the strap while her thoughts dance like butterflies across her face, each one clearer than the last. "If I were you," she says at last, not looking at me, "I'd use this time to think about how you want this to go forward. Because you know how I'm feeling. I don't think we're going anywhere. And unless you can show me otherwise pretty fucking soon then you know what's going to happen." Despite the swear word, her tone is calm and sad. If she's talking to anyone, it's to herself.

The thought is vaguely reassuring. *If you can't even look me in the eye*, I think, *don't think you can tell me what to do.* And soon it's like it's never been said at all.

Eddie gallops into the room. Red shirt, blue shoes. Before I know it he's launched himself against me, his head butting into my stomach. It hurts, like most things do now. I wince, drawing him back by the shoulders. His arms are reaching out, squeezing around my neck. "Bye, Daddy." A moment of wide-eyed contact. He's the only person left in the world who doesn't judge me and it's only because he hasn't got the tools for it yet. He's not old enough to know better. But sooner or later his eyes are going to narrow with suspicion and his lip is going to twist with distaste and he's going to turn his back.

The door slams and they're gone. I prod my feelings, a sharp stick digging into the mud of the riverbank. Loneliness. Relief. Two sides of the same coin. I hate to be alone and yet it feels natural, inevitable. Two days. I check the pill packets stuffed down the side of the sofa and take a few. I start to count what's left, but I can't keep the numbers in my head. Better be on the safe side. It's not like they do anything anymore—I remember the hit they used to give, the swooping high that has eluded me for months, like it's the sweet memory of an old lover—but all the same they're necessary. They punctuate my breathing. Make it possible.

I send a text to one of my sources and ask him to set something aside. Can't afford it but it makes little difference now. Something tells me I won't be around to sort this all out. The last time I checked my bank balance it seemed crazily high, until I saw the little minus sign. When I'm lying here, sometimes I see the figures rising in negative, cycling and whirring like silent-spun wheels. A whole parallel world, growing while reality recedes.

I get up and go to the window, breathe in sweet, warm air. I have a session today. Young teenage girl who's been coming for months. I was helping her, at first. Could cancel. I mostly do, these days. But all of a sudden there's a strange little burst of energy and the thought of getting on the train and going to the clinic feels doable. Kind of fun. Maybe I was lying when I said there was no hit. Sometimes there's still something, even if it's hard to predict or define. Might as well ride the wave.

~

By the time I'm at the clinic the window that opened up inside my head for a few minutes has closed again and the shutters are dark. Cold in here despite the heat outside; yellowing carpets and musty walls, faded lampshades. I shouldn't be here. The walls are rearing up at me like sentinels, slanting grimly inward and blocking out the light and space in my head. This place doesn't want me in it.

But it's too late now and I'm walking into the counseling room and seeing everything laid out neatly just the way it should be. Box of tissues on the little low table. Jug of water with two small glasses. Lamp glowing in the corner. And she's pattering in after me, the girl. Can't remember her name. I glance at the pink crib sheet poking out of the top of my folder. Melody. Not really a name. Means something else, though right now I can't quite think what. Doesn't matter.

"So," I'm saying, "how are you?" My voice sounds different and strange in my own head. Kind of muffled, filtered through several layers of sound. The girl cocks her head and I have to repeat it.

"Oh," she says blankly, like she thought I'd said something else, something better. "I'm OK, I guess. Not so great this week overall, though. Some stuff happened with my mum again." She's off, drawing me through the marshlands of her memory, raking up the mud. I try to listen. Something about a fight, some raised and unkind words. Digging up old wounds, making her wonder if the relationship can be saved. The words are going in but my mind is throwing them out again, because my heart is thudding fast and my palms are wet with sweat and I know that this stuff used to matter but it doesn't now because no one matters but me.

She's still talking but her eyes tell another story. They're raking over me as if she's wondering who the hell this man is that she's trusting with her secrets. I haven't shaved in weeks and I can't remember the last time I had a shower, and there's a stain the size of a handprint halfway down my shirt.

My fingers are rattling against the edge of the tabletop. Stop. Looks like I'm impatient, like she's boring me. "Say that again," I say, because she's paused and it seems like I should be giving her something in return but I have no idea what she's just said.

"I said," she repeats, and just as Caroline did, she slows her words down and leaves a lot of space around them. "I said, it feels like I've been born into the wrong family."

"Interesting," I say, and actually this is interesting, and my mind is suddenly speeding up and thoughts are rushing around it at a hundred miles an hour, brightly colored lottery balls falling into the slot at random without thought or design. "Because, you know," I say, "your mother might well be thinking the same thing. That you've been born into the wrong family. That she's given birth to alien spawn. Some kind of incubus." I'm warming to my theme, but the girl draws back as if I've hit her and her eyes fill with tears, and before I know it she's leaped up from her seat and flounced out.

I stay sitting in my chair. That's never happened before. A lot of firsts, today. Outside in the corridor I can hear the distant echo of her voice, raised and tearful, and a soothing murmur coming back. It carries on for a few minutes. Then the girl sweeps back past my door again, not bothering to look in, and bangs her way down the stairs and out onto the street.

"Francis." It's Sara, with her hooked horn-rimmed glasses and her wispy hair, her floaty dresses. She's like a hippie without any of the free love or the fun. The thought amuses me and I wonder if I should share it. But before I get the chance she's talking again, her voice relentless and smooth, arms folded across her chest. "I can't quite get to the heart of what you just said to Melody, but she's very upset."

"Upset?" I think back, struggle to understand. What I said was interesting, thought provoking. Nothing personal. I'm an incubus myself. I don't belong anywhere. Not in the smug, gentrified space my family inhabits, not in the would-be-perfect nuclear little bubble with my wife and child. Maybe I should have said that.

"Yes," Sara says firmly. "And I have to tell you that this isn't the first complaint that's come in about you in recent weeks. Not to mention all the cancellations. It's a very difficult situation, as I'm sure you understand. We all care about your well-being, but you're in a position of trust here. We need to be sure that you're capable of upholding that position. There is support available, if you need it. You of all people should know that there's no shame in . . ."

And that's the point I switch off, because it's obvious where this is going. Her mouth is still moving and the sounds are coming out. Sharp eyes, soft words. She's wrong to think she can reason with me. Give me a loaded gun and I'll pull the trigger.

"Fuck this," I say, standing up. "I'm out." Push past her. Barely touched her but her mouth is rounded in a shocked little O of surprise and she's clutching at her side like I've stabbed her in the ribs. It's only her pride I've hurt and people so easily hurt shouldn't be allowed to live.

Out on the street, back onto the train, the walk down the road toward home. Noise is pounding in my head and my limbs are sore and tight. Bursts of color are lurching out of the air, people sliding past like they're on ice. That's done with. No more putting on a mask, no more pretending I'm someone who can listen to your problems and pull you out a solution, or even that I've got the means to listen at all. Dust my hands off and on to the next thing. Whatever that is.

At home I switch on the television and stick a pizza in the oven. I eat the whole thing in five minutes flat, oil clinging to my fingers and the cheap artificial taste flooding my mouth. There's a program on about the Grand Canyon and as I watch it, the sweeping panoramic views and the knowledge that there's a whole world out there to which I don't have access sends me hurtling down into my own canyon, a place I know so well now that it feels more like home than these four walls. I send Caroline a text: **Remind me to tell you about the black canyon.** A few months ago this kind of cryptic non sequitur used to throw her into instant fearful meltdown. **What's up, Francis? Are you OK?** Cutting her nights out short sometimes, to hurry back to my side. I kind of liked it. Showed me she cared. But this time the phone stays silent and it just sits there like a brick next to me, and there's no one else to call.

I sit on the sofa for a few more hours and I run my fingernail down the new packet of pills, pop them out and swallow them one by one, and then, when I think I should stop, I take some more until the world blurs in front of my eyes and I lose my grip. But all that happens is I wake up fourteen hours later with a splitting headache like my bones are painfully sharpened points, digging into me like knives from the inside out. Because anything else would be too easy. And it seems that even now I can't take the easy option.

I *shouldn't have sent the photograph. It was a snap decision. I sup-*
pose that with the number of emails she was sending, something was
bound to hit home and goad me eventually. A monkey rattling away
on a keyboard might produce Macbeth *after a few hours or a few mil-*
lion years, and in the grand scheme of things it didn't take her long to
find a weak spot. It was the challenge of inactivity that did it. The
casual assumption that I was hanging around, impotent and passive,
waiting for something to happen. And of course, like all the best insults,
it hurt because I was afraid it might be true.

It took me awhile to understand why the tone of her messages had
changed—terse queries; veiled, confused threats—but when I looked
again at the photograph I saw my own telltale shadow in the corner
of the shot. In the end, all it took to break her romantic fairy tale was
an intangible blur of reflected light. It's rocked her equilibrium, shone
an unpleasantly harsh spotlight on her own assumptions. While I
was Carl, she could kid herself that the only reason anyone would
infiltrate her life in this way was because they couldn't bear to be
without her. Now she can't. And she still doesn't understand. This is
how completely she's overwritten the past. She still can't accept that

so much more was lost back then than the thing that she's made everything.

Still, I can't sit stewing over it now. I've got visitors to prepare for. I have to get the house looking perfect, at least the parts that they might see. I've polished the surfaces, tidied away the detritus. Taken down all the photographs in the hall that featured her, which admittedly doesn't leave many, but I'm hoping they won't notice. And now I'm doing the dishes, cleaning and scrubbing, and all the while thinking about the instant when they step over the threshold and we're here in the house together. It's become a perfect moment in my mind: a flawless little tableau, in a suspended bubble of time. I don't know what to do with it yet. But the closer it gets, the more I think that the way will be shown to me; that some kind of divine inspiration will descend and suddenly I'll understand how to make everything right and wipe out the past two years and start again.

AWAY

Caroline, May 2015

I'm in the last place I want to be. A neon-lit madhouse buried in the bowels of a concrete shopping center, with the air suffused with the smell of frying chips and the sound of thudding bass and children screaming. Francis has decided that we should take a trip down memory lane and visit the bowling alley we used to go to occasionally together years ago when we were living in London, before Eddie. When he came into the bedroom to make the suggestion, I was still staring at the emailed photograph, trying to focus, blood rushing in my head. I was in no state to say no. For a crazy moment I almost thought that it might be good for me—to take a break, clear my thoughts, and unpick this complex mixture of disappointment, relief, confusion, and fear. But there's no chance of that in this chaos, and every thump and screech jars on my nerves.

"Right!" Francis is briskly weighing balls, finding the right sizes. "I'll start. Prepare to get whipped." He strides up to the alley and throws the ball with more force than precision, sending it skittering into the gutter with a rattle that sets my teeth on edge. "Yeah, well . . . ," he says, shrugging and casting a rueful glance over his shoulder, "it's been awhile. Just need to get back into the habit of it."

I try to smile, but my mouth feels tight and frozen. Despite the number of bodies packed into this space it's cold in here, the air conditioning pumping brutally through the room and bristling the hairs on my arms. I take a ball, walk up to the mark, and force my arm to swing and release. I watch the ball rolling, a bright orange sphere heading for a bull's-eye, but at the last moment it swerves and veers, knocking two or three pins as it drops out of view.

"Unlucky," Francis crows, giving my arm a mock pat of sympathy as I return.

"Luckier than you, anyway," I say automatically, and a kind of desperation overtakes me as I listen to our banter and I know that I should be enjoying this, that I should be able to relax and have fun with my husband without these shadows crowding the air and these horrible, ugly thoughts forcing their way between us. I reach for his hand where it still rests on my sleeve, and curl my fingers between the warm flesh of his own. This is what is real, and yet I can't rid myself of the knowledge that it could all crumble into dust if I said the word, even now. It would only take one revelation, one decision, for everything we've carefully rebuilt to pop and vanish. Whatever you do, all it takes to make it worthless is for one person to turn his back and walk away.

We carry on with the game, and all the while thoughts are pounding relentlessly through me. You and the woman in the photograph you emailed me are linked somehow; you must be. Have you cooked this up together between the two of you? Is she in love with you, willing to do your dirty work? But that doesn't make sense—if you wanted to be in my house, understand where I lived, then there would be no point in sending someone else in your place. Unless you're there together. But those pictures in the hallway . . . it doesn't strike me as the sort of thing you would ever do, or even approve of. It's too subtle for you, too threatening. Even if you wanted to hurt me, the bottom line is that I can't believe you would do it like this. You wouldn't cloak it in this kind of deception and trickery. Which can only mean . . . that you aren't the one behind this at all.

But that doesn't add up either. I can't believe that it can be a coincidence that you are living across the street from where I am staying. No matter how I look at it, I'm driven 'round in circles, brought back again and again to the same point of incomprehension. Who the hell is this woman? Why is she in my house, and what does she want?

Something is rising darkly in the back of my mind, and I push it down, clenching my fists with the effort. The room shimmers around me, the faded psychedelic pattern of the carpet suddenly rising up and rolling beneath my feet like waves.

"Strike!" Francis is standing with his arms aloft in triumph at the end of the alley. "What a way to end it." He jogs back to my side, gives me a commiserating kiss. "Never mind, eh. You didn't do too badly . . ."

I look up at the scorecard, realizing that I have absolutely no idea how the game has gone. I seem to have racked up 68 points, though when I cast back I can't remember a single ball I've thrown since that first one. I've lost the time again, stepped outside my life. Like any addiction, it seems this appetite for self-destruction has been gnawing at my defenses with steady, unwavering determination, finally breaking through.

Making my voice light, I congratulate Francis and give him a hug, breathing in the familiar smell of his aftershave and clinging to his reassuring solidity. "Are you hungry?" he asks. I nod, even though I can't imagine eating and the smell of oil and grease in the air is making me feel sick. "OK," he says. "I'll go and get us a couple of burgers. Maybe see if you can nab a table?"

He heads off down the neon-lit corridor toward the cafeteria, and I follow at a distance, blankly scanning the rows of yellow tables. I see a spare one in the center and make my way toward it, slipping into one of the hard plastic chairs. Next to me, a family of five is wrestling over the last portion of chips, children complaining and squealing at each other across the ketchup-spattered table, and a baby in the high chair drumming its fists and screaming. The sound scrapes at the edges of my already frayed nerves, and I look 'round for another spot, but the tables are all jam-packed and I give up, letting my shoulders slump.

My phone buzzes in my pocket and I feel the familiar clench of apprehension. For an instant I think it might be Amber, telling me that you have returned—perhaps that she's told you everything, that you're appalled by the idea that I might have followed you here. But the name that flashes up on the screen is Jess's. I stare at it for a moment, jolted. It's a signal, a white flag in the wilderness, reminding me that there's more to me than all of this.

I open the message. **Hey there! Having a good week? How are things with you and F? Saw your FB profile pic—bit weird?! Am I not getting the joke? LOL. Anyway speak to you soon I hope. Xx**

I frown, trying to remember. My profile picture on Facebook is a shot from last summer—on the beach with Eddie, when we made a day trip to Margate. I haven't changed it for ages. I barely even use the site now, except to lurk and satisfy an occasional curiosity about former acquaintances.

A tiny premonitory trickle of instinct is traveling over me, making me shiver. Quickly, I load the Facebook app on my phone, then click through to my profile. At first I can barely make out the picture. It's a jumble of lines and shapes, blotches of darkness and color. I enlarge it, peer closer. And then I see. It's a car, mangled and misshapen, thrown at the roadside like a crumpled toy. The windows are shattered, shards of glass littering the layby, and through the dark hole of the front windscreen the seats are darkly streaked with blood.

This time the shiver that racks me is powerful and intense, sending the breath hissing through my parted lips. Out of the corner of my eye I can see Francis, weaving his way toward the table, carrying a tray heaped with burgers and fries. I should put the phone down, but my hand is clasped rigidly around it, unable to let go. Because I can't hide from it anymore. It's staring me in the face and as I stare back I realize that on some level I've always been aware of it—that it isn't surprise but guilt that's paralyzing me. I may not know exactly who has done this yet, who is in my house. But I know why she's there.

HOME

Caroline, July 2013

Eddie and I have a good run down on the train, and my mother meets us at the station, waving gaily through the window as she steers into the carpark. Eddie spots her instantly, jumping up and down on the spot with frenzied impatience.

"Nanny, Nanny!" he squawks, pulling at my sleeve, beaming up at me. As soon as the car glides to a halt in front of us he runs forward and tugs at the door, squeaking his hello and launching himself into the backseat.

"Well, bye then," I say with mock outrage, leaning in to strap him into the car seat.

My mother laughs, glancing back at Eddie. "Sure you won't come back with us for a bit?" she asks.

"No, I'd better get on." My mind skates uncomfortably around the lies I have told. Even to me this disguise feels thin and not thought through. There's nothing to stop Francis from calling my parents' house and asking to speak to me, and if he does there would be no innocent explanation I could give. All the same, I don't really think it will happen, and even if it does, I'm not so sure that it would be a bad thing. More and more in recent weeks

I've felt the threat of an oncoming explosion building inside me, tensing and tightening. Sooner or later, something has to give.

"Suit yourself," my mother says cheerfully, leaning back in her seat and revving up the engine again. "Say bye-bye, Eddie," she calls as they pull away.

Eddie looks through the glass, smiling faintly at me, his eyes clear and untroubled. "Bye . . ." I hear him calling faintly, blowing a kiss.

For an instant, I don't want him to go, and I almost run after the car and flag it down. I could go back with them, spend the weekend with my son and my parents with a clear conscience. It would be simple. Soothing. But while I'm standing there they have turned out of sight, and I'm left clutching an overnight bag that is stuffed with expensive new underwear and pretty bikinis and clothes I've modeled in badly lit changing-room mirrors, imagining how Carl will look at me when he sees me in them, how they'll soon be invisibly imprinted with his hands. And before I know it the weight in my heart drops away and I want to be with him so much that everything else fades into nothing at all.

I take the train up to King's Cross and hurry out onto the main road, looking for the car he's told me he'll be hiring. His friend's birthday party is in the middle of nowhere, twenty miles from the hotel we'll be staying in. I scan the street anxiously, not seeing him. For an instant I wonder if he's changed his mind. Going away together, even for such a short time, feels out of step with the way we've conducted things so far: snatched evenings in his flat, the odd hour crammed in around the rest of my life. But then I hear the sound of a car pulling up behind me and when I turn 'round he's there, smiling through the open window and patting the seat next to him. "Hop in," he says.

My heart lifts and I scurry 'round to the passenger seat, sliding in and kissing him. He's had his hair cut since we were last together and I run my fingertips over the newly shorn nape of his neck, feeling the way it scratches softly against my skin.

"Like it?" he asks, swinging the car out into the road.

"Very much."

He's steering one-handed, his left hand straying across into my lap, running lightly up my thigh and smoothing the thin fabric of my skirt. In the rearview mirror, his gaze slides to meet mine.

"Good," he says mildly, and I feel the muscles of my stomach contract with desire, a quick visceral shudder. I stretch my hands out in my lap, gripping my knees with my fingernails, grounding myself. When I glance to the side, he's watching me again, his eyes flicking between me and the road. "You've taken your rings off," he says. "Mean business, do you?"

"I thought we might use the swimming pool," I say quickly; it's a half-truth. I remember sitting on the train, easing the rings 'round and 'round my knuckle. The tightness of them, the angry redness of my skin when I finally managed to pull them away. They're zipped up in my wallet now, safe and out of sight. I'm not sure what prompted me to remove them, when I never have before. But now when I look at the bareness of my left hand there's a sudden defiant surge of freedom and elation.

"Right," he nods, but there's a spark in his eyes that tells me he isn't fooled.

"Not that I want you to think I *don't* mean business," I elaborate, "because I do . . ." My hand snakes across the space between us now, slipping 'round to the inside of his thigh and feeling the tautness there, creeping slowly higher until he hisses through his teeth and bats me away.

"Control yourself," he says. "I want to get there alive." He switches the radio on and music floods the car, and suddenly we're both laughing, high on the tension between us. Sunlight is streaming in and dazzling the windowpane, and in this moment all the sadness and complication burns up and everything is perfect.

We reach the hotel just after two; a small, unobtrusive place with low brick walls and a dark green awning, a badly painted logo and the words *Silver Birches* stamped in looping script onto the whitewashed entrance doors. I stand next to Carl as he checks in and chats to the receptionist about the opening times of the restaurant and the pool, all the while looking for some kind of suspicion in her eyes, which isn't there. She smiles as she hands over the key, and it hits me that here, we're just a normal couple like any other. The thought is intoxicating, and as I hurry after him along the corridor toward our room, it swirls around and around in my head, so fast that I can barely form it into words even to myself: the idea of us together, fresh out of the box, and starting on a journey that is anything but a dead end—that is going to go somewhere, that could make us both happy for a long, long time.

"Not too bad, is it," he says, swinging open the door. Dark red walls, a double bed covered with a duvet in the same color and pillows edged with white piping. There's a picture on the wall above the headboard: an abstract field of poppies, their petals splashed across the canvas like blood. The air is warm and the curtains are drawn, lamplight shining dimly next to the bed. My heart is still thumping with the force of the thoughts rushing through me. I toss my overnight bag onto the floor and move forward into his arms.

"I like it." I press my body up toward his, tilting my hips slightly upward to press against the hardness of his crotch. His lips graze against mine once, twice. "So," I say, "shall we go and have a swim?"

"Sure. If that's what you want," he says. His hands are working their way slowly down my body, sliding underneath the waistband of my skirt and slipping slightly inside the bikini bottoms I already have on beneath my clothes. I'm shivering, but I nod. I don't want this to happen quickly, not today. I can wait just as long as he can.

He looks into my eyes and in the darkness of his pupils I see my own reflection. A long moment, and then he smiles and exhales. "Good girl," he says, and then he pulls away, affecting disinterest, lazily doing up the buttons of his shirt that I hadn't even realized I had undone.

We go down to the swimming pool—a small white-tiled room flanked with green waxy-leaved plants that look shinily plastic, the pool a glittering splash of bright blue. It's cold and I ease myself in in stages, exclaiming as the water inches over my thighs and soaks into my suit. Carl is already in, making his way down the length of the pool, sending droplets scattering in his wake. I set my teeth and submerge myself. When I surface, I know I'm grinning stupidly with the weird, giddy pleasure of floating that always hits me when I'm in water. I swim over to him and he pulls me into his arms, my limbs coiling wetly around his. I wipe the hair back from his eyes, slicking it back across his scalp.

"I love this," I say. "I always have."

"I can see. Funny. I didn't know that about you."

His tone is light but I can't help thinking that we really know so little, both of us, about each other. I move onto his lap and kiss him, resting my legs gently on his, suspended in the water. For a moment I want to tell him everything I can think of about myself, good and bad—pour it all out and have it done with, make him know me as well or better than anyone ever has. But I have no idea where to start and in the end I just bite my lip and twist out of his arms, swimming away down the pool.

We stay in the water for almost half an hour, chatting about the week we've had and unimportant programs we've seen on TV, then spend a few minutes in the sauna. The wood is so hot that it feels as if it's branding my back, etching ridges of memory into my skin. He's watching me from above in the dim reddish light; the darkness of his stubble shadowing the bones of his jawline, his eyes glittering blackly down at me. Sweat is trickling over me and impatience makes me shift restlessly back and forth—wanting his mouth hot on my skin, his tongue licking the path of my sweat down my body, giving me what I want so much now that it feels almost impossible to deny it any longer. I'm dizzy and defenseless, the walls of the small, hot room lurching uncontrollably around me.

"Christ," I say, scrambling up. This desire is too much; scares me, almost. "I need to get out."

Outside the sun is shining but the breeze blowing through the propped-open window is blissfully cool, and when we've dressed we go for a walk in the small grounds, wandering across the lawns and finally coming to rest on a bench at the far edge of the rose garden. He puts his arms around me and I lean back against his chest, looking back at the hotel behind us. I have the strange sense of these moments being both fleeting and lasting; the knowledge that whatever happens, I won't forget this.

"I wish you could come with me tomorrow," he says suddenly. It's the first time he's mentioned anything like this. Despite our deep connection, our lives are fundamentally divided. We've never met each other's family or friends, never been able to announce our relationship publicly—never done any of the things that would make it real in the eyes of the world, or perhaps even to ourselves.

"I wish I could, too," I say. There's a sudden lump in my throat. I know that if I suggested I could come after all, he'd laugh and dismiss it. As far as he's concerned, I don't exist for him anywhere but in the private spaces we've carved out for each other. He knows the score, and he's made his peace with it. For the first time, I wonder what this really is to him, this no-man's-land he's created. I imagine him lying awake at night and thinking about what the hell he's doing, how he's just wasting time with me. I wonder if he wishes he'd never met me at all.

"Hey," he says, smoothing the hair back behind my ears, "don't look so sad."

"I am sad." My voice is so quiet that it would be easy to pretend I hadn't spoken at all, but I force myself to speak louder, looking up straight into his eyes, only inches from my own. "I don't want this to end."

He sighs and continues stroking my hair, his hand moving rhythmically and tenderly across my skull. "Nor do I, Caro," he says, "but it has to happen soon. We could go on like this for ages, but it doesn't make any sense. This isn't . . ." He pauses, tries to sort his thoughts into words. "You must see I can't be in a long-term relationship with someone who's married."

I feel the breath draw up through my body, and it's the closest I've ever been to telling him. That I'm really not sure what Francis and I are still doing together—that the way we live now reminds me of two strangers skating 'round each other on thin black ice, unhappily circling the rink of our marriage. And that now that I'm here with him I'm surer than ever that I'm in love with him, that I'm terrified I'm going to regret it for the rest of my life if I let him go. I don't know why I can't say it.

Tears are blurring my eyes and I see their echo rising in his own, and by the time he kisses me we're both crying and I can feel the wetness on his skin.

"Come on," he says after a while, wiping his hand across his eyes. "This is stupid. We're not here for long, and we should enjoy it. Let's go back in and get an early dinner. OK?"

"OK." I dry my eyes with the back of my sleeve, blinking the last of my tears away. I know he's right. Whatever the time is for this conversation, it isn't now. As we stroll back over the lawn together, his hand in mine, I feel the happiness sweeping back, ironing over the last few minutes as if they were never there. I won't think about them. Not now.

We eat our dinner in the near-deserted restaurant, laughing at the awkward plastic flowers poking out of the tabletop vase, taking our time poring over the laminated menus and in the end choosing almost at random. When the elderly waitress brings a bottle of wine, she smiles indulgently at our clasped hands, radiating bonhomie and approval. I could change her expression, I think, if I told her what was really happening here. As I taste the wine, cool and crisp, the idea of being some sort of scarlet woman suddenly seems funny. It isn't who I am. It's not how this feels.

"It's all right, this, isn't it," Carl comments halfway through dinner, indicating his food with an air of mild revelation.

"It's actually really nice." I up the ante, widening my eyes in surprise. The food is pretty bog standard, if I stop to think about it, but in this moment everything feels amplified, ten times better than it actually is. "Not as good as your cooking, of course." My sole experience of his cooking has been a hastily-cooked pasta one night in his flat when we were both too wired and strung out on sex to want to go out for dinner, but he nods as if accepting his due.

"Yeah," he says with no attempt at false modesty, "I'm pretty good at that. Pretty good at most things," he adds, smiling wickedly across the table.

Abruptly we're standing up and walking fast across the restaurant, pausing only to give our room number to the waitress and ask her to put the meal on the bill. My heart is beating fast and my legs are weak as I follow him down the corridor. He unlocks the door and I'm barely inside before he's slammed it behind me and pressed me up against it, forcing my body back against the hard wood. He takes my hands and pins them up above my head, keeping them there with his hand gripped around my wrists as he kisses me hard, his tongue in my mouth and his teeth biting at my lip, the smart of blood bursting in my mouth for an instant. "Tell me you want it," he says into my ear, and I hear myself saying things I thought I'd never say, the words tumbling out as I impatiently arch my hips up to his and he pushes down my skirt with his free hand, ripping it away.

He picks me up into his arms and in another moment we're on the bed, and I catch sight of us in the long mirror on the far wall, my hands tangled in his hair and his body on mine, the strong lean muscles of his shoulders rolling as he eases out of his shirt. The curtains are still drawn and the lamplight casts our shadows onto the wall, moving together, and I can hear my breath coming fast and urgently as I wrap my legs around his and he pushes his way inside me. We move slowly at first, his hands unhurried and intense on my body. He says something I can't catch. *"Harder,"* I say, *"yes."*

"Ask me nicely," he says, his eyes burning intently into mine.

"Sorry," I whisper, "please," and I feel his body tense, and after that he does what I want without my having to ask because he knows what to do with me and he always has, even without being told, because this chemistry between us is something that can't be taught or explained. "I can't get enough of you," I find myself saying, and he smiles that teasing smile that says I don't have to say it out loud because it's so brutally obvious that a blind man could see it.

We lie in the bed together afterward talking, and when the sky outside has darkened and I can hear the first beginnings of rain pattering onto the window, we move into each other's arms again and I climb on top of him, my hair hanging down and brushing over his chest, his hands reaching up warm and hard on my skin. I tell him that I love doing this with him, and he says it back, and it would take so little to slip over this boundary and say what I really mean but I still don't do it—and when, much later, he's fallen asleep beside me and the rain outside has deepened into a hot summer storm, I lie awake half the night staring at the shape of his face in the dark and I say it then instead, knowing that he can't hear me and that I don't have to wait for him to reply.

*W*hen the buzzer sounds I don't quite believe it at first. I've been
sitting in the living room all afternoon, unable to concentrate on anything for more than a minute at a time. I've just been here. Waiting.
Breathing. These two things suck up as much effort as I've got to give.
In the back of my mind, I'd accepted that they wouldn't come. But now
the sound jars through the air again and I'm crossing to the intercom
and saying, "Hello?" and hearing a voice that I know now sounds like
Caroline's spilling out explanations and justifications even though I've
invited them in the first place.

I let them into the building and then I listen to the sound of Eddie's
footsteps pattering eagerly up, his grandmother's following more slowly
behind. There's no time to prepare myself. They're here, framed in the
doorway, the little boy glancing at me briefly and then losing interest
almost as quickly, dashing to the hamster's cage in the corner of the
room and unlocking the top.

"Thanks for letting us pop in," Caroline's mother says. "He's been
talking about it all day at school, apparently. We won't take up much
of your time." The words are polite but her eyes are darting around all
over the place, betraying her uncertainty. On some level, she knows

there's something here she doesn't trust. And by a process of elimination, she knows it must be me. The silence lasts a fraction too long, long enough for me to understand that I should have filled it. "I'll make us a quick cup of tea," she says at last. "I know where everything is."

I listen to her moving around the kitchen, briskly filling the kettle, clattering the mugs on to the worktop. Without realizing it, I've moved closer to Eddie. He's crouched down on the floor, cradling the little silvery hamster in his hands, cooing and muttering some babyish private language to it as it sniffs the air. His fair hair falls over his forehead.

"He's mine," he says suddenly and clearly, not looking at me, but raising his voice so that it's clear who he's talking to. "I look after him."

"I can see that," I say. I pause, testing the next words that have come to me inside my head. They gather in the air, like delicate balloons. "And who looks after you?" I ask.

He shrugs, still intent on the little creature in his hands. "Lots of people," he says.

"Your mummy?" I ask, and he nods. "What would your mummy do for you?" I ask. And at last he looks up at me, his large gray eyes clouded by a confusion and suspicion that seems far older than his years, alerted to the fact that something in my voice has changed and that this means something, even if he doesn't understand what. He stares at me unblinkingly, silently, still and watchful. Blood is pumping in my head, making me dizzy.

"Would she kill for you?" I say.

AWAY

Caroline, May 2015

Somehow I make it through the lunch, swallowing mouthful upon mouthful of food past the lump of nausea in my throat, and with every bite, I'm thinking of her. A woman without a face I can see, sitting in my home. Someone who knows me better than I can understand.

By the time I have trailed after Francis 'round the nearby shopping mall, then for a walk in the park, and we make the train journey back to Chiswick, with Francis keeping up a steady, chirpy stream of chatter, it's almost five in the afternoon. As we walk back from the station he glances over at me, then leans across and taps his fingertips gently against my forehead. "Hello," he says. "Anyone home?"

It's an innocent enough turn of phrase, but it makes my throat constrict. "Sorry," I say. "I know I've been quiet. I'm just tired."

Francis shrugs. "If you say so."

I look back over my shoulder at him as I unlock the front door. He meets my gaze steadily, unflinching. He knows, I realize, that I am lying. He just doesn't know what about.

"Sorry," I murmur again, and as I speak I'm aware that I can't stumble through the next day in this tense state of limbo, turning my fears over and over until they become huge and suffocating. I'm going to have to do something. Once again, I think about going home. Now that I've seen that profile picture, it doesn't feel safe being here. I don't want this woman in my house. I have no idea what she might do.

"Francis . . . ," I begin, but instantly I bite my lip. We've been here before, and I know I have little chance of persuading him to set off for home early. And besides, what would happen if we did? I picture us stepping into our flat together, his look of incomprehension as I try to turf this woman out of our house while telling him nothing. I can't do it. I have to keep this to myself, and the safest way to do that is to ensure that his path never crosses with hers.

All the same, I have to do something. And suddenly I know what it's going to have to be, and I know I have to act on it before I lose my nerve and change my mind.

"You know," I say abruptly, "I think I need a bath. I'll feel better afterward. That place was pretty sticky." It's only half a lie. There's a strong urge to strip naked, climb into the hottest water I can manage, and attempt to purge myself of all the things that I know I can't really get rid of—not now, not ever.

"All right." Francis shrugs, half mollified. "Well, you do that and I'll start getting something on for dinner."

I head quickly upstairs and run the bath, pull off my clothes. I don't get in. Instead I sit by the foot of the bath and reach for my phone, and I dial the number of my own landline. I count the rings, shivering with the phone pressed to my ear. Six. Seven. Halfway through the eighth ring the voice mail kicks in. I hang up, but some instinct makes me dial the number again straightaway, and when the same thing happens I do it again.

The third time I call, it rings four times and then there's a click as the line is picked up. There's no discernible noise on the other end, except for what might be the quietest of breathing. Drawing in my own breath, I prepare to speak. I haven't got this far in my imagination, let alone in reality. The silence grows and swells, pricked only by the faint crackling of static. She isn't going to crack first, but she's listening.

"It's Caroline," I say at last.

There's a pause, a tiny shift of movement at the other end of line that could be the rearrangement of clothes or a hand brushed across a forehead. "I know."

The voice is soft and low in tone. There's an evenness to it, as if all the emotion has been flattened out. As soon as her voice stops, I'm unable to recall the way it sounded.

"I don't want you in my house," I say, and I haven't even known until now that this is the way I'm going to play it: cold, a little imperious, the outraged middle-class wife and mother. "I would suggest that you leave and that you don't contact me again," I continue. "I could call the police."

This time there's a little exhalation that sounds like amusement, but nothing else. I realize the stupidity of what I've said. This woman has made almost no contact with me, except to respond to my own messages. Entering into a house swap is not illegal, and when I look at the facts I could lay out, they're so intangible that I can barely even make sense of them in my own head. Veiled clues and reminders of a past that means nothing to anyone but me. No threats, no intimidation. And besides, she of all people must know that I would never involve the police in this situation; that it's the last thing I would ever do. She doesn't know that even now, when I see a policeman in uniform on the street my mouth dries and my legs threaten to buckle. She doesn't know that for months I dreamed of cool, faceless corridors, cells boxed in by heavy metallic doors. But she knows that I'm hiding, that my whole life these days is an exercise in turning a blind eye to myself. She's never met me, but she knows me.

"I'm sorry," I say then. I can hear the crack of tears in my voice, swallow it down. "I don't know what to say to you." Silence, keen and insistent. She isn't hanging up. "Who are you?" I ask.

"There's no point in asking questions," she says. "When you already know the answers."

And as soon as she speaks I realize that of course I do know—that there's only one person who could do this, who could care enough and have the will to see it through. I think of Eddie; the clearness of his gray eyes and the perfect curve of his cheek, the way his face has changed and refined over time and how if I close my eyes I can still see him the way he was, a litany of snapshots reeling back through the years to the baby I first held in my arms. "You're her mother," I say, "aren't you."

Silence again, but this time it feels as if something in it has snapped, a tension broken and released, and what is left is a mist of loss and sadness that curls its way down the line and infiltrates my heart, filling me up so that it's hard to breathe. And now the tears are running down my face and I've lost count of the times that guilt and pain have made me cry this way, the number of times I've sat alone and tried to force these thoughts away, but I make myself stay quiet because I know that the last thing she wants is my self-pity.

"You never let go of that man," she says at last, "did you? You were good at putting everything else in a box. Packing it away as if it never existed. But not him."

With humiliation I think of the messages I sent her, when I thought she was you. The neediness that seeped out of them, the desperation for contact. I wonder if she realizes that part of the reason I have been unable to get over you is that if my thoughts are full of you, then they can't be full of the demons that really haunt me. I've needed you and the pain of missing you there in my head, to block them out. But I press my lips together and stay quiet, and after a while she speaks again.

"Do you believe in justice, Caroline?" she asks.

"I . . ." The question feels like a trap. Whatever I say, she'll be able to twist it. "I believe in a lot of things," I say. "Justice, redemption, repentance." *Forgiveness*, I almost say, but I bite it back. "But beliefs aren't always the same as reality." It's the best I can do.

She pauses again, seeming to mull this over. "Tomorrow, this will all be over," she says eventually. "I don't intend to talk about this to anyone. I don't want to see you. I don't want to speak to you again. This is the last time that our lives will cross."

It should be reassuring, but with every word she speaks I feel unease growing; something not right, some subtext that I can't catch. And before I have a chance even to open my mouth to reply, she hangs up.

Slowly, I lay the phone to one side, rake my fingers through my dampened hair. The heat from the bathwater is curling up into the room, misting the mirror and the window with condensation. My skin is lightly covered with a film of sweat. I wipe the back of my arm across my eyes, and when I look at it it's smeared with streaks of mascara and tears. The conversation replays itself: the sparseness of her words and the meaning all glittering in between them, threaded finely through the silence. She knows exactly what happened that night. I have no idea how, but she knows.

My head swims and all at once I know that if I don't get some fresh air I'm going to faint. I stand up unsteadily and push the bathroom window halfway open, kneel in front of it with my arms folded on the ledge and my face upturned to the bright sky.

After a few moments I feel more stable, but I don't move. Instead I look down at the length of the street, its symmetry and stillness. Sun is slanting off the red-washed roofs, giving them the air of having been recently polished. Below, the gardens unroll in neat little lawned rectangles. I see the shadow first, cutting across the grass, passing swiftly and surely down the road. There's something in the way it moves that catches me before I even realize I've been caught; my heart pounding with recognition and a fresh wave of heat pouring across my naked body. The figure is walking with purpose, not wavering or looking back, heading straight to the doorway of number 14.

The sun dips behind a cloud and I press forward, my fingers clenching on the windowsill—and I should have been prepared for this but now that it's here in front of me I realize that there's no amount of groundwork that could have stopped my pulse thumping through me or the tears of an emotion I can't even name rising afresh to my eyes. It's you. You're home.

HOME

Caroline, July 2013

Carl is doing up his tie in the mirror, watching my reflection as I sit on the bed behind him. He's already late leaving. It was only ten minutes ago that he started getting dressed, and even now he's only suited from the waist up; white shirt and dark jacket, and nothing else but a pair of black boxer shorts. I know that if I tried, I could make him stay—a little longer, at least. But my limbs are aching with sexual exhaustion already and, besides, I know this isn't the goodbye he thinks it is.

"What time will you go?" he asks. "Fucking hell." He fumbles with the knot, letting the tie fall apart again impatiently. "Can't get this right."

"Can't concentrate?" I ask, stretching luxuriously on the sheets, and he smiles. "I'll probably go in an hour or two," I say idly, hugging my secret to myself. Right from the start, I'd decided that I'd be here waiting for him, an unexpected surprise when he returns from the party. I'm not due to pick up Eddie until tomorrow lunchtime, and I've got nothing else to go home for.

He pulls his trousers and shoes on and runs his fingers through his dark hair, angling this way and that in the mirror. "Better go then," he says flatly. There's sadness in his eyes as he comes to sit next to me, and for a moment I think about telling him that we'll have another night together, but I bite my tongue. I want to see the pleasure on his face when he returns.

"Bye," I say, pulling him down for a kiss and running my fingers lightly over his jacket. "Very nice," I murmur. "You know I like you in this kind of stuff."

"I know, Caro, believe me I know," he says, wrenching himself reluctantly away. "Maybe I'll send you a little picture later when I get back."

"You do that." The urge to confess rises up again but I squash it back down, and then he's backing away toward the door, turning 'round for a last look, and then pushing his way out into the corridor and letting it close gently behind him.

When he's gone the room feels emptier than it should, as if by leaving he's taken all the energy out of it. These walls are thick and soundproofed, and even if I listen hard, all I can hear is a faint hum of static, a tiny suggestion of water moving through pipes. The storm from last night has cleared and the sun is out again, shining through the thin red curtains and warming my naked body as I lie in a shaft of light. I haven't thought about this part—about what I'm going to do for the next ten or eleven hours until he returns. No car, no shops for miles around. I haven't even brought a book.

I switch on the television and spend a few minutes looking through the channels, but nothing catches my attention and I can't focus. Although it's the last thing I want to think about, I keep coming back to the idea of Francis sitting alone at home, without his wife and son nearby; taking stock of things, thinking about the fact that this is how it would be if we weren't together and that on his own he doesn't have a damn thing to occupy his time. For a crazy moment, I think about calling him. But I have no idea what

I would say and I dismiss the thought. My mobile is on silent—I've deliberately cut myself off from him, not wanting anything to intrude on this time away. Unwillingly, I glance at it, half expecting a barrage of incoherent texts, but there's nothing. I'm not sure if the feeling that twists through me is relief, surprise, hurt, or something in between the cracks of all these things.

Shaking my head, I force myself to get up. I'll go down to the pool, spend some time swimming and in the sauna, and then maybe ask at reception if they have any magazines I could borrow for an hour or two. This enforced solitude feels strange. Once I would have loved the idea of a day to myself at a hotel, but right now all I want is for Carl to be here. I picture him driving, his eyes narrowed in the sun; a flicker of indecision crossing his face, his hands on the wheel turning the car around, coming back to me. I can see it so clearly that when I push open the door and the corridor is empty and still, I am almost surprised.

The hours pass slowly, falling like stones. I check the time every five or ten minutes, barely able to believe that it has moved on so little. I have some lunch in the hotel restaurant, go for another swim until my hair is saturated with chlorine and I have to wash the smell out in the shower afterward. I lie back down on the bed and think about last night until I'm humming with desire and I touch myself swiftly and mechanically, exploding the tension in seconds and putting me right back where I began. I order a bottle of wine and drink it in the space of an hour or so even though I don't really want it, just for something to do. It's nine o'clock by the time it starts getting dark. My head is lightly blurred, and I don't think I've moved in hours.

When I hear the footsteps approaching outside the door it's a red alert, setting all my senses on fire. I sit bolt upright, suddenly anxious. All at once the possibility hits me, dreadful and unforeseen, that he isn't alone. He's seen a girl at the party across the dance floor, made eye contact. Kissed her in the darkness of a hallway, offered her a place to stay for the night. I've never asked him if he has seen anyone else in the past six months, because I know that there's nothing I could say to justify how I feel when I think about the idea of his hands on some other woman's skin. I don't want to have to confront it, but now in these few seconds when I hear the click of the key card in the door and see the handle turning, I wonder if I'm going to have to.

The door swings open and he's standing there. Alone. We stare at each other in silence. The first emotion that flickers over his face is shock, but in a split second it's given way to the kind of happiness you can't fake: his mouth breaking open into a smile, his eyes crinkling with delight and surprise.

He comes forward into the room, places his bag carefully down onto the dressing table. "Well, well," he says. "And what are you doing—" but he doesn't even finish the sentence before I've leaped up from the bed and launched myself into his arms, and I can tell from the way he clutches me to him instantly—the wholehearted force of it, the quick dip of his face into my neck—that he's abandoned the idea of playing it cool. "It's so good to see you," I think I hear him saying, his voice muffled in my hair, and I'm saying it, too, pulling back to trace my fingertips over his temples and take him in, wanting to etch this moment onto my memory for good.

"I can't believe you're here," he says. "You know, it was all right today, but I kept thinking about you, about how much I wished you were there with me, and in the end I thought, there's no point in staying, I may as well come back and be fucking miserable in the room by myself." He laughs, self-mocking. "Now I wish I'd come back hours ago. Why are you here?"

"Because I want to be," I say simply, and suddenly it all rises up, my heart in my mouth, and I realize I'm going to tell him that I want us to be together, that I'm never going to turn away and pull on my clothes and leave his room at midnight to go home to another man, ever again. I'm going to tell him tonight.

"Are you OK?" he asks, because my thoughts have choked my throat and I'm silent, staring into his eyes and trying to read what's in them, wondering how this will go.

"I'm fine," I say. Restlessness is sweeping through me—the exhilaration of these feelings, after the long aimless day; the desire to get out, clear my head before I say what I want to say. "Look," I say impulsively, "let's go out. I haven't eaten. We can drive to a pub or something, there must be something nearby. Sit outside. By the river, maybe. Come on," I encourage urgently, tugging at his sleeve.

He smiles, but rubs a hand over his eyes, half flopping back onto the bed. "I don't know," he says. "I'm pretty knackered. Been driving for the past hour, and it's felt like a long day. Besides, I can think of things I'd rather do than sit in the pub . . ." He reaches for me, sliding his hand up underneath my top, his fingers stroking a gentle path of exploration over my skin and reaching the base of my bra. His eyes are dark and shining, inviting me to agree.

I'm tempted, but I can't quite shake that sense of needing to be somewhere else, if only for a short while. It's only now he's here that I realize how oppressive these four walls have been. The air is thick with the day's torpor, and I want this to be perfect; I want to look him in the face and tell him I love him, shout it out into the open air. I'm flooded with the power of these words and what they mean. I've never felt like this before—the world suffused with light and color, the sharp brightness of possibility.

I leap up from the bed and pull on my shoes and coat. "I'll drive," I say. "You don't need to do anything. Just sit back and let me take you."

He stands up and comes over to me, and I can tell that whatever this is that has gripped me, it's infectious. Excitement is shifting behind his eyes and he's looking at me as if he's never seen me before. "OK," he says, "if you say so. Whatever you want, baby." He pulls me toward him and kisses me hard. His lips on mine, his tongue in my mouth. "Not for too long, though," he warns me, "and when we come back, I expect you to behave, right? Can't have you thinking you're in charge."

"You're the boss," I tell him, and we're both smiling, unable to resist these games we play. I grab the car keys from his top pocket as we walk quickly down the corridor and out into the carpark.

"You sure about this?" he asks as I scramble into the driver's seat.

"Yes," I say quickly, "it's fine." As I start up the engine, I suddenly remember the bottle of wine I've drunk. I hesitate for an instant. I don't want to tell you that I've been drinking—don't want you to think that anything is clouding my judgment or my decisions. My head feels completely clear; in fact it feels like I haven't thought this clearly in years. And the roads will be practically empty at this time of night, especially here.

Uncertainty is twitching at the back of my mind, but I push it aside. I'm filled again with that sense of power, the knowledge that everything is finally coming together and nothing can stop it. I switch the headlights on, and the road coiling ahead away from the hotel is illuminated in pale yellow. Shadows are shifting on the horizon, the blowsy branches of trees swaying darkly in the faint wind. I steer the car out onto the road, and there's a rush of air through the open crack at the top of the window, setting the hairs on my arms on edge.

"We'll go to that town we passed on the way," I say. "There's bound to be something open there. OK?"

Carl laughs, leaning his head back against the headrest. "I don't have a say in this, remember?" he says. "I'm putty in your hands." He stretches out his hand and cups my knee, pushing the fabric of my skirt up toward my thigh. "This is crazy," he says wryly. "Driving out into the middle of nowhere when I could be fucking your brains out right now."

The words send another jolt of electricity through me—savage, dirty, a fierce pulse of need—and for an instant the road ahead blurs. I shake my head slightly, tighten my hands on the wheel. Out of the corner of my eye, I see the needle on the speedometer quivering, and I pull the car back. Shouldn't go too fast. There's a strange, itchy feeling spreading through my bones, telling me I'm not entirely in control.

"Don't," I say. I hear the breathlessness in my voice and I find myself gasping, sucking in a sharp, cold burst of air.

He's watching me. I can feel his eyes on me, traveling over my body. "I love how much you like this," he says. "I don't just mean the sex. I mean . . ." He trails off, turning his face to the window, staring out into the night.

I know what he means, even if he doesn't, and all at once I'm willing him to say it, wanting to hear him say he loves me before I have to say it first—and I'm twisting my head to try to catch his gaze, my eyes sliding away from the road ahead. And in another moment I catch a flash of something right at the corner of my vision and I realize there's a bend looming ahead, tucked away from the streetlights.

My eyes snap back and my body floods with adrenaline. I realize in an instant that I'm going to have to turn fast, and my hands tug at the wheel, swinging the car sharply to the left—measuring in a split second that I'm going to veer onto the pavement, but that I'll be able to stop before we hit the side of the road. It's going to be OK. But

Carl is sitting up in his seat and I hear him shouting something I can't quite decipher, and as he does I see her, walking fast along the pavement with her head ducked down and her hands in her pockets, her dark hair and her green scarf blowing together behind her in the wind, and with a sickening lurch of instinct I realize that she's too close, that there is no way I am going to be able to get out of her way.

I'm slamming the brakes on and the sound of my screaming is filling the car, and I hear and feel the impact in the same moment— the sudden speed and force of it, the way she smashes against the windscreen and slides down instantly, the bright spatter of red that splashes across my field of vision. The car has jerked to a halt and we're sitting in complete silence and stillness but it's too late.

My hands are shaking crazily and there's an ache shooting up the entire length of my spine. My eyes are fixed on the wheel. I can't raise my head. "Jesus Christ," I hear myself say, "fucking hell." It doesn't sound like my voice at all.

"We have to get out," he says, and I drag my gaze over to him and see that he's bleeding, his hand cut sharply by glass from the fractured windscreen. "It might—she might—"

I'm unfastening my seat belt, opening the door with hands still shaking so much that I can barely wrap them around the handle. As soon as I see her I know there's no hope but I drop to my knees anyway and bend forward, forcing myself to look. Her arm is un-naturally twisted, flung across the length of her body. The right side of her face is caved into a bloody mass, lacerated almost to the bone. She's young. Sixteen, seventeen. A dark streak of mascara is pooling down the untouched side of her face and her green silk scarf is streaked with red. The impact has knocked her scarlet high-heeled shoes off her bare feet. She's completely still. Her eyes are half open. Every detail comes in flashes—brutal snapshots, fired one after the other, then snatched away.

He's checking her pulse, bending his head. I don't have to ask.

For a few moments we're crouching there together in silence in the dark. My mind is blank and buzzing. "What do we do?" I ask. "What the hell do we do?"

His face is white, drained. "I don't know," he says. "I suppose we have to call the police."

I nod slowly, fighting for breath. Now my thoughts are working at a hundred miles an hour, cycling frantically through what is going to happen. I've gone out driving in the dark, several units over the limit, miles away from my family, with another man. And now this girl—this girl with the green scarf and the long dark hair and the makeup that she probably applied carefully in her bedroom only hours before—is dead. I've killed her. I've killed her.

"Caro," he's saying, and his tone is harsh and almost angry. "You need to go."

I raise my eyes to his. "What are you talking about?" I whisper.

"You need," he says, "to get the fuck away from here, as soon as you can. I will call the police. I will deal with this. Do you understand?" When I don't reply, he draws in breath sharply. "This car is hired in my name," he says. "The hotel room is booked in my name. There's nothing to connect you with this. There's no reason for you to be involved."

"What are you talking about?" I'm almost screaming, and suddenly tears are pouring down my face. I'm choking, vomit rising bitterly in my throat. "I can't do that," I gulp. "I'm responsible for this. I can't just—"

"For fuck's sake, Caro!" he shouts. We're both standing now, surreally facing each other, with the girl lying there at our feet; the road deserted, the wind whistling coldly between us. "You're not stupid," he bites out. "You know how this is going to go for you.

You've been drinking. I knew it, and like an idiot I still let you get in the car. You're not going to get off scot-free from this. You'll go to prison, maybe for years. You've got your son. You've got a life. I've got fuck-all. And I'm sober. It was an accident. It makes sense," he shouts, and his voice is roughly edged with hysteria. All at once, standing before me with his fists clenched, he looks incredibly young. "You know it does, so don't try to martyr yourself. Just get out of here. Please."

"And then what?" I force out. The tears are still streaming down my face, and they feel cold now, the wetness collecting damply on my skin.

"Then nothing," he says. There's a moment of silence. "This is it," he says. "It's over. It's time to say goodbye and walk away."

The words hang between us, draining the energy out of the air. The dark landscape shifts and sways around me, and for a moment I think I'm going to faint. "You don't mean that," I whisper. "We have to do this together. We can't do it without each other. We can't just . . ."

"Yes, we can," he interrupts. With horror, I hear the determination in his voice—the steely edge to it, the warning that there is no point in arguing. "This is the only thing to do," he says. "It was always going to happen. And now it needs to happen more than ever. I mean it. No calls, no texts. You need to keep completely away from this. From me."

"I love you," I say, and it's not how this was meant to be—the sourness still in my throat, the shocking hot scent of blood in the air, my body shuddering with trauma. "I love you."

"Caro," he says quietly. For the first time there's a tenderness trembling in his voice. "I don't think you should say that. There's . . . there's no point." He frowns minutely, passes a hand across his forehead. "I don't know," he says. "I think I love you, too. But that's partly why this has to happen. And I'm not going to change my mind."

It filters in slowly. A strange, dreamlike sense of calm descends. I realize I can't fight this. Everything has ground to a halt around us. My eyes flick to the ground again. She's lying there, the blood still pooling from her head and soaking into the granite. I'm half waiting for her to raise her head, open her eyes. But it doesn't happen and suddenly my tears have stopped and I'm quivering with shock and nausea, and taking the first step away from her.

I look up straight into his eyes and I see the pain cross his face, raw and visceral. I can barely believe this is all happening. Before I know it I'm raising my face to his and his lips are on mine. I close my eyes. He's kissing me slowly and gently and I know that it's the last time.

When it's over I feel a bizarre lift of hope, the senseless thought that I must still be able to turn this all around, find some magic words that could bring the girl back to her feet and catapult us back into the future I'd planned, the one that was so close I could almost touch it. But there's nothing that can change this and I'm turning and walking slowly down the dark empty road, every step echoing in my head.

When I reach the next bend I look back. He's facing away from me, and I see the screen of his phone shining as he raises it to his ear. I try to think about the words he will be saying. Think about how it will be for him when they arrive: the blunt inquisition, the looks of disgust and suspicion and reproach. I can't get my head 'round it. I'm still walking, one foot after the other. The nearest train station is five miles away. It will take me over an hour. And when I get there, there's no place to go but home.

Still walking. I'm on my own. I don't yet know how it will be. About the dozens of messages I'll send and receive no reply to, about the dreams that will shake me from my sleep, about the sense of helplessness and guilt that will pulse through me so hard and so relentlessly that it feels impossible to survive. But I know that some things burn their way into you and scar you from the inside out. No recovery, no escape. The only way out is going to be to bury these memories so deep underground that they are almost impossible to access. Find some way of pretending to start again. And with a jolt of sick surprise, I realize this will be possible. That it's almost frighteningly easy. Already it feels as if the last ten minutes have belonged to some other life. That woman back there in the car—already she's disappeared. It wasn't me. It wasn't me. I've left her there with him, and she's gone for good.

W̲ould she kill for you?" The boy is staring at me, trying to understand. These words are ones he knows, but they have never been arranged in quite this formation—and I can tell from the gravity of his gaze that he realizes they mean more than the sum of their parts. We are both quiet and still, enclosed in our little bubble. His hands clasped neatly in his lap around the hamster. The slow sweep of his eyelashes as he blinks. The faint scratch of the carpet bristles on my legs as I kneel in front of him. These tiny things are filling the room, leaving no space to breathe.

It's a revelation, a curtain drawn swiftly up from a dark stage as the lights snap on. The sudden ruthless clarity of it hurts me. I understand why I'm here, and why I have asked them to come. It makes sense now. When someone is responsible for your misery, you want to hurt them. You want to do to them exactly what has been done to you. That's justice. Not the sterile courtroom she evaded, with its inadequate pronouncements and punishments. Something deeper, more primal, than that. If an animal lunges at you in the wild, you don't stop to think. You fight back. This woman ripped my life to shreds with her carelessness. She strolled away from what she had done without looking back. You take from me, I take from you.

I'm rising to my feet and going to the floor-length window, unlocking the catch and stepping out onto the balcony. Air rushes up coldly into my lungs. I'm looking at the swarming cars and the street, three floors below, and I can feel the force of gravity—almost see it—wrenching the whole world down. And when I hear the sound of footsteps I'm not surprised that he's there, sidling up beside me, drawn to this force, his head tilted very slightly to one side. His eyes are wide and steady, gazing up at me. Every second expands and stretches. I take a small step toward him. This next part will need to be quick. A jolt of time, swift and instantaneous, changing everything.

My hands are millimeters away from his shoulders when he moves. He doesn't quite understand but he's backing away, into the safety of the room, and I'm alone on the balcony with the wind in my face and the tears have come so fast that I'm choking with surprise and I can hardly breathe, because of course I can't do it. Because I'm playing at being someone I'm not and can never be. Because even the thought is ridiculous. Because there are no answers here or anywhere else, and the idea of taking life away revolts me as much as it always has, and the enormity of the knowledge that there's nothing I can ever do to fix what has been broken is slamming into me hard and fast without compromise, and for the first time.

AWAY

Caroline, May 2015

I stay at the bathroom window for some minutes after you've gone inside—staring at the windows of your house, trying to make out some flicker of movement behind the glass. I think about you crossing the living room, making yourself a drink, settling down on the sofa. Amber next to you, sliding her legs onto your lap as she lies down and asks you how your week has been. Or perhaps you're leaving the conversation for later and you're upstairs together, not talking at all.

I realize that I'm shivering. My skin is speckled with goose bumps and when I glance behind me I see that the bathwater looks cold and clouded, congealed suds of foam floating on its surface. Mechanically, I drain it and pull my clothes back on. In the bathroom mirror, my reflection evaluates me. My makeup has started to run, and I can feel my foundation getting oily. I move my hand up to rub it away but even this small action feels too complicated and in the end I let my arm fall back down limply by my side.

The woman's voice is replaying in my head—the soft evenness of her tone, her dispassionate final words. A voice down the line, hundreds of miles away, coming to me from my own home. She is there and I am here, with you disturbingly, electrically close . . . and suddenly it seems that everything is in the wrong place. I don't want her there, and I don't want to be here. I want to go home. Not in a couple of days, but right now. In the back of my mind, a thought half stirs, an ugly unexpressed fear. I'm thinking of Eddie, and although I know that he's with my mother and that he's safe, I still don't like the idea of this woman being so close to him, not now that I know what I know.

The thought gives me the surge of energy I need. I fling open the bathroom door and hurry through to the bedroom, pulling my suitcase out from underneath the bed. At random, I start snatching up my clothes, bundling them haphazardly inside. I'll tell Francis that we just *have* to leave. That there's been some kind of emergency and we need to get back. My head is fuzzy and I can't work out the details, but I'll think of something. I'm still snatching up handfuls of our possessions when I hear the doorbell ring downstairs.

I stand motionless for an instant, listening, and then Francis's voice floats up to me. "Can you get that, Caro? I'm cooking."

I look 'round at the half-packed room. I'll see who is there, then come back and finish it off. I run downstairs, glimpsing the figure through the opaque glass; female and slight, long hair falling over her shoulders. As I pull the door open I see that it's Amber. She looks as if she hasn't slept in days, her eyes sunken into their sockets and the surrounding skin bruised violet with exhaustion.

"Carl's back," she says with her customary directness, as soon as I open the door. "I've told him you're here."

Even though I have expected it, something shudders through me at her words. "What did he say? How is he?" I ask.

She spreads her hands out silently. "Shocked," she says at last. "He's trying to make sense of it—understand how it could have happened. As we all are," she adds, cool evaluation briefly flashing in her gaze. "Anyway. Can we go out?"

Wrong-footed, I hesitate. An image of the woman in my house flickers again at the corners of my mind. "I need to get home," I say. "You were right."

"That's as may be," she counters swiftly, "but I need to talk to you first." There's a kind of savage intenseness to her tone, and somehow from her the word *need* feels stronger, overturning mine. I look at her, and there are still so many unanswered questions in my head, pulling me toward her. And there's still you, just across the street, only meters away.

"It won't take long," she says swiftly, sensing my weakness. "We can just go to the park or something. Francis?" Her voice is suddenly gaily raised. "It's Amber. I'm just going to borrow Caroline for half an hour, if that's OK? I want her advice on something."

There is a pause. "Errrm—OK," he calls back at last, his tone tinged with confusion.

My eyes meet Amber's, and she shrugs. There's nothing to do but pull on my shoes and follow her as she turns and walks briskly down the road, weaving through the backstreets toward the riverside park. She doesn't speak as we walk, and I'm unable to help second-guessing what she wants to say. I know she still believes I came here deliberately. That I've followed you like a pathetic stalker, desperate to be close to you again.

"I'm not what you think I am," I find myself saying. My voice is brittle and I have to stop and breathe for a second to quell the tremble that might signify weakness. "I'm not trying to come between you and Carl."

Amber is twisting 'round, looking for a suitable place for us to sit. "Here," she says, walking swiftly over to a bench shaded beneath a canopy of willow branches close to the river's edge. She curls up at one end, drawing her knees up to her chest, waiting for me to join her. "I have no idea if that's true or not, Caroline," she says. "I've got no way of knowing. But that's not really the reason I wanted to speak to you."

Slowly, I sit. She's not looking at me as if I'm an object of her hatred, or even of her pity. Her expression is more one of cautious evaluation, as if she's wondering whether I am the last piece of the puzzle that she's trying to put together.

"What is it?" I ask.

She brushes her hair back from her forehead and runs her hand down its length, grasping it into a fist and tugging on it gently. The mannerism looks familiar and I find myself wondering if I do it myself. "I wasn't really honest with you, that first day we went to the coffee shop," she says. "When I said that I didn't know Sandra."

"Sandra?" I ask, but as soon as I've said it I know who she means. The shape of the word lingers oddly in my mouth. I'm not sure I've ever said it before.

"Yes," Amber says. "The woman at number 21, the woman whose house you're staying in."

"OK," I say, and now my heart is thudding for a different reason. "So you . . ." And I realize that I don't know what to say next.

Amber frowns minutely, knitting her fingers together and staring down at them. "I've always been aware of her," she says. "She moved in not long after us. You know, I see people on this street around all the time, but right from the start I saw her more than most people. She always seemed to be there, when I was out and about—just passing outside, or out in the front garden. We didn't speak much, but she seemed friendly, and when you move somewhere new . . . I don't have friends here, or family, and Carl was working away such a lot. I started to feel like I knew her." She shrugs, glancing at me for my reaction.

I look back at the regimented rows of houses stretching away from us. In this kind of place, familiarity feels like more than it is. The sight of the same people moving in and out of your eyeline from day to day seems to add up to more than the sum of its parts. "Yes," I say, "I see."

"It wasn't easy between me and Carl, when we first moved here," she says. The flicker of unwillingness in her eyes tells me this must be important—that she wouldn't say this to me unless she had to. "Our relationship had gone a long way in a short time. I hadn't really got to grips with him yet. At times I felt that I'd moved in with someone I barely knew, and he didn't always help that. To be honest," she says, her voice rising now and her words coming faster, "I don't think he was over you, or what happened. Not at all. He'd told me everything almost at once, when he barely even knew me. It was like he needed to pass it on to someone. I don't think it really mattered who. I'm not saying he doesn't love me," she adds warningly, flashing me a quick look. "But back then—I don't know. It was a strange time."

"I can understand that," I say automatically, because she's paused and she seems to be expecting something, but all I can think of is you—washed up in this place with a woman you fell for to save your sanity, spending your days and nights trying to deal with the fallout of everything that had happened. I don't know why I never thought of you this way before. All along I've seen you as self-sufficient, impenetrable. I told myself that you would cope, that you had washed your hands of me and never wanted to see me again. In my darkest moments I almost thought that you had been glad of the chance to do it while playing the sacrificial lamb, in a way that so completely exonerated you of blame. I was the damaged one. There was no space to think of you as being the same.

"Anyway," Amber continues, "one day I invited her over for coffee. We hung out at my place for a while, just chatting. Nothing deep, you know . . . just small talk, but it broke up the day. It got to be a sort of routine, whenever Carl was away for a few days. She was a lot older than me, but I kind of liked that. It sounds stupid, but it was almost like she was looking after me. I was lonely, you see? I just wanted someone to talk to."

She spreads out her hands unconsciously as she talks, opening up her isolation to me. "And one day—Carl and I had had a fight over the phone while he was away, and I'd said to him that I wasn't sure why we were bothering, that I wasn't sure if he would ever be able to let go of the past. He didn't even answer me—he just hung up. I'd just got off the phone with him when Sandra turned up at the door. I'd forgotten I'd invited her, and I was in tears. She asked me what was wrong, and I . . ."

"You told her," I finish, because suddenly I understand what this is about and the pieces are falling into place, and I can feel the hairs on my arms rising against my sleeves. "You told her everything."

Amber nods. "You don't understand what it was like," she says. "It used to go 'round and 'round in my head, everything he'd said. The way he told me about your affair, and about the accident, it was like reading his way through a script—all the words there right next to the surface. Like I said, he needed to pass it on. And I wanted to do the same."

I try to put myself in this woman's place. Imagine myself sitting in my home opposite Amber, listening to her tell me about how my daughter died. Understanding that the man I had thought was responsible was little more than a front for someone else. Someone who had walked away scot-free. I can't really do it—can't get out of my own head for long enough to climb inside hers—but for an instant I think I glimpse the edge of it, a brief flash to the corner of my eye, and it's enough to make me shudder.

"What did she say?" I force myself to ask. "How did she react?"

Amber shrugs minutely. "It was hard to tell," she says. "She's very . . . controlled. She didn't say much at all. But when I look back, that's when she started behaving differently toward me."

"How do you mean?" I ask. My voice is trembling slightly, and I breathe in deeply, trying to ground myself.

"It's hard to explain," Amber says. "The best way I can describe it is that she just became a lot more—intense. We usually met up once a week or so while Carl was away, but she started turning up more and more, almost every day at one point. I started realizing that we didn't actually have much in common. When we were together so often we had nothing to say to each other, but she kept on coming. And—I know this sounds a bit crazy, but I started noticing a few things going missing. My favorite umbrella, a jumper I liked, one of Carl's aftershaves. I mean, I had no proof that she'd taken them, but . . ."

"I understand," I say quickly. I think of the shock of my fingers closing around that bottle, the first hint of its scent. This has been delicately planned. A subtly plotted treasure map of hints and clues and red herrings, designed to lure me in.

"I didn't like it." Amber cuts into my thoughts. "The past couple of months, I've tried to distance myself. Been out at the times she normally called, cut our meetings short. It's worked, in as far as we don't see each other very much anymore. But she's . . . still there." I see a quick shiver rack her body, her eyes lost as she stares somewhere into the middle distance. "And then," she says, pulling herself back, "of course, then you turned up."

"Is that why you spoke to me in the first place?" I ask. "Because you thought I knew her?"

"Well . . ." Amber looks briefly awkward. "I don't mean that was the only reason—I mean, under different circumstances, maybe we could have been friends—"

I think the absurdity of trying to cling to social niceties in this situation strikes her as much as it does me, because for a moment her lips curve into a half smile before her face straightens again. "But yes," she continues. "I suppose I thought that I might be able to find out more about her somehow, through you. But then you told me that you didn't really know her, and I thought it was better to say that I didn't either, because of course I didn't know if you were being honest with me or not, you didn't even know me, and at one point I even started thinking that Sandra had sent you as a kind of plant just to find out what I was saying about her when she wasn't there . . ." She stops, takes a breath as she listens to the echo of all these hastily spilled-out words.

"I was telling the truth," I say. "I've never—" I am about to say that I have never even spoken to her, but then I remember the phone call, the soft, clear, even tone of her voice down the line. "I've never even seen her face," I finish.

Amber nods. "I'm not saying I don't believe you. But there's something here I don't understand. I'm not imagining it, I know I'm not. There's something odd about her. You know, when I came 'round to see you the other day, that was the first time I'd ever been into her house. We'd always met at mine. I had a quick look 'round and I couldn't find most of the things that were missing, but I found the umbrella. She had it hanging up like it was some kind of shrine. Why the fuck would you do that? I don't know, I just . . ." She stops, collects her thoughts. "It's not about the umbrella," she says. "It's everything."

Abruptly she stops talking, hugging her knees to her chest again. Through the fine blond strands of hair straying across her face, her green eyes are narrowed and watchful. The line between her brows is creasing and deepening, her expression flickering with uncertainty. In this moment I feel sorry for her. She's walked into something she doesn't understand and can't change. She knows something is wrong, but she doesn't know what, and I don't want to tell her. That's your job, if it's anyone's.

"Have you told Carl about this?" I ask. "Does he know Sandra, too?"

Amber shakes her head. "Like I said, I used to meet up with her when he was away. I might have mentioned her to him once or twice at the start, but not recently. I knew he'd think I was an idiot for letting her latch on to me. He always says I'm too soft." Abruptly, she stops, as if she's realized that I don't want or need to know these details. She's right. Even the thought of you chastising her, telling her she's too kindhearted for her own good, is painful.

My silence is unsettling her; she looks at me head-on, steeling herself. "She has something to do with all this, doesn't she?" she asks. "With why you're here? With you and Carl?" When I don't answer, she shifts uneasily in her seat. "This is frightening. I don't want to feel like I'm being watched."

The words unlock something and I realize that of course this is what this is all about. This woman has tracked you down here because she wanted to watch you. Some people turn away from tragedy and force it underground, and others stare it in the face. She wanted it close. Perhaps it's the only way she can cope with it, to feel that she's taken back some tiny amount of control, even if it means torturing herself every day with the reality of what has happened. But what she's been doing with me goes beyond watching. It's shifted up a gear.

Amber is still waiting, biting her lip. "No one's watching you,"

I say. It's as close to the truth as I can manage. Her eyes are shining with the threat of tears and all at once I just want her to fade away. "It's OK," I say, "honestly."

She frowns, shaking her head. "It doesn't feel like it."

"Really. This is all going to be over soon, Amber. I promise." Strangely, I believe what I'm saying. There's a sense of things gathering, time sharpening to a point of decision, even if I don't know yet exactly what it might be.

She opens her mouth as if to argue back, then slumps back. She wants this comfort—enough to accept it without further complaint or question. "I hope you're right," she says quietly.

We sit there a few more moments in silence, drained. "Come on," I say finally. "Let's head back."

"OK." As she stands up and we begin to wander back I can see a certain looseness in her shoulders that tells of relief, despite the lack of resolution in our conversation. She's passed the burden on again. This is the way our lives are, I think—shifting pain back and forth between each other, expanding it, diluting it. Waiting for it to stretch and thin so much that it's barely visible.

As we turn into Everdene Avenue, I sense Amber stiffen and hear her rapid intake of breath as she looks up the street. She's seen it before me. You and Francis, standing on opposite sides of the pavement, staring at each other. The sunlight is falling across the two of you and it's impossible to see the expressions on your faces. Neither of you is making a move toward the other, but you aren't moving away either. It's as if time has stopped.

And then Francis looks up and glances down the road, and he sees us standing there. In the next instant you glance up, too, and you're turning, walking fast up the pathway toward your house, and Francis is walking in the opposite direction, back toward number 21. In that split second, there's a violent sense of wrenching. I want to tear myself in two. But my feet are already turning toward Francis and following him to the other side of the street, and as I look swiftly back over my shoulder I see Amber running toward you, your eyes meeting mine for an instant before you look away and your hand brushing her shoulder as you steer her inside.

HOME

Francis, August 2014

A new day. Day one, every time I open my eyes. A clean slate. Sixteen waking hours that I can use however I want. I can work, go for walks, watch television, listen to music, spend time with my family or my friends, travel across the city, go to museums. I can do anything I want as long as I don't take the pills.

The sunshine is warm and soft on my face as I move back and forth in the bathroom, taking a shower, brushing my teeth, pulling on my clothes. In the mirror I see the lines of my cheekbones newly revealed. My skin is smooth. My eyes are bright and clear. It's happened slowly, but now, thirteen months in, I can see myself again. I look well. The knowledge is sweet and simple.

I push open the bathroom window and the summer breeze curls gently into the room, and I realize that today it's going to be easy. The kind of day when I feel confident that I can keep myself on this course and achieve whatever I want—carve out successes, fix the broken relationships. It isn't always this way. Some days it still feels as if I'm walking the most fragile of tightropes, that there's no way that the violent batterings of my mind can be contained by this thin shell I live in. There are days when it seems that I'm fighting a battle I can't possibly win and even the effort of existing is a black cloud that I can't get out from under, the darkness of it pressing down on me so hard that I can hardly speak. But not today.

"Daddy, Daddy," I hear Eddie singing next door, and I push open the nursery door and see him lying in his bed, grinning and waving, his fair hair tousled and tangled on the pillow. When I first started to surface from the dream I'd been in for the past two years, his presence was a shock. He had been there all along, but I hadn't. Suddenly we were in this together, father and son, and to my surprise I found that the weight of his expectations on me was easy to carry. I'm patient with him. Firm but fair. I take him to the shops or the park and he trots along beside me, his small fingers curling their way around mine. When I tuck him in at night his breath is warm and sweet on my downturned face. Small things. Before, if I noticed them at all, they were daggers to the heart—just more reminders of a life that couldn't be enjoyed and that was irretrievably out of reach. Now I build my world around them. It's a smaller world than most, but that suits me. For now.

"Morning." Caroline appears behind me, slipping her way into the nursery and leaning against the wall, smiling. She's wearing a dark green vest top that barely skims her thighs and a small pair of black knickers underneath. An image of the night before flashes into my head: her face turned to one side on the pillow in abandon, her legs hotly clasping mine. The thought gives me a surge of desire and I have to stamp it back down. These days it sometimes seems I can barely think of anything else. It was one of the first things that came back, after I stopped the pills. The delirious realization that this was still something I could do—the bizarre novelty of fucking my own wife. She's watching me, looking as if she's reading my mind. "Are you off soon?" she asks.

I nod. "Got that early appointment." It's a new patient, a last-minute request. I've been building back up slowly. A new clinic, new practice. Another clean slate. Not taking on more than I can handle, not caring what other people think. Giving myself the space to breathe. I'm doing this right. It hasn't been perfect, but it's still moving in the right direction.

"Well," she says, moving over to Eddie and taking his hand to pull him out of bed into a cuddle, "I'll be around when you come back. Day off, remember? I'll take him in to nursery and then maybe we can have lunch together or something?"

"Sounds good," I say. There's an unexpected stinging across the bridge of my nose, the hint of approaching tears. My emotions aren't always predictable. Sometimes I have no idea where they have come from or what they mean. I've learned to sit back and let them take over when they want to, and then to pack them carefully away in their boxes. Take your feelings out to lunch, my sponsor said to me awhile ago, and then tell them to fuck off. That's what I do. So I give myself a moment, let the strange tenderness and sadness linger, and then I toss it away.

Caroline comes with me to the front door and winds her limbs around me, pressing her body up against mine. She's clingy at the moment, desiring. I don't mind. It's a change from all those months back in the dark times when she was slippery like mercury and shrank away from my touch. "See you later," she murmurs.

"See you," I say, kissing her. I pull back and look at her for a moment, taking her in. There are lines on her face that weren't there a few years ago and I can see the tiredness in her eyes, but she's still beautiful. More so to me than ever, really, now that she's mine again.

I stride down the high street toward the station in the bright sunshine. The trees are still laden with lush, green leaves and the sky is blue and cloudless. It's a film set, a picture of perfection. I'm thinking of Caroline and the smell of her perfume as she wrapped her arms around my neck. Something tremors at the edge of the image. I let it stay there, knowing I shouldn't ignore it. These memories are still there, and it's useless to deny them. Now and again it still comes in a rush of bitterness and surprise: the knowledge that another man has been inside her and made her believe that she loves him. Every time it feels like the first time. It isn't going to go away. It has to be lived with, just like everything else.

I carry on walking and now I'm thinking about that July night, so long ago, when she came back crying and wouldn't tell me why. Standing in the middle of the lounge with tears streaming down her face, lost in some private space that she couldn't explain and that I had no way of reaching through the fog that was suffocating my every breath. It should have been a wake-up call, but it only drove me further underground. The weeks that followed were a disjointed montage of broken sleep, slurred insults, and abortive attempts at reconciliation, punctuated by the pills at every hour until I had completely lost any lingering sense of who or where I was. And finally, the calm stillness of the September evening when she came to me and told me she was leaving. *I'm taking Eddie down to my parents in the morning, and I'm leaving you. I've had enough. I don't want this life anymore.*

What cut through was the relief. Hidden in the pale tense lines of her mouth, the half-defiant lift of her chin. She'd made her decision and at least part of her was happy. Strange that that's what it took for me to see that I couldn't let her go. I stayed up all night and I didn't take any more pills. It was the first time I'd gone more than a couple of hours without in weeks. I'll never forget that bizarre, dreamlike sense of surfacing—the first bubbles of air popping into my body and dragging me up and out, skinned and reborn.

It took hours to persuade her not to go. Hours of talking in the gray dawn, convincing her that now was the time for change. But as soon as we began to speak I could tell that although the decision was made, it could be undone. She hadn't managed to sever the bonds as entirely as she thought, and I could see almost at once that even though she didn't really believe what I was saying, she wanted to, and that was half the battle.

Six a.m. and I had unfolded myself as much as I could physically bear. The pounding in my head, the weird starkness of the objects in the room around us, revealing themselves to me after weeks of sitting around them and seeing nothing but shadows. And when I had finished talking, she began. *If there's any chance of us doing this, then I need to tell you something, too.*

The affair with Carl was hard for her to speak about. I'd never seen such sadness in her eyes, such reluctance. It was more serious than I had thought. It had been months, and in her head she'd worked it up into a grand passion. I didn't know—still don't—how real it was. But I knew she felt it was, and that was enough. It had ended, though she wouldn't tell me how, but it was clear she wasn't over it. It didn't matter. There was no pain, no anger. That came later, but in that moment there was nothing but the sweetness of revelation. We had spent more time talking to each other in those few hours than we had in months, maybe years. The facts were out on the table for inspection and our marriage was a fucking mess. But the air was sharp and clean and I was breathing in and out and we were both still alive.

I've been so lost in thought that it comes as a surprise to find that I'm sitting on the train and we're pulling away from the platform. The sun against the window shines onto my hands folded in my lap. My wedding ring is much too loose now, but I'm still wearing it. For now at least, we seem to have survived.

~

The woman who enters the counseling room is in her late forties: dark hair cut into a bob, a slight narrow frame, smart neutral clothes. I've had barely any chance to skim the notes that I've been sent from her assessment. It sounds like fairly standard depression. And yet as soon as I see her I get a strange feeling that nothing about this is going to be standard at all.

Maybe it's the way she stops when she's halfway across the threshold, looking intently at me, and then around the room. People don't usually focus their attention on these things. They're driven by their own suffocating concerns—that's why they're here. But she looks around so carefully and her gaze lingers on my desk: the small red-flowered potted plant, the framed photograph of Caroline and Eddie. I keep it turned inward toward me, so all she's staring at is the back of the frame, but she looks at it as if she really wants to know what's on the other side. Her hands are twisted together in front of her and I can see the tension in her jawline, like she's gritting her teeth.

"Good morning," I say, "Sandra, isn't it? Come in. Take a seat."

She edges farther into the room and her gaze flits around the couple of chairs available to her. At last she chooses the one closest to mine and draped with a purple throw, next to the window. She slides into it in silence. Her eyes are dark blue and unblinking, as steady as glass.

"If it's OK with you," I say, "I like to start by just letting you talk. Telling me a bit about yourself and what's been going on."

Almost imperceptibly, she nods, as if this has reconfirmed what she expected to hear. When she starts to talk I have to strain to hear her at first. Her voice is level and soft, almost hypnotic. She sketches a picture of a fairly unremarkable life. She and her husband were divorced several years ago, but she speaks about it without passion or regret. Since then it's just been her and her daughter, Robyn.

It takes awhile for me to realize that the way she speaks about her daughter is strange. She refers to her at times in the present tense, at others in the past. She slips between memories, blurring the years. When she tells me that Robyn has been dead for over a year, it's almost like an afterthought. She doesn't think she needs to spell this out, because to her it's part of her DNA. It's written across every second and every breath.

"I'm sorry," I say to fill the brief jagged silence, but she doesn't respond and she begins to tell me how her daughter died. I'm listening, but at the same time a trickle of panic is slipping down the back of my neck, stiffening my muscles. I'm not a bereavement counselor. I specialize in relationships, family tensions. How the hell has this woman been assigned to me? I'm almost certain that there was no mention of any of this in the assessment notes I hastily scanned. But it hardly seems conceivable that she wouldn't have mentioned it in her first appointment. Clearly, this is why she's here. Why would she hide it?

"I spent a long time looking for sense in what happened," she's saying. Flatly, without apparent pain. "But I was looking for something that wasn't there. The car had been coming too fast around the bend. It must have been. But there was no reason why Robyn was there at that precise instant. No reason why a few moments of inattention ended up destroying her life, and mine. You can only go so far down that road. It leads nowhere."

I nod. I think about saying something around the idea of acceptance and how this realization can be part of it, but something tells me to stay quiet. Besides, whatever she's feeling, acceptance isn't it. I can see it in the set of her muscles, the strange way she's half bent forward as if she's poised for flight, and in the haunted look in her eyes that seem miles away from me even as they're looking straight into mine.

"I watched the man who was responsible in the dock," she says, "and I thought, he's barely started to live his own life, and already he's ruined mine. Does that sound unfair?" I say nothing, moving my head to one side in noncommittal encouragement. "He was young. Repentant—shell-shocked, even. He didn't seem like a boy racer. I wanted to hate him. I did hate him, in a way."

She stops for a minute and looks intently out of the window at the drifting clouds. When she speaks again it's with her gaze still trained there, spilling her thoughts out into the open air. "He got six months, but he was out in three. It's not surprising, really. It was an accident, a mistake. But still. It was laughable. Nothing could have compensated, of course, but that . . . it didn't even scratch the surface of the pain he'd caused. I don't mind telling you," she says with mild, disarming frankness, "I became a little obsessed with him. Let's just say I've followed his progress. And it's taken a long time, but I've seen enough to know that I don't think he's happy. Not really. I couldn't have borne that. I was starting to think that it was time to let it go. I don't mean forget her, or forgive him. But it seemed that there was nothing more to think, nothing more to feel. I'd got to the end of it."

"But something changed," I prompt, because she's looking at me again now and I can see the expectancy in her face and the command for me to speak.

For the first time, she half smiles. It's a strange, shifting experiment of a smile and it looks wrong on her, but it briefly transforms her and suddenly I can see that she would have been attractive once, charming. "It did," she says. There's a note of praise in her voice; I've picked up on her unspoken implication. It's not the first time a new patient has tried to test me this way, but it's the first time that I've felt such intense eagerness radiating from another person in response to my passing the test—a real hunger to reward me with her secrets. "Like I say, the sentence was negligible, but when I heard it I thought, well, it's something. At least it's something. But recently, I discovered that things weren't as they appeared. I discovered that the whole thing had been built on a lie. The man who had been held responsible—he wasn't alone. In fact, he wasn't even the one driving the car. There was a woman. His lover. He lied to protect her, I suppose. I don't really care why he did it. But I do care about justice. And it seems that that's something neither of them knows much about. Especially her."

Her voice is louder now and she's speaking with passion, violence—her eyes burning, her hands clenched hard on her knees. "Do you think that's something that should be allowed? To turn your back on the mess you've created and slip back into your own life with barely a ripple? Do you understand what I mean? Do you understand why it's wrong?"

These aren't hypothetical questions. She's firing them at me like gunshots, and all at once I'm wondering if she's actually deranged—a complete fantasist—and how much, if any, of what she's saying is true. "I understand what you mean," I say at last. "And I can see exactly why you would feel that way."

As soon as I've spoken I see her visibly relax. The fury that has been pulsating from her shrinks and disappears. She leans back in her chair and takes a long breath. "Good," she says. "I thought you would." There's something uncomfortably personal about the way she's looking at me. "I don't think she deserves what she has," she says. "This woman. This Caroline."

When I hear the name there's that tiny reflexive jolt of familiarity, the same way there is when anyone says a name that means something to you, that runs through your own life. On this woman's lips, it's tinged with reflective bitterness. It hangs in the air between us for a moment before she speaks again. "I think of her often," she says. "Her, and her lover. Carl Jackson."

This time the name hits like a blow to the head. Over the years I've learned to keep my expression composed in the face of the most outrageous and wild pronouncements that patients have thrown at me. I've received tales of obsession and betrayal, deceit and insanity, with studied neutrality. But right now I can't stop myself from flinching, and the fierce glint in her eye tells me two things. First, she knows exactly who I am. And second, she's not lying. This is real.

In the few seconds of silence that cycle lazily through the room before I speak, a lot of thoughts flash through my head. I'm thinking of those weeks and months after Caroline came back crying, the way she often got up in the middle of the night and I'd find her standing in the hallway, staring at nothing. I'm thinking about the feel of her limbs, feverish and slicked with sweat, when she used to wake up from dreams that she couldn't or wouldn't share. I'm thinking of the way she told me that she was selling her car because she didn't want to drive anymore, bluntly and without explanation. And yes, it fits. But I have absolutely no idea yet how I feel or what it means. All I know is that this can't continue.

"Our time is up," I say. The clock still has twenty minutes to run, but we both know what I mean. I stand up, moving toward the door. "If you would like to make another appointment, please talk to reception. But I'm afraid I won't have this slot in future. In fact, I'm completely booked up."

She stands up slowly, her small figure neat and composed. "I don't want another appointment," she says. "I've done what I came here to do." There's no vindictiveness in her tone anymore. Just a flat encroaching sadness, as if even in this moment she's realizing that it hasn't measured up to how she thought it would be. That it won't ever be enough.

She shakes her dark hair back behind her ears, and she leaves quietly. As she passes me, she turns her head quickly back toward my desk, and I can see her gaze seeking out the photograph, taking it in for a cool instant. The last I see of her is her face in profile as she turns away, moving out of my orbit and down the corridor. Her pale skin is stretched tight across her high cheekbones and the planes of her face are oddly beautiful.

When she's gone I lock the office door from the inside and sit down again. I stay there for a long time. Thinking about my wife and the life she's led away from me. The secrets that she keeps holed up inside her because she doesn't trust me with them. Wondering if things would have been different if she had driven in another direction that night, and if it would have taken her right out of my life, away from me.

I want to feel angry, but I don't. I feel sadness, and pity. And there's something else—a surge of conviction, rising from somewhere too deep inside to pinpoint; the knowledge that what this woman thought might break us will have the opposite effect. I'm strong enough now. I can carry a burden without it destroying me. I can understand my wife better than she knows. And I can wait for her to be honest with me. However long it takes.

*C*aroline's mother is back in the room and everything is speeding up, a jerky roll of film sputtering in front of my eyes. She's moving fast toward Eddie, taking his hand, and snatching the hamster's cage with her free hand—standing there in the doorway with her possessions, her eyes wide and uncomprehending. I think she asks if there's anything she can do. I can't speak through the tears and in another moment she's pulling Eddie away, hurrying with him down the staircase. She closes the front door softly, as if she wants to escape as quietly as she can.

I stand and wait. Maybe she's calling the police right now and telling them to come here to take me away. Funny, the rush of calm that thought gives. Someone to take control and sort everything out. I can see us now, me and Robyn, watching the policemen march up to Buckingham Palace when we visited for her fourth birthday. "Who are those men?" she asked, and I told her that they were the police, that they were in charge. Her little face, earnest and accepting, her head nodding under her woolly hat, the faint steam of her breath escaping into the cold air.

I wish I could forget her. I want to be purged and to wake up *mindless and new. Instead for two years I've been picking around the edges of these people's lives, playing with fantasies that won't come true. Watching Carl and his new girlfriend go about their daily business. Sitting opposite Caroline's husband in the therapist's office. At first I hoped that somehow I could change things just by being there. Just by existing near them. But I couldn't, and even now, when I've spent this time in her house, and thrown my pointless little grenade into her family, I still can't.*

Somehow I've fetched the little piles of photo print from the bedroom and I'm back kneeling on the living room floor, looking at the tiny slices of her face. I reach into my pocket and pull out the crumpled yellow letter I've carried around for months. I look back and forth, from her smiling mouth to the desolate words she wrote to him, trying to match them up. I think about what happened every day, *she* wrote, and I can hardly bear it, and without you I'm not sure I can bear it at all.

She's just a woman. Not the devil I've imagined—calculating, merciless. The truth is much harder to swallow. I stare into her eyes and I think about all the times I've imagined what I would say if we came face-to-face—the cutting streams of vitriol, the words that would stay with her for the rest of her life—and I realize now that if I ever saw her I can't trust that they would come out, and maybe I'd end up saying nothing at all.

The quality of the light in this room is sharp and strange. Sun shining through the thin curtains and brightening the air. There's an ache in my head but my limbs feel limp and relaxed, finally at peace, because at last I realize that I've had everything the wrong way 'round, and I know what to do now.

AWAY

Caroline, May 2015

Francis slams the front door an instant before I reach it, and I have to fumble with the key, forcing it into the lock and then hurrying into the hallway, trying to work out which way he has gone. I find him in the kitchen, standing with his back to the door, his fists clenched on the worktop, staring intently at the wall.

"Francis," I say, my breath catching in my throat.

He wheels 'round and I can tell at once that he is angry, more angry, perhaps, than I have ever seen him—his jaw set in a grim unmoving line, his mouth twisted with disgust and suspicion. "What?" he says roughly. "You've finally come to tell me what the fuck's going on?"

Any vague, desperate hope I might have had that he didn't recognize the man who had been standing across the road from him a few moments before evaporates. He's seen you, and there's no avoiding this. "Francis," I say again, "I know this must be a horrible shock. I promise you, none of this has been done to hurt you."

He stares hard at me, unmoved. "What is he doing here, Caro?" he asks, then stops, shakes his head roughly. "No," he says. "What are *we* doing here? That's what I really want to know. Is this some kind of sick game? Coming for a little holiday across the road from your lover? Sneaking out for a quick shag whenever my back's turned? Is this the sort of thing that turns you on?"

"Of course not," I stammer. Heat is flooding my body, making my head spin. "He's not my lover, not anymore. And I promise you, I didn't arrange this. I had no idea he lived here, I—"

"Interesting," interrupts Francis scornfully. His tone is harsh but contained. I would rather he were shouting expletives at me, losing control, but that isn't his style. "So the fact that when I pop out for a minute to put out the bins, I bump into him, is just an amazing coincidence. Of all the houses we could possibly have stayed in across the entire country, we just happen to rock up a mere ten meters or so from his. Extraordinary. It's the kind of thing that makes you believe in fate, doesn't it? Like it's written in the stars that—"

"Please, stop." I take a deep breath, preparing to speak, but the enormity of it—of plowing back into the past and spilling out the ugly truth of that night at Silver Birches to him, and everything that has come from it and led us here—overwhelms me, and I close my eyes for a moment.

When I open them I see that his expression has changed. He isn't sneering or contemptuous anymore. His face is twisted with worry and confusion, not knowing whether to be hurt or angry or something else entirely, and there's a vulnerability to it that is painful to see. "I don't understand any part of this, Caro," he says. His voice is still angry, but quieter; he's trying to give me space to talk.

I force myself to look at him steadily. Although I know I will have to give him what he wants eventually, I don't think I can do it right now. I can't tell him the truth when he's already on the edge, when his world has been so savagely rocked.

"I don't understand it either," I say, and I don't blink.

He looks back at me for a long moment, trying to read my

expression. "Then it's him," he says simply. "He's engineered it in some way."

I shake my head. "No."

Francis gives a quick exhalation of frustration. "I don't see any other explanation."

"No," I say again. "It makes no sense. He doesn't want me here. You saw him just now—he didn't want to speak to me. He just turned around and left." A stab of hurt, lightning fast but unmistakable. I push it away, but something of it must show on my face, because his own expression twists with sudden pain.

"Do you still love him?" he asks.

I've half expected it, and I realize that for days now I've been silently asking myself the same thing; turning over our memories, prodding them to test the sharpness of the hurt, letting them suck me back in. The denial I know I should give rises fast to my lips, but I hold it back. He's right—he deserves this honesty, even if I'm not sure I have the answer to give.

After a long while I say, "I still miss him. I'm not sure I can tell the difference." I pause, thinking. Francis is listening intently. "I don't know him anymore," I say. "But there's something I can't seem to let go."

It can't be what he wants to hear, but Francis doesn't seem angry. If anything, the look in his eyes is one of pity. Somehow, I've drawn closer to him and my hands are reaching out for his and my fingers are locking around his own. I press my face into his chest, listening to the quick thump of his heartbeat against my forehead. "I still love you," I whisper, but I'm not sure he hears. "You know that, right?"

After a few moments, he pulls away. "Well, that's the thing about you, Caroline," he says lightly. "It's never easy to tell when you're lying."

I bite my lip, but have the sense to stay silent. He glances at the oven, and I realize that the pasta sauce he was cooking on the hob is smoking, reduced to a sticky volcanic mass. Francis reaches out and turns it off. He passes a hand over his forehead, gives a sigh.

"I can't handle trying to make sense of this anymore tonight," he says. "I'm going to bed. I need to lie down."

I think about the packing I have started, the desperate need I felt earlier to get back; about Sandra prowling through our home. I already know that I can't force him to make the journey to Leeds tonight, not after everything that's happened. "OK," I say quietly, swallowing down my discomfort. One more night. Already I'm counting down the hours. "I'll come up soon."

He nods, then moves toward the door.

~

The night passes slowly, punctuated by drifts of light, uneasy sleep. I lie watching the shifting shadows outside the window, the gradual strengthening of light through the curtains.

In this quiet space, it's as if nothing has happened. You, Francis, Amber . . . they've all receded and there's nothing left in my head but the pictures that I've been blocking out for years, and which are finally breaking through my defenses. Whenever I lose my grip on consciousness for even a few seconds the girl is there—walking softly through the room, threaded through the thin line between reality and dreams. Her long dark hair blowing out behind her, her green scarf slung over her shoulder. It replays again and again, this procession, and the split second that I have never been sure if I have imagined or not: the wide-eyed moment of connection as she spins 'round in the instant before we collide and it explodes in a burst of splintered glass. And the impact wakes me, jolts me brutally up and out of this strange space of memory into the dark bedroom, until the next time. Over and over again.

At some point I must have fallen asleep for more than a few minutes, because when I open my eyes again it's daylight and Francis is no longer next to me. Instead there's a note lying on the pillow. **I'm going out for a walk to clear my head. I won't be more than a couple of hours. Just need some time alone. I'll see you soon.** I'm not surprised, but all the same my heart drops. I have no idea what he's thinking or how he's feeling, how the long night might have warped our conversation the evening before.

I drag myself out of bed and get dressed, then wander aimlessly down to the kitchen. I stand quietly for a few moments, wondering what to do. It's bizarrely silent and still—a shaft of sunshine piercing the windowpane, minuscule dust motes shimmering faintly in its light. When my phone beeps it sends a brusque jolt of shock right through me. I snatch it up and look at the screen. The message is from a number that isn't in my phone, but as soon as I see the digits I recognize them.

> **If you want to talk, we can. I'm on my way now to the Garden Café on Castle Street. Come if you like.**

Somehow, I'm not surprised. Perhaps because the message is so typical of you, so familiar in tone, that it doesn't feel unexpected. You haven't changed; the way you've framed it in terms of what I might want, as if your own desires were irrelevant, or maybe nonexistent. Back then I found it charming and thoughtful at first; then, later, frustratingly oblique. I never really knew—still don't—if what you wanted matched up with what I wanted, or if that mattered to you at all.

I'm already out of the house, walking swiftly down the street and turning out onto the main road toward the street you've named. I walked past the café a couple of days ago, dimly registered its dark green walls and soft-hued lighting. I remember noticing two leather sofas tucked into the back corner and shielded from the rest of the room, and I already know that's where you'll be.

It's only when I've turned onto Castle Street and spy the café toward the end of the road that it even occurs to me that I didn't have to come—shouldn't have come. I could have sent a polite dismissive message back, suggesting that there was nothing between us that needed to be said, or simply ignored it. These options were there, and yet they weren't.

I'm pushing open the café door and turning toward the sofas at the back, and as I see you there—hunched over a newspaper, your head dipped intently over a page that I know you aren't reading—there's a sliding sense of inevitability, the pieces clicking into place and the knowledge that this was always going to happen one day, and why not today.

I stand in the doorway a moment, watching you, drinking in the sight of you at close range. You're taller than I remember, your face narrower. You look older, your features somehow more defined. Your hair is shorter than it was the last time I saw you. You're wearing a dark green jacket I've never seen before, and despite all the differences you fit exactly into the picture in my head that the years had blurred. It clicks into place with a sense of rightness, as if you had never been away.

I'm only a couple of feet away when you look up and your dark eyes meet mine. Without meaning to, I smile, and you smile back. It's a strange little twitch of instinct, a throwback. For an instant, it's as if the past two years have been erased and we're right back where we were, perhaps in June of 2013, at a time when being together was sweet and precious.

Something in my face must change, because you blink, your expression rapidly turning to awkwardness and confusion. "Hi," you say, motioning for me to sit down opposite you, and stupidly I feel the threat of tears rising and stinging along the bridge of my nose because your voice is just as I remember.

I slide into the seat. We're sitting face-to-face, and the soft low light casts shadows across you, hollowing out the skin beneath the ridges of your cheekbones, throwing the line of your jaw into stark relief. I realize that I'm barely blinking. There's a hunger growing inside me, the violence of which surprises me—the desire not to miss an instant of this, the knowledge that it's important and that I've been waiting for it for so long that I can't afford to let it go. I can feel myself trembling with sudden adrenaline; not knowing how to process this, unable to look away.

We sit in silence for a few moments, and then you sigh and push your hands out across the tabletop, palms down; a gesture of defeat or supplication. "This is fucking strange," you say simply. "I don't know what the hell's going on. Tell me honestly, did you follow me here?"

"No," I say quickly. "I can see why you'd think that, but no, Carl, I didn't. Even if I had known where you lived, I wouldn't do that. Not after all this time." Not ever, I think, but I don't say it. You know as well as I do that I could have done anything back then, half crazed by your absence, and that it was only fear that stopped me.

You look at me hard, your eyes glittering and liquid in the soft lamplight. I've never been on the receiving end of it before, this cool appraisal of yours that I've seen you employ with others many times. I don't like it. "OK," you say finally. "It seems like a big coincidence, that's all."

"I didn't say it was a coincidence." I take a breath, and I don't know where to start; can't do this here, so unprepared and with so little knowledge of what I want to say. "You know the person whose house I'm staying in? Number 21?"

You frown, jolted. "Well, no, not really," you say almost instantly. "I don't know anyone on the road well. Why?"

I take a deep breath, and I realize that there's no point in prevaricating, and that the truth is all there is now, with no reason to hide it away. "I'll tell you," I say, and almost at once there's a sense of release.

I tell you about the message I received, inviting me to exchange houses; the series of prompts and memories that began almost the instant I arrived; the emails exchanged and the dawning realization that what I had thought was one thing was quite another. I tell you about the woman in my house, and why she is there. I tell you that we have both been wrong in thinking that we could close the door on the past and lock it away, because it isn't only our past that we have been dealing with, and that it isn't only ours to turn our backs on.

You listen in silence, letting me talk. A couple of times you look sharply at me, your eyes widening in fear or surprise, but you don't speak until I have finished, and even then you let the silence stretch for a good half a minute.

"This is a lot to process," you say blankly at last. Absently, you scratch the stubble on your chin, and I know exactly how it feels under your hand, the physical memory leaping to life with unbidden clarity. "I realize that's an understatement. But it is."

I try to imagine myself in your position—how it would feel to have the information that has been drip-fed to me in agonizing stages dumped into my lap in the space of a few sentences. "I know," I say.

"I have no idea what to do," you say, as if to yourself. "I can't—" You exhale, almost impatiently. "I can't think about this now. I haven't thought about any of this for months. Years."

"I can't believe that," I say quickly, although as soon as I've said it I realize that I can. You know how to switch things off: pack them away in their box and throw away the key. It's a gift.

"I don't mean that I didn't care about what happened," you say sharply. "I was in prison for three months, you know. I had time to think about it then. And believe me, I did. It focuses the mind, being somewhere like that. It was . . ." You trail off briefly, frowning. "It was like the worst kind of Groundhog Day, the same soul-destroying routine over and over again. So there wasn't much to do *but* think. I even used to dream about it, you know—the impact, the blood. The sight of her on the ground. But when I finally came out, I thought to myself, I'm damned if I'm going to ruin my life over something that I can't change. It doesn't mean that I didn't care about it," you say again, and there's a brief sharp pause before you meet my eyes and the next words come out as if you're not aware you even meant to say them. "Or about you," you say.

"You never replied to my messages." I can't help saying it. I think of that last long love letter I wrote to you, and all the emails I sent for weeks afterward when I realized I had no way of knowing if you had read the letter or not. I put tracking receipts on those emails, and I know you read them. You read every single one. Sometimes over and over again. But you never replied.

"That's because I meant what I said," you say carefully. "It had to end there. You know that. I know you thought I'd change my mind, but I couldn't help that. I knew I wouldn't. And I didn't."

Your tone is defensive, but tinged with pride. You've always considered it one of your most admirable qualities—this single-mindedness, this ability to stick to your guns. No one has ever told you that just because you can stick to something, it doesn't mean that it's the right thing to do. Or if they have, you haven't wanted to listen.

My eyes are stinging and I force them open wide, knowing that the tears will fall if I blink. I'm trembling, thinking of myself hunched over the table in the middle of the night, scribbling the story of our affair out onto those yellow lined pages, desperately trying to find the words that would force a response, that would make you miss me so much that you couldn't help but want me. And suddenly something stirs in the back of my mind, some nebulous suspicion. "Have you kept the letter I sent you?" I whisper.

Your face shadows, and you look briefly uneasy. "I did keep it," you say, "even when I moved here, although I don't really know why. But I don't know where it is now. I haven't looked at it in months. I guess it's in my things somewhere."

I can't say for sure that you're wrong, but I feel it in my bones. All the little details, the ones that no one but us would have known. The pale pink roses in the bathroom, the song playing on the radio, the picture of the park where we lay together. When Amber told me about the things that had gone missing from their home, she could tell me only about the things she knew existed. There's a kind of mental click, an internal calibration as the last piece of the puzzle slots smoothly into place. I try to imagine those yellow pages in Sandra's hands, and I can't feel anything but pity.

"I've never forgiven myself," I say, "for being so stupid and thoughtless in the first place, for deciding to drive when I'd been drinking, and most of all for walking away from what I'd done. I should have faced up to it. I owed it to that girl. I walked away—I walked away like she didn't matter." It's the first time I've said these words out loud.

You shake your head. "Don't," you say. "There's no point. You can't undo what happened. You're right, you were stupid, and so was I, for not stopping you. I can't make you feel better about it. But as for what came afterward . . . if it helps, I still think you did the right thing by walking away. Even now. I'm not saying I never felt angry or resentful. But I never really doubted that it was better for me to take the blame than you." You speak with such conviction. I always envied you this—this inner knowledge you seemed to have that your own decisions were the right ones. You never seemed to suffer from the uncertainty that gnawed at me almost constantly, making me turn my own thoughts and motives inside out.

"I'm glad you feel that way," I say slowly, not sure if I mean it or not. Part of me wants you to feel the same way I do. There's no room in that serene complacency for doubts or longings. And yet I'm thinking of Amber, and the way she talked to me about you, before she knew who I was—the picture she painted of a man whom she couldn't even quite reach, who had fenced himself off into his own distant space—and I wonder if the thoughts that come to you in solitude are quite the same color and shape as the ones you are giving to me right now.

"Are you happy?" I ask. I know it's out of the blue, but there's no time to soften it or pretend that I don't feel I have the right to ask.

You half frown and your shoulders twitch, a quick gesture of exasperation. You brush your hand through the air in front of us, and for a fraction of a second it grazes against my own hands where they rest on the table. You snatch it away again as if I've scalded you. It sets off a shiver throughout the length of my body, and I'm thinking how strange it is that you used to lie next to me naked, hold me against you so close that your sweat soaked into my skin, and now you feel like you can't allow any part of your body to touch any part of mine.

"Sure," you say. "As happy as I'll ever be."

"With her?" I ask. "With Amber?"

The frown deepens. You don't like me saying her name. For a moment she's a ghostly presence with us, slipping in beside you on the sofa, curling her slim body up into a question mark. Someone doesn't belong in this picture. Her, or me.

"Yes," you say. "We're happy." You're watching me carefully now, trying to measure my reaction, to determine what's behind the question. In those few seconds of silence, something shifts. It's as if the barrier has cracked open and all at once I can't stop thinking about the way it used to be between us, and I can see in your eyes that you're thinking the same. "It's different than how it was with you," you say quietly, your voice so low that I have to strain to hear. "More—real," you qualify. "Less . . ." You stop. "I don't know," you say. "Less something else."

I nod, and I can't find the word either, but there's a tightness in my chest and I'm thinking about the sweetness of putting my arms around you and your lips coming down onto mine, and I know that whatever this something else is, it's something that won't come again, not for you and not for me either, no matter what else might be in its place.

"So you and Francis worked things out," you say. It sounds like a non sequitur but we both know it's not, and even now you can't quite rid your voice of the edge of dryness and contempt that shouldn't really be there anymore.

"We're still doing that," I say carefully. All at once, I'm seized by the violent desire to make you believe that my marriage is happy. I want to tell you about all the ways Francis has changed, the efforts he's made, the journeys we've been on. I want to prove that he's worth it. But I'm not sure you'll care. Why should you?

"It isn't easy," I say, and this is true, too. "There are good times and bad times." The days that I wake up to find a stranger with my husband's face prowling in the living room, gripped by anxieties and neuroses that he can't even bring himself to talk about. The strange, mercurial lift and swoop of his moods, impossible to predict or steer. The knowledge that every day is a new one, and that he still has no real idea how each one will go. I think of these things and there's a sudden strange throb of vertigo, making me grip the edge of the table for an instant and briefly close my eyes.

When I open them you're watching me again. "Well," you say, "you're an adult, Caro, you make your own choices."

I nod, not trusting myself to reply. There is no way of forming these thoughts into words, and in any case they're not yours to deal with, not anymore.

You pass a hand slowly through your hair, scraping it back from your forehead. The lights above our heads seem to dim further, and I'm conscious of the tiny distance between us, the ease with which I could reach out and take your face in my hands. "I did love you," you say at last. "I want you to know that."

"I know," I say quietly, and suddenly all the weeks and months that I have spent turning over this question seem crazily wasted, because I've always known this really, perhaps more clearly than you ever did yourself until this moment right here and now.

You're getting to your feet and with a sick lurch of realization I understand that the conversation is over and you're preparing to leave. My legs are shaking but I force myself to stand beside you. You smile, and you're reaching out, placing your hand on my shoulder and turning my body in toward yours, bringing me into a hug. My face is against your neck and I'm breathing in the smell of your aftershave, and the feel of your skin on mine is so familiar and strange that the tears are falling now because I know that this is the last goodbye.

"I'm glad we did this," you say, your words muffled in my hair.

"Me, too," I'm saying, and we hold each other, your body pressed close against mine. Our lips are inches apart and for a moment I think that we're going to turn toward each other as easily and smoothly as we always used to. I can remember the way it felt to kiss you as clearly as if it were yesterday, and the possibility is so insanely close that it makes my head swim. Your arms are suddenly rigid, locked around me, your breath coming hard and fast. And then you swallow and we're moving apart and I have no idea who made the first move to do so.

"Goodbye. Take care of yourself," you say, and you're walking quickly away.

I don't want to see you leave. I stare down at the table, my eyes still blurred with tears. At the last minute I change my mind. I look up sharply, but it's too late.

You're gone, and the sense of resolution and serenity that I felt for a few seconds is already draining away. Because this is how it goes, I realize. There are no words in existence that will ever make this story feel finished. We could see each other every day and talk long into the night, and I still wouldn't make sense of it. I'm tired of searching for answers that aren't there, or struggling to define what kind of love I felt or feel for you or how much it means. It doesn't matter. It is what it is.

GOING HOME

Caroline, May 2015

It's probably only five more minutes that I stay sitting there in the café after you leave, but when I force myself to stand up again and walk toward the exit, my eyes hurt with how bright the world outside seems. There's a faint, cool breeze blowing as I make my way down the street.

I'm still shaking a little, and there's a soreness in my limbs. I almost welcome it. I'm ridding myself of the last vestiges of a fever that has gripped me so hard I can barely believe I've survived. Senseless euphoria is surging through me as I replay the last few minutes in my mind. My thoughts are crowding each other out, leaving nothing but white noise.

I carry on down the high street, taking the left turn down the road that will lead me back to Everdene Avenue, and as I do so I'm aware of my phone vibrating. I pull it out and see that there's a voice message, left only ten minutes earlier. I dial my voice mail and listen. When the message kicks in there's silence for a couple of seconds—a frustrated little intake of breath, and then I hear my mother's voice. *Hi, Caroline.*

As soon as I hear it I know something is wrong. I stop dead on the pavement, immobilized. It must be only a split second before her voice begins again, but in that tiny, compressed rush of time I'm thinking—*Eddie. Something has happened. My mother is calling to tell me my son is dead.* And the force of this thought is such that it sweeps aside everything else in my head and burns its way into my brain, makes me lean back against the wall and close my eyes.

I don't want to worry you, my mother's voice continues, and although her tone is still tense and strained I know that this is not how a tragedy is introduced. I breathe in sharply, sucking the air jaggedly down into my lungs as if I've been saved from drowning. *Eddie and I went to your flat this afternoon—it's a long story, but anyway, we met the woman who's staying there, and to be honest, she seems very disturbed. I'm not sure what's going on, but it doesn't feel quite right, Caroline, and I wanted to speak to you. We're fine, don't worry, but—well, just call me when you can.*

My heart is thudding as I redial the number. She picks up almost at once, and I launch straight in, with no time for preamble. "What happened?"

My mother sighs. "I don't know how to describe it," she says. "This woman—we bumped into her by chance and she invited us to come and see Paddy. She seemed perfectly nice, but while we were there today, she just—broke down. She was crying, and I couldn't make sense of anything she said. I have no idea what was going through her head. Maybe it's silly, but I feel uneasy about her being in your place. I know you're coming back tonight anyway, but I just thought you should know, and—"

"I'm coming back now," I say. "I'm packing up my things and we're coming back as soon as we can. I should be there in three or four hours."

"Well, maybe that's a good idea," my mother says, clearly

relieved. "I'm sorry, I didn't want to disturb you on your holiday. Have you been having fun?"

My throat closes up and I find that I can't speak, the tears that have dried up only minutes before rising up again to choke me. I grip on to the phone, listening to the low buzz of the line. Before I can make myself reply, I hear a scuffling sound and the sudden loud breathing of my son at the other end of the phone. "Mummy," he says, and with the word the tears shrink back and I find myself saying his name in return, clear and strong.

"I miss you," he says.

"I'm coming back," I tell him. "Daddy and me. We'll be back today."

"That's good." His voice is oddly adult for a moment, reflective and thoughtful. "Because then you can put me to bed."

"That's right," I say. I'm filled with the desire to say something to him that he won't forget—to make him realize that I understand what matters, even if I've lost sight of it for so long. "I love you," I begin, but before I can say any more he's pressed the wrong button and cut the call off.

I think about calling back, but I find that I'm shoving the phone back into my pocket and running, my footsteps thudding in my head. I can't wait any longer. I run down the street to number 21 and fumble for the keys, wrenching the front door open. As soon as I come into the hallway I see Francis through the open living-room door. He's bent over his suitcase, zipping it up. When he hears me he straightens up, dusts off his hands. He looks me straight in the eyes and I look back, feeling a jolt of connection. We understand each other.

"We need to get back," he says, and I nod silently, flooded by the sudden strangeness of this shared purpose, the way we have both arrived at the same conclusion from poles apart.

I glance 'round the room, looking at the bareness of the walls, the flat gleaming surfaces. I don't need to try to imprint these things on my memory. Already I know that they'll be here with me for a long, long time. For a moment I wonder if I should leave some message or symbol for the woman whose house I have been living in, but I have no idea what it might be. So I just reach for my handbag and follow my husband out through the hallway and close the front door behind us, not looking back.

Francis crosses the driveway to the car, unlocking it and preparing to get into the driver's seat. I haven't planned it, but I find the words rising unstoppably inside me. "No," I say. "I'll drive."

He stands very still, his hand still on the door handle. "Are you sure?" he asks.

"Yes."

I move forward and take the keys from his fingertips. They feel cool and smooth against my skin. I slip into the driver's seat and slide the key into the ignition. Place my hands on the wheel. Look through the windscreen at the road ahead.

And then I'm moving the car forward, and it's easy. Strange, but easy.

I drive slowly at first, watching the road carefully, conscious of nothing else. It's the first time I have driven outside my dreams in almost two years. In those nightmares my hands have dripped with sweat and my head has pounded, and I have known even in my sleep that this will end badly. It isn't that way now. I'm driving and everything is clear and calm and it's like I never stopped.

We're onto the motorway before I speak again, and when I do I don't move my head, not wanting to look away from the road or meet his gaze. "I need to start telling you something now." I have no idea how I will begin. "Something that happened when Carl and I ended things," I say. I draw in a breath, tighten my hands on the wheel. The skyline spilling out ahead is vast and blank, punctuated by gray drifting clouds.

"Caro," he says. "You don't need to tell me."

I do look at him then, a swift glance in the mirror before I snap my eyes back to the road. He's staring at me with sadness and tenderness, his green eyes narrowed with concentration. "I already know," he says. "About the accident."

I shake my head, unable to process the words. "No," I start. "How could you?"

"I've known for a while," he says. "Look, the important thing is to get home. We can talk later. But a few months ago, I had a visit from a new patient. The girl . . . it was—"

"Her mother," I finish, because from the moment he started speaking I realized that there are only three people in the world besides myself who have known the truth of what happened, and that she is the only one who can have reached him, the only one who would have wanted to.

I tighten my hands on the wheel. "We have to talk about this," I say quietly. "We have to—"

"I know," he interrupts, "and we will. Trust me."

I bite down hard on my lip, struggling to know how to reply, and then there's a rush of sudden peace and I realize that I don't need to, not now. All I need to do is drive.

Trust me. The words echo in my head as I lean forward in my seat and steer the car down the road. There's no rhyme or reason to trust—it's there or it's not. And now it's there—soaking through the silence between us, warming this small, private bubble. We've spent almost every day in each other's company for the past two years and this is the first time that I've really felt this intimacy.

The knowledge is fierce and sad. I'm thinking of the way another man's arms were around me less than an hour before, and I know that there's no point in clinging to a dream if what I have right here in front of me is something I want to keep. I have no idea where we will be in five years, or even five weeks, but I want to live in the present, with my family. I'm tired of walking through my own life like a ghost, giving them my body when my head is elsewhere.

We don't speak another word for the rest of the journey. The hours blur, the miles whirring silently past. It's almost three in the afternoon by the time we reach home. I pull carefully into the parking space and switch off the ignition. My hands are trembling. I've done it, but this isn't over. I peer up at the third-floor windows of the building, and I try to determine if she's still there.

The thought fills me with nausea, but there's no going back now. I turn to Francis, stretch my hand out to cover his. "I need to go in first," I say. "Just please wait here for me."

He opens his mouth as if he might protest, then abruptly closes it and nods. He leans his head back against the seat, his eyes intent and reflective. He knows as well as I do that something is coming to its end here. That once it's past we'll be left with a life that is a different shape, and that we'll start to discover if it's worth having.

I climb my way out of the car and slam the door, folding my arms tightly around my chest as I walk up to the building. I climb the three flights of stairs to our flat, listening to the sound of my footsteps in the silent hallway. I'm half expecting to find her standing there waiting for me, but the door is closed. I reach into my pocket for my keys and unlock the door, letting it swing gently open.

As soon as I step into the hallway I feel it—a sense of otherness, a presence that is intense and strange, and yet not quite a presence at all. The air is heavy and thick, as if suffused with invisible smoke.

The door to the lounge is ajar. I walk up to it, softening my footsteps. My lips form a question. *Are you there?* But I barely have the chance to begin before a flash of something through the crack in the door catches my eye—a flutter of green, whipped across the gap and then withdrawn—and the flat of my hand is pressing against the door and opening the room to me.

She's hanging from the ceiling light, swaying slightly in the breeze that blows through the open balcony window. The scarf that I last saw illuminated by headlights, blown darkly back by the wind, is fastened tightly around her neck.

She's about fifty years old and she has shoulder-length brown hair and slim limbs. She's wearing a discreetly stylish shirtdress, pale blue, the same color as her open eyes.

I stand there motionless for a minute, and then I sit down on the carpet close by and watch her. I watch for the slightest uncurl of her fingertips, a minute twitch of her eyelids to show me that it's not quite over. There's nothing. She's left me her last message.

I say it then.

I'm so sorry.

The word is small and clear in the silence. It isn't enough, but it still needs to be said. I stay there next to her for a while—looking at her face, the sad lines of her mouth—and I wonder who she once was. Before she became a mother without a child. In her place, I can't say I wouldn't have done everything that she has done. I have no idea what it might have driven me to.

I get to my feet and go to look out of the window, down to the car below. I think about calling Francis, calling my mother, calling the police. I know that when I do, these moments of silence will snap and the calmness of this shock will dissolve. Everything will change. I don't yet know how. All I can see ahead is mist and shadows, and I'm walking into the darkness and the strange freedom it offers—opening myself up to it, and giving myself to my future on trust.

LEAVING HOME

Caroline, September 2015

The estate agent arrives bang on twelve—a sharp suit and a slicked-back haircut, looking barely out of his teens—and hovering behind him, a young couple smiling shyly, the woman's hand resting on her pregnant stomach.

"Still all right to take a look 'round?" He's elbowing his way through the front door, throwing out an expansive hand to showcase the living room as if he's the one who owns the place.

"Sure," I say. "If you want to know anything," I add, turning to the couple, "just ask me."

I linger in the hallway, listening to the salesman patter: great south-facing light, original features, sound foundations. I'm not even sure how much he knows of what has happened here, but if he's aware he gives nothing away. A suicide doesn't make for a great sales pitch, even one that has been wrapped up so neatly and smartly by the authorities; filed away and dismissed, with no need to probe further beneath the surface. Nothing to see here.

From where I'm standing, I can see the couple moving from room to room, and I'm watching the woman's face and the emotions flickering across it: her eyes keen and thoughtful, narrowing as she takes in the space as if she's imagining it stripped of every-thing it contains and filled with her own things, molded into someplace new.

They finish up in the living room again, and the estate agent retreats to take a call on his mobile, barking instructions to some even more junior colleague. The couple are talking quietly to each other—gesticulating and sizing up, reading each other's reactions. I watch the woman drift over toward the balcony window and stand beneath the ceiling light, and for a moment her expression blanks and she half shudders, as if someone is walking over her grave.

"I think I'd paint this side of the room paler," she says, "lighten it up a bit more." As she speaks, she glances over toward the door-way, seeing me in the hallway beyond, and her face flushes, caught criticizing. "It's a lovely place," she says, louder, smiling tentatively at me.

"Thanks." I take a few steps forward, hugging my arms around myself.

"Are you staying local?" the woman asks.

I half nod. "Renting around here in the short term," I say. "Just seeing how things go."

"I see," she says, though of course she doesn't, not at all.

Outside there's the sound of scuffling; Eddie's excited voice raised high and talking fast, his fists banging on the door. The key turns in the lock, and Francis comes in, letting Eddie run ahead of him to embrace me. I bend down and pull him against me, feeling the sturdy warmth of his body, his hair soft and sleek against my cheek.

The estate agent barrels back into the room, tucking his phone back into his pocket. "Sorry about that," he says. "All done?"

The couple murmur their agreement and make their goodbyes,

thanking us as they go. Francis turns to me, eyebrows raised. "What do you reckon?" he asks. "Did they like it?"

"I think so," I say. "It's hard to tell."

"I guess we'll see." He hesitates fractionally, then leans forward, drawing me against him and kissing the side of my mouth in a belated hello. I kiss him back, our lips not quite touching. Four months on, we're still careful with each other—careful to the point of slight awkwardness. We don't quite fit together yet, but it seems that the rough edges are being sanded off, eroding and smoothing into something more than serviceable.

Another brief pause, and then he nods toward the phone sticking out of my shirt pocket. "Anything today?" he asks, his voice light.

I shake my head. "No. Almost a week now." I think of all the messages Amber has sent me in the past few months; dozens, maybe even hundreds. At first I thought she was practicing the principle of keeping your enemies close, but lately I've started to wonder if the reason she wants to keep these links alive is because, just as I once saw an echo of myself in her, she now sees herself in me. I'm the only other one who's been close to the person she loves, and she's starting to realize that what she's taken on isn't easy. I never reply to her messages, but I haven't blocked them either, and I know exactly why. I think that someday I'll be strong enough. That I won't want this connection anymore.

Francis lets it pass without comment. "I'll get the lunch started," he says, raising his bag of shopping. "Eddie, do you want to come and help out?"

He scampers after him to the kitchen, still chattering about the film they've seen. I listen and feel a smile lifting the corners of my mouth, feeling suddenly suffused with love for him, and hot on its heels is the dark weight of guilt that is its chain reaction; the fear that what I have is so much more than I should and that this precarious tightrope of luck is one I don't deserve to walk. I'm used to this now. I close my eyes and breathe deeply, and wait for it to lift.

When it does I wander over to the balcony window and look out onto the street. The young couple are still waiting at the bus stop down the street, bodies turned toward each other, chatting animatedly. The woman's hands are making shapes in the air, as if she's slotting the pieces of a puzzle into place.

I think of her face as she stood here, the sudden vacancy of it and the way she shivered. It could have been a coincidence, but deep down I believe that some trace has been left—some remnant that won't be purged by coats of paint or pretty lampshades. I feel it often in the middle of the night, this force field. The presence of the woman who was once here, the pull of it drawing me magnetically to this window from my bed in the dark. And sometimes I wonder if the same is true in that other house, hundreds of miles away and just across the road from where you still are; if some hint of the few days I spent there lingers, and if some ghost of me shakes awake whoever lives there now from uneasy dreams, filled with love and loss.